AUTUMN
SECRETS

AUTUMN SECRETS

SUSAN C. MULLER

Autumn Secrets
Copyright © 2017
Susan C. Muller

Published in the United States of America by
Stanford Publishing Company

Cover design by
Najla Qamber Designs
http://www.najlaqamberdesigns.com

Interior Design and Formatting by:

www.emtippettsbookdesigns.com

Books By
SUSAN C. MULLER

PROLOGUE

S HE DIDN'T WEIGH much. A hundred and ten, tops. But it was hard work carrying, as they called it, dead weight.

If he didn't have a place prepared, he'd be tempted to drop her beside the road like the trash she was.

But he'd done the necessary groundwork.

He'd spent days driving aimlessly around Houston, scouting the perfect location. One that met his specific criteria.

No cameras recording suspicious activity. No neighbors glancing out an upstairs window. No headlight beams from oncoming traffic.

Then one June night, under a sky so clear he didn't need a flashlight, he'd found the spot. Right under his nose all the time.

His heart swelled in anticipation, and he sang to himself as he dug in the barren soil.

The moon at night
It shines so bright
I'm right at home here in Texas.

Not exactly the way he'd learned it at his father's knee, but better. New and improved.

Then again, sometimes what *not* to do was the lesson.

Like get caught.

His father needed three tries to wise up. First, his mother took her own life when she caught him diddling the nanny. Wife number two took his money. Finally, wife number three didn't care who Daddy diddled, as long as she got her monthly allowance and wasn't bothered with domestic duties.

So he'd watched and learned, and unlike Daddy, hadn't been caught. He took his cues from the Boy Scouts. Always be prepared.

And he was. For months to come. Which was good, because he liked Houston. The people were friendly, trusting, yet not too inquisitive. Each suburb a separate municipality. Even in the city there were plenty of open spaces. Dead end roads.

He stopped to catch his breath and laughed at his own pun.

After here, who knew? He couldn't go back to Austin. And didn't want to.

Not Huntsville. People actually noticed when college girls went missing.

Dallas maybe, or Amarillo. He'd always liked the sound of Seguin. Definitely not Galveston.

On an island, you could get trapped.

CHAPTER ONE

A FTER SIX WEEKS of "officially encouraged" vacation and four weeks back on the job, Noah Daugherty was accustomed to his office and the constant *beeping, whirring, ringing* of phones, printers, and computers. They were white noise that didn't register on his conscious brain.

But he hadn't gotten used to seeing dead bodies. Maybe he never would.

He stood, knee deep in weeds, not half a mile off I-45. The ship channel bridge was visible in the distance. Big-rigs belched past. Drivers leaned on horns as rubberneckers slowed to look at the gathering of squad cars, ambulances, and crime scene vans.

News helicopters hovered overhead.

The vultures had descended with amazing speed. And he wasn't thinking of the winged creatures who alerted a fisherman to the presence of the decaying body.

He should be searching the scene, but there was nothing more to see here and he'd already trudged through enough gumbo mud to coat the bottom six inches of his pant legs. Instead, his mind kept returning to his forced time off and the peace he'd felt. He longed for those hours of silence. Entire days when he spoke to no one except Sweet Pea. The five-pound Yorkie never answered him, but her expression spoke volumes.

Unfortunately, the criminals of Houston hadn't spent the summer on vacation.

This discovery made two bodies found less than a block apart. From what he could see of her condition, she pre-dated the other by several months.

The first had been left inside an abandoned apartment building two weeks earlier. She'd still be there if a county employee hadn't been given a clipboard and a list of derelict buildings with instructions to decide if they posed an danger to the community and should be demolished, refurbished, or ignored.

But someone had taken time to bury this one's remains. And last night's rain had opened her shallow grave.

The first cool breeze of autumn did little to blow away the stench.

If she was the perp's earliest victim, there was a good chance he'd made mistakes, left trace evidence this time.

If she wasn't, there were likely more. Waiting. Someone's daughter or mother or sister or even a wife, left to rot a few feet below ground.

Waiting to be discovered. Waiting for justice. For retribution.

While at home someone waited for that phone call or knock on the door. Waiting even while knowing the news would end all hope.

Noah slapped at a mosquito as his partner bowed his head over the makeshift grave. He never knew for certain whether

Conner's prayer was for the victim or his own ability to bring her justice.

A moment later, he approached, memo book in hand. Noah's fears that fatherhood would force Conner to transfer to a less demanding department had never materialized. Yet he knew his partner's five a.m. jog had turned into a six o'clock speed walk around the neighborhood pushing a baby carriage. The dark circles under his eyes hinted even this might not last much longer.

"The M.E. says early summer, best he can tell. He'll know better when he has her on the table."

"Don't suppose the illustrious Dr. Mackie is willing to comment on cause of death. Or if she's related to the other one." Would Noah rather have one guy going around killing young women, or two different sleaze bags working the same area? None of the above didn't seem to be an option.

Conner slipped the memo pad into his shirt pocket. "You know better than to ask. I was lucky to get that much out of him."

They'd be lucky to get an identification any time soon, considering she was only wearing the skin she was born in.

He'd bet his pension on manual strangulation. This guy liked it up close and personal. Looking into their eyes as the light of life faded.

If it was the same perp, he didn't know his victims. He'd dumped them like a piece of garbage without the decency to lay them out. With only two feet of dirt to cover their nakedness.

Conner's voice brought him back to the present. "What now?"

He looked over the vacant lot, the size of a football field. What were the odds? He'd shucked his coat, rolled up his sleeves and loosened his tie, but sweat ran down the back of his neck and his shirt stuck to his skin.

It would take a dozen academy rookies—something they weren't likely to get—to do a proper grid search, but he and Conner were there, dirty and miserable.

"Want to walk the field, see if anything else washed up?"

An hour later, Noah regretted his suggestion. His slacks were clammy and clung to his legs like yoga pants. He'd stepped out of his shoes in the thick mud twice so even his socks were wet.

Every step through a new batch of weeds or yaupon stirred up a fresh swarm of mosquitoes. He'd have quit, but he didn't want to give up before Conner.

His fastidious partner didn't seem to sweat or get bitten by the veracious bloodsuckers, but at least his expensive slacks were filthy from the knee down and that gave Noah a perverse sense of pleasure.

He took another step and his foot sank ankle-deep into the mud. He stepped to the side to pull that foot out when the other plunged in even deeper.

"Hey, partner. I think I'm stuck. Is there really such a thing as quicksand?"

Conner eyed him, standing shin deep in the mud. "I don't know, but if there is, you found it. Let's get you out of there and call it a day."

Praise the Lord and pass the biscuits. He never thought he'd live to see the day Conner quit first.

His partner yanked up several handfuls of the tall weeds and laid them on the edge of the muddy area. He placed one foot on the grass, grabbed Noah's wrists, and tugged. Noah came out, but one shoe didn't.

Now what? Limp home?

They had worked their way close to the crime scene techs so he yelled to them. "Hey, guys. I need a shovel over here."

The youngest tech, a kid he could have sworn wore a Bozo the Clown fright wig, brought the smallest shovel Noah had ever seen. Not two feet long, it couldn't possibly scoop up more than a handful of the gooey muck at a time.

The tech—his name tag read Benny Schroeder—smiled, and Noah swore under his breath. If that kid dared laugh, he'd make his life miserable as long as he worked for the department. Maybe longer.

Two shovelfuls later, Noah's shoe reappeared. But so did something else.

A hand. Red fingernail polish still visible.

For once, Noah and Conner had taken a motor pool car to the crime scene. They sat in the front seat, caked in mud, smelling like old fish left in the sun, and let the air conditioning blow in their faces.

It wasn't much, but it helped.

Noah almost felt human by the time Benny trudged up and tapped on the window. "You might want to come see this," he said and swung around to trudge away again.

He glanced at Conner who closed his eyes and sighed. "I guess we have to."

Damn, he could get used to this new Conner. Sure, it was only temporary. One day, the baby would start sleeping through the night and Conner would be his old self again.

Until then, the slight feeling of superiority was the kick he needed.

The midday sun had driven away any clouds and the hot air slapped Noah in the face as he opened the car door. The first of October and eighty-five degrees at least.

He scraped an inch of mud off the bottom of his shoe, but really, what was the use? It would be back again after half a dozen steps.

The M.E. squatted next to the shallow grave. "We've got a problem."

Noah stared down at the body. Long hair, blonde under layers of filth, covered the face of the nearly-intact woman. Other than another body, ten feet from the one they were investigating, what could possibly be wrong?

Doc M pointed to a bone next to the woman's arm. A femur, yellowed with age. "She's not alone."

Conner's hands dropped. He didn't even bother to take notes.

Noah looked again. He could make out portions of a skull and other parts of a skeleton hidden beneath the blonde with the red fingernails.

His stomach threatened to rebel. He was supposed to investigate homicides, not discover them. While he'd always had empathy for witnesses, some part of him would secretly will them to grab hold of their grownup panties, pull themselves together, and give him the information he needed to find the killer.

Now he truly understood, and he didn't like it one bit.

This was bad. How was he going to solve this case? No

neighbors to question. No businesses nearby that might have security cameras. No firm date of death to know who'd gone missing.

As backed up as the lab was, he couldn't expect DNA anytime soon. And were fingerprints even possible after this length of time?

The only good thing about this entire day was that the news media had gotten tired and gone home before he stumbled into the second grave. That wouldn't last. They'd find out and be back.

He turned to Conner, disillusionment weighing heavy on his shoulders. "Let's head to the office, write this up, and wait for the autopsy to give us some direction. If we can get anything that says even two of these are the same guy, I'd like to push for one of those cadaver sniffing dogs or ground penetrating radar. Look around this field. See if they had any more company."

"Do we even *have* those things?"

"Damned if I know, but it might be worth finding out."

"Her hyoid bone is not broken." Glacial blue eyes peered at Noah from under the M.E.'s surgical cap.

Noah had always hated the morgue. Who wouldn't, with its chemical smells, near freezing temperatures, and disgusting sights? Well, apparently not Doctor Mackie and his merry band of part-vampire helpers. But since the day, little more than a year ago, he'd had to identify Betsy's body, it held a special spot in his places-to-avoid list.

So why did he always seem to be the one tasked with attending post mortems?

Because he'd kept that secret, along with many others, from

his partner.

His gut churned and he longed to be away from the building and back outside, no matter how gray the day.

"Are you saying she wasn't strangled?" One time he'd like to have Doc M spew out the pertinent facts and let him leave before the stink settled into his hair and clothes.

"Oh, no. She was manually throttled. You asked me for similarities in the deaths. I assumed you wanted differences as well. On the other girls, the bone was broken."

"So the doer wasn't the same person." Okay, he wasn't searching for one douchebag but two. Maybe more.

"I didn't say that."

Shit. "So what are you saying?"

"The hyoid is only fractured in one third of strangulation cases. There are multiple causes for this. In children under ten, the bone is not yet fused. In adults over forty, ossification may occur."

There were people all over the world, millions of people, who went through their entire lives never learning this stuff. Right now he wished he was one of them.

"Also, the amount of pressure is significant. Compression of the carotid arteries or jugular veins indicates less pressure while the trachea, which is crushed in all four victims, takes as much as six times the pressure."

Yep, more information he could have done without. "I'm not studying for an exam, Doc. Can you keep the lecture to this victim and how she compares to the other women?"

"You realize I'm estimating the age by teeth and bone structure." The doc stopped abruptly. Disappointment flooded his face.

For one moment Noah felt like an ass. Doc M had missed his calling as a teacher or some kind of professional negotiator. But this was work, not a hobby, and he had four dead women waiting for identification.

"Numbering the victims by the order in which they died, not by when they were found, victim number one, the skeleton, was probably twenty-two and had been in the ground for ten years."

Ten years was a long time between kills if this was the same doer. Did he know where the grave was and used it again, or did a second mope stumble on it and decide to add to the collection? Hell, there could be four murderers out there, waiting to strike again.

He'd say he'd lost faith in humanity, but that ship sailed a long time ago.

"Victim number two was the young woman you went to the field to investigate. She was approximately twenty-one and had been in the ground about four months. She's the one without a broken hyoid. Victim number three is the poor soul who had to share her grave. She was the oldest at twenty-four and the only Hispanic. Estimated death, late August. About six weeks ago. Which leaves us with your fourth victim. The one discovered in a vacant apartment building."

Not his victim. She was Lefty Bob's case and he was welcome to her. Three deaths in one day were plenty for him.

"She was dead about two weeks when her body was found, placing her death in mid-September. She was most likely no more than seventeen."

Fuck. Only a girl. Not even a woman yet.

"Fortunately, I was able to retrieve a DNA sample from

victim one, the skeleton, and sent it to the lab along with that of victims two and three. Victim four's was sent in last week."

"What about fingerprints?" The bodies were in bad shape. He didn't hold out much hope, but the doc was an expert.

"No chance on victim one, but three and four were manageable. Victim two will be a little tricky and may take me a while but I should be able to come up with something for you." He motioned to a body on the table. "I've already removed her hands and put them in a formaldehyde solution to reconstitute them. In time, I'll be able to take off the skin and slip it on like a glove to retrieve the prints for you."

Holy shit. He could never tell that to the girl's parents. He was sorry he heard it himself.

"Is there anything else I should know?" Please let the answer be *no…*

"Using maximum pressure, a person will lose consciousness within a few seconds. It's impossible to tell for certain on the first victim, although she did have a broken wrist, but the other three lasted long enough to suffer from air hunger and fought back vigorously. Whoever killed these women took his time, making their deaths last as long as possible."

He'd have been so much happier if he hadn't asked that question.

CHAPTER TWO

DRIVING HOME IN Lola, his beloved truck, Noah tried to put his visit to the morgue out of his mind. He didn't want to think about the four unknown women and their last hours.

He didn't want to think about the morgue at all.

Yet, despite his hatred of the place where he'd identified Betsy's lifeless body, he hadn't suffered the stomach cramps that usually preceded his visits. Had offering to be the one who attended the autopsies finally paid off by hardening him to the building, its long echoing corridors, and offensive smells?

Or had it all happened on August 26, the one year anniversary of his wife's death, the day he'd dreaded most in the world?

He'd planned to spend the day alone, with only Sweet Pea for company. After all, the little Yorkie had known Betsy long before Noah barged into their world. It had taken months for them to accept each other. Now they were inseparable.

But his family and friends would have none of that.

Conner, Jeannie, and baby Betsy had showed up at his door by nine o'clock carrying breakfast tacos complete with chorizo sausage and salsa. Later they dragged him over to Rachelle's house where his sister had obviously instructed Emma and Iris their job was to make Uncle Noah laugh.

And against all odds, they had.

The two girls ganged up on him in the swimming pool and tried their best to dunk him. Later, as his brother-in-law, Frank, grilled vegan hot dogs and hamburgers, they'd pop out unexpectedly from behind a bush and soak him with water guns. He'd chase them, growling, and scoop them onto his shoulders.

Even Sweet Pea had fun, running and playing.

In the weeks since, each day he'd felt himself grow stronger. Maybe that's why today's trip to the morgue, while unpleasant, hadn't been devastating.

And why he could go home, play with Sweet Pea, take her for a walk, eat some of Rachelle's vegetarian lasagna, and not obsess over dead young women.

There'd be plenty of time for that tomorrow when he could actually do something about it.

Lieutenant Jansen glared at Noah from under bushy eyebrows knitted together into one line, like the sleeve of a woolen sweater after a cat attack. "You want me to do what?"

"Check with the Chief. See if we can get a cadaver sniffing dog or one of those ground penetrating radar things. There are more women buried in that field. I can feel it in my bones. This guy's been up to no good for a long time."

"As much faith as I have in your bones, the Chief may want

more proof."

Conner stepped in to back him up. About time he pulled his weight. "There's circumstantial evidence to indicate the woman found in the deserted apartment building and the ones in the field were killed by the same person. All were murdered by someone who was careful to leave no trace evidence."

"So your evidence is that there's no evidence? That should go over well."

Damn Conner, hadn't he learned? You always start with the sexy stuff. Don't bury the lead. "All were strangled, slowly for maximum effect, even though the trachea was broken, indicating the perp was strong enough to finish the job quickly. He then washed away any evidence and left their nude bodies hidden with the expectation they wouldn't be found for several years."

"Yet they were found within a few months."

"That field was in a hundred-year flood plain. He wouldn't have expected her body to float up, and that apartment building should have been a safe disposal site. The county is covered with demolition projects that will wait decades before facing the wrecking ball. Still, I think the fact that one was left aboveground and two shared a grave indicates the perp had lost track of where his other bodies were buried."

"You're saying that site's a killing field?"

Conner's voice was soft, an indication he was serious. "That's exactly what we're saying. He could have spent the last several years perfecting his craft and filling up the available space."

Good. Conner was always cautious. If he'd convinced him, his wild theory maybe wasn't so wild after all. "Victims three and four were killed quite recently and only a couple of weeks apart, yet victim number two died four months ago and victim one has been dead for ten years. Why the different time frame? I believe he didn't change his M.O. We just haven't found the ones in between."

The Lieu visibly shivered at the thought. "I'd like to help you guys, but I'm not even sure HPD *has* the things you're asking for."

Noah leaned in, pressing his point. "No one else is, either. If not, let's call the FBI. They always have the latest toys."

"You'd be willing to work with those guys?"

"Yes. I am." And wasn't that a sign of his new attitude toward life?

"It's barely eight o'clock. The Chief's not in yet. Give me an hour to research this and I'll get back to you."

Tom Meyers stood over the apron-front porcelain sink with his first cup of coffee and a toasted bagel. The coffee was too hot to drink, so he set the china cup in its saucer on the granite countertop and switched on the TV. His own image filled the screen.

Not the best photo he'd seen—his mouth was open. And not the most recent—that tie had to be ten years out-of-date, and the suit looked more Men's Warehouse than Armani. Hell, there were areas of brown in his trademark white hair. But definitely him. Still a baby lawyer, first starting out, before he hit the big time.

Normally he'd be overjoyed with the free publicity, but this didn't feel right.

He was plenty busy—filing affidavits, taking depositions, interviewing witnesses, researching, schmoozing with possible clients—but not one of the multiple cases on his desk was newsworthy at this point.

He lifted the coffee and blew on the hot liquid before taking a sip.

And where was that photo taken? An official-looking hallway, but not the Criminal Courts Building, or City Hall or police headquarters. If it was one of the outlying stations, he didn't recognize it. The hall was grubby, but not filthy enough to be the Harris County Jail.

The camera panned to the side and he caught a glimpse of a hauntingly familiar face before the scene changed and the traffic report came on with the woman forecaster whose smile made Houston's abominable traffic almost, but not quite, bearable.

He waited, frozen in place for one nanosecond, while the face registered. The gold-rimmed cup slipped from his fingers and shattered in the sink as his phone chirped.

Three texts. One from his secretary. One from his junior partner. One from his mother.

This couldn't be good.

Noah busied himself with paperwork while he waited for his boss to call. He tried, but failed to keep his eyes from straying to the phone on his desk. The hands on the old-fashioned clock over Lieutenant Jansen's office crept forward so slowly he worried the battery had given out.

When his phone rang he grabbed for it, knocking over his Styrofoam cup and spilling cold coffee over his desk. "Yes?" He didn't bother to identify himself.

"Detective Dougherty?"

Shit. It wasn't Jansen.

He scrambled to rescue papers from the spreading puddle while balancing the receiver against his shoulder. "Yes." A bottom drawer held paper towels and he built a dyke to protect his keyboard.

"This is Tom Meyers."

Silence.

"Conner Crawford's attorney in the Aldo Rogers case."

He knew who the shyster was. He just didn't want to speak to him.

"Something's come up that I'd like to consult with you about. Could we meet in my office later today?"

Hell no. "I'm rather busy at the moment. Can't you tell me about it over the phone?"

"It's a very delicate matter. Perhaps I could buy you lunch at a restaurant near the courthouse."

And take a chance someone would see them together? According to that fucking clock, it had only been twelve minutes since he left the Lieu's office. It would be a cold day in August before the Chief made it to his desk by nine-thirty. And who knew how long after that till he took the Lieu's call or gave him an answer.

"I can come over right now if you guarantee I won't sit there cooling my heels for an hour."

"You have my word."

Conner shot him a questioning look, but he simply shrugged as he swept the last of his spilled coffee into the trashcan. "I have to run a quick errand. Text me when you hear from the Lieu."

He lied to suspects every day. He didn't like it, but that came with the job. Lying to his partner was out of the question.

Omitting a fact wasn't.

No way would he let Conner know the lawyer he trusted with his future had a problem.

Conner glared at his partner's retreating back. All this secrecy caused him to wonder if he'd made the right decision about returning to Homicide. Maybe he should reconsider the offer of a transfer to Internal Affairs with its regular hours and lower stress level.

Betsy's colic had both him and Jeannie exhausted. Heading home at five every night sounded like Heaven. If Jeannie went back to teaching in January, it would be essential.

Some cops acted like Internal Affairs was the kiss of death. He didn't feel that way.

In Homicide, you might bring a sense of justice or closure to a victim's family and friends, but their loved one was still dead.

Working IA would allow him to take bad cops off the street—protecting the public—and clear good cops—saving their careers. Both of which would give him absolutely as much satisfaction as spending his days surrounded by the scum of the earth.

Especially if he had to waste energy trying to decipher his partner's hidden agenda.

CHAPTER THREE

"I DIDN'T GROW UP in Houston, you know."

Tom Meyers wasn't a big man, probably five ten, but he looked imposing as he sat behind his polished mahogany desk in a room filled with framed certificates and photos of him shaking hands with two different presidents and various celebrities. A monogramed dress shirt with the sleeves rolled up just so, a silk tie, and a full head of snow-white hair added to the image of accomplishment.

He wasn't as old as the hair made him seem. Only forty-seven.

Noah knew this because he'd Googled the guy. He also knew where he was born, where he went to law school—SMU—and where he started his career. But if that's the way the lawyer wanted to play the game, Noah would bite his tongue, sink back into the butterscotch leather chair, drink coffee made from the finest Arabica beans, and let the guy tell the story his own way.

"My father had a very successful law firm in Austin. He was

also active in the Republican Party. At one point, he was on the short list for a federal judgeship."

Your father was a damn crook who got caught with his hand in the cookie jar.

"My mother was a former Dallas debutante, a member of the DAR, the Junior League and every other organization that coincided with her high standards. They met at SMU and, from what I could see, were quite happy for the next thirty years. I joined my father's firm straight out of law school and made junior partner in two years."

Yeah, yeah. Get on with it. I need to get back to work.

"The firm specialized in business—contracts, negations, etc.—with a side order of keeping politicians out of trouble. Of course, we wouldn't be caught dead representing your common thief or murderer, but sometimes one of those business men or political leaders, or their children, needed a little discreet help. That's where I came in. My mother was horrified, but little by little, I was sucked into the practice of criminal law."

Noah glanced around the office with its thick carpet and stunning view of the Houston skyline. *It's a shame how much you've suffered.*

"Then one day my father ran into some trouble himself. Seems he liked to bet on college football and baseball and the ponies and maybe play an occasional game of high-stakes poker. He'd been skimming a little here and there from different accounts until a client died and his widow demanded an audit. His firm covered it up, of course. Paid off all debts. But rumors got out. He was done."

It wasn't all covered up. Charges were filed, but dropped. Everybody knew. Good thing it was only a poor widow. If it had been a politician, he'd have been in the federal pen.

"He retired to their place on Inks Lake where he fished and golfed and Mother berated him daily. He died after four years. *In the end, your name and reputation is all you have,* as my mother was fond of pointing out."

The guy actually made quotation marks with his fingers. Did people really do that?

"The Meyers name wasn't worth shit in Austin, so I moved to Houston and started over."

Noah couldn't take it any longer. "I hate to rush you, but what does any of this have to do with me?"

"I want you to look into one of my old cases."

"I'm a homicide detective. Not a private investigator. I work for the City of Houston. No one else."

"I wasn't planning on paying you."

What the fuck? I should help you out because what, we're such good friends?

"Your partner, Conner Crawford, still owes me $8,000.00. And that's after the discount I gave him and the money you collected. Which he will never know about, as promised."

Noah felt his face turn red and Meyers must have seen the steam coming out of his ears because he held up his hand in a *stop* motion.

"I realize that must seem like a lot, especially since Internal Affairs cleared him in the death of Aldo Rogers and the man's family dropped their suit, but you have no idea what went into making those things happen. I flew to Nashville twice, hired a court reporter and videographer to record Paige Reimer's deposition. By the way, she asked after you."

Ah shit. Now he really felt bad.

"I also traced down the young officer—Nguyen—that Rogers shot. He left the department and is working on a shrimp boat with his cousin in Victoria. At least I didn't have to spend the night there."

"I didn't realize Nguyen had quit the force."

"He claimed getting shot once was enough. He'd take his chances against Mother Nature from now on."

Nothing like being shot point blank to encourage a change of career.

"I invested a lot of man hours here in Houston, also. I took depositions from Roberto "Lefty Bob" Hernandez and Earl Sparks. I had several meetings with your legal department, which, I must say, didn't impress me. Then there's the Rogers family. I should charge you the $8,000.00 for having to deal with them alone. I'm still fumigating my office."

The whole batch of them were scum, no doubt about that.

"So, what do you say? Do me this one favor, which falls well within your area of expertise, and I'll wipe the debt clean. I'll tell him it's a baby gift."

Tom Meyers watched Noah wrestle with his decision. He'd spent many hours with the detective's partner, Conner Crawford, while preparing his defense after he'd killed a man to save Noah's life.

He'd even spent some time with Noah, taking his deposition and questioning him on the events that led up to the shooting.

He knew Conner well, but had a fairly good handle on Noah's personality, also. In fact, he'd made a dossier of both men.

At thirty-seven, Conner was the oldest by one year, yet

Noah was lead detective because Conner had spent two years in Seminary before joining the force.

Both men were fiercely loyal to each other and the citizens they served, although Conner might have showed a bit more respect for their top brass. Noah seemed quicker to anger, but that didn't make Conner a pushover.

Physically, they were both imposing men. Conner stood about six feet tall with a trim, athletic body. Noah sported two more inches and twenty pounds of muscle. They both had brown hair and eyes, but Noah's edged closer to black.

And those dark eyes glared at him, lava-hot.

"I don't fix cases. Not to help you, not to help Conner, not for any reason."

"I would never ask you to do that. I was hoping you could check over one of my old cases. See what you think."

"Same answer. I won't feed you confidential information."

"Don't need any."

"If I find anything incriminating I'll turn it over to the DA."

"I wouldn't expect anything less."

Tom could almost see the wheels turning in Noah's head.

"Which case is it?"

"I can't tell you. Attorney client privilege."

"How am I supposed to know where to look?"

"I'm betting $8,000.00 you can figure that out."

"Is your client in jail?"

"Nope."

"Any open charges?"

"None."

"And all I have to do is read over the evidence and tell you what I think?"

"Well, I'd like you to do a little investigating. Don't take any information at face value. Other than that, you don't even have to tell me. Simply satisfy yourself."

"I'm working on an important case right now. Your job might have to wait until I'm finished."

"Don't let it wait *too* long, but at this point a few more days won't make any difference."

Well, that was interesting.

Noah's drive back to the office was short and he spent it considering everything Tom said.

Eight thousand dollars wasn't an insurmountable amount for Conner, but with the extra expenses surrounding Betsy's difficult birth and resulting health problems for Jeannie and the baby, he might need time to pay it down. The guys had already chipped in and Noah wasn't about to ask them for more.

He'd made a substantial contribution himself and could pay another thousand or two, but if Conner already had the bill, he'd know and that couldn't happen.

So, was Tom's "favor" something he'd be willing to take on?

Not once had the lawyer asked him to do anything illegal or immoral or even questionable. That was no guarantee the subject wouldn't come up later.

Noah had disliked Tom Meyers the moment he set eyes on the dapper lawyer. Why? Because he showed up at an outdoor crime scene at ten-thirty at night wearing a twelve-hundred dollar suit and a ninety dollar silk tie? Or because his air of entitlements allowed him to breeze past the crime scene techs while they stopped Noah in his tracks?

Those were shallow reasons, but face it, the real one was worse. Tom Meyers helped Conner when Noah couldn't.

Shit. Wasn't self-examination a bitch? No wonder he tried to avoid it whenever possible.

So, after listening to the guy's sob story about growing up rich and privileged, did he now like the lawyer, or at least no longer dislike him?

Maybe. But if Tom pulled anything shady, Noah was perfectly capable of giving the guy the finger and dropping the case mid-stream.

The whole idea was intriguing. Starting with figuring out which case he wanted investigated. Or was the son-of-a-bitch that sneaky? Hooking Noah with a mystery before he got to the mystery.

Well, it worked. He was willing to dip one toe in Tom's polluted pond. He'd at least try to figure out which case kept the lawyer up at night.

Over his career, the man must have represented hundreds of clients. So how was he to find the right one?

By the process of elimination.

Was Tom worried an inadequate defense had doomed an innocent defendant? No, the client wasn't in jail. Plus, the high-toned lawyer would never admit to being inadequate.

Whoa, there's that initial bias slipping in again.

Was Tom considering taking on a new client who might be keeping secrets? All clients lied to their lawyers, like criminals, witnesses, and family members lied to the cops. That wouldn't even slow him down. The claim of no charges filed could change by tomorrow, but twice he'd mention something about an old case, so not a new client.

Okay, how old a case?

Tom Meyers was one of the top lawyers in Houston. He never said a word without a good reason. But he'd spent half the interview reciting his life story.

A smile played across Noah's face. Ten minutes and he'd narrowed hundreds of cases down to a manageable few. He was looking for a client Tom represented in Austin. Not one of his business clients, but one of his fewer criminal cases.

Noah flipped on his blinker and turned into the parking garage.

Set Earl Sparks on a computer search and he'd winnow the field further. They were looking for a guy—no, he never said guy. Keep an open mind—who had never been or was now out of prison.

The smile slipped away, replaced by a clamped jaw. The lawyer was worried someone he got off was now up to his old tricks. And that frightened him enough to call for help.

Tom was obviously carrying a shit-load of guilt over something and that meant it was worth Noah's time and energy. However, he'd said himself his case was old and could wait.

The one Noah was working now came first. That son-of-a-bitch was killing a woman every couple of weeks.

CHAPTER FOUR

THE BLINDS ON the window between the squad room and Lieutenant Jansen's office were open, usually signaling his good mood. This time Conner wasn't so sure.

He watched as his boss hung up the phone and dialed the next number on his list.

Conner had started keeping track when the Chief called the Lieu. He didn't *know* it was the Chief, but if the big boss came in at his usual time, spoke to his secretary, got a coffee, checked his calendar, and returned calls in the order of importance, 9:37 was about right.

Add to that, the Lieu sprang up straight, feet square on the floor, back parallel with, but not touching his chair and yes, the call was from the Chief.

That's when Conner sent his first text to Noah.

Chief's in.

Not exactly telling him to get his ass back to work, but his partner knew him well enough to decipher his meaning.

Noah didn't answer, but that was okay. He wouldn't if he were in the parking garage, or the elevator, or anywhere close.

Jansen's eyebrows weren't dancing across his forehead, so odds were the Chief didn't give him an outright *No*.

The Lieu's next call was internal. Conner knew that because he pushed a button on his desk phone. Probably the K9 division. That call lasted longer but wasn't much more successful, judging by Jansen's posture. He must have gotten a few leads, though. He held the receiver against his shoulder and jotted down something, nodding occasionally.

Leaving the receiver in place, Jansen disconnected and dialed a number from the list he'd been given. His left eyebrow began to twitch.

Conner sent a second text in case Noah thought he had more time.

Any minute now

Jansen crossed off the first number and held the pencil between his teeth as he dialed the second number. Both eyebrows were dancing now. Good news or bad, the Lieu's mood barometer was set for the day.

Conner absently took a sip of cold coffee and almost spit it out. Where the hell was his partner? If Noah thought he'd cover for him, he was dead wrong.

Maybe he was tired. Maybe it was the stress of a colicky baby. Or maybe he'd had it with a partner who kept a trunk-load of secrets and liked to play Lone Ranger, but Internal Affairs was looking mighty good.

The third call went better. The Lieu hunched over his desk and took copious notes, then leaned back and put his feet up, nodding as if the person on the other end of the line could see him.

Two minutes later he hung up and stood, shoving his chair back. He crossed to his door and leaned his head out. "Crawford, Daugherty, my office." He glanced around the squad room. "Where the hell is Daugherty? He drops this pile of shit in my lap and disappears?"

A voice answered from the back of the room. "Right here, sir. Just getting a cup of coffee."

The knot in Conner's stomach eased, but the pin-prick of anger in his brain didn't.

Jansen slapped a slip of paper on the edge of his desk, in front of Noah. "It's not what you asked for, but it's what you got."

The aroma of the hair product Jansen used in a failed attempt to stop his advancing baldness swept over Noah and he lifted the paper and took a step back.

The paper contained almost illegible chicken scratches. Noah had worked with Jansen for years. He could decipher his boss's handwriting.

A name and phone number.

The Lieu liked to make a guy guess, but Noah could out wait him.

"This is a group from Colorado who've been in Mexico training a new batch of search and rescue dogs before avalanche season starts. Apparently, sand and caves aren't the same as snow and ice so they left early. They're stopping in Houston for a few days—their van needed new brakes—before heading back to Colorado. They'd love a chance to work their dogs here."

"So we don't even know if these dogs are capable of finding

bodies?"

"It's what I could come up with. Take it or leave it. But with four unidentified bodies, if I were you, I'd take it."

"Three bodies. The woman in the apartment building belongs to Lefty Bob."

"Not anymore. You think they're connected, you got 'em all."

Shit. Exactly what he didn't want. One more murder to study. One more family to notify. One more creep to hunt down.

There was a time when he'd have wanted another notch on his belt. After Betsy died, he feared he wouldn't be allowed to join her in Heaven unless he atoned for his sins. And he had plenty of sins requiring penance.

He'd misremembered an old Sunday School lesson about forgiving not seven times but seven times seven and set his sights on putting away forty-nine truly evil bad guys.

Lately, he'd realized this was nonsense which was good because he Googled the quote and it was seventy times seven. Four hundred and ninety was more than he could handle in a long lifetime. Certainly not in the fourteen months he'd originally allowed himself to decide if life was still worth living.

At any rate, it didn't matter now. They had Lefty Bob's case and an untrained pack of dogs. They'd have to make the best of it.

Noah reached into his pocket, pulled out a quarter, and slapped in on Conner's desk. "I'll pay you to call Lefty Bob."

"What, you don't want to be the one to tell him we stole his case?"

"I'll take the dog handlers. They're likely to be a little on the *woo-woo* side anyway. Coming from Colorado, smoking weed."

Amusement flickered in Conner's eyes and was gone. He dropped the quarter in his pocket. "You're on."

Good, he didn't have to deal with Lefty Bob and Conner was letting go of the mad he'd been carrying around since he slipped out to see Tom Meyers.

When he heard footsteps behind him, Noah realized Conner had put one over on him.

"Good thing this is Homicide instead of Burglary. I'd have to arrest you two for stealing my cases." Lefty Bob held out a thin manila folder. "Have fun. Her prints aren't in the system and no one's reported her missing. Bruising says she was raped but no semen, hair, or trace evidence. Good luck to you."

Two seconds later, he was gone. Talk about hit and run.

Conner had a full-out grin. "I'll go get a sandwich while you call the dog handlers. I assume you got something to eat during the hour and a half you were gone."

Well, shit. Conner was mad at him. The Lieu was mad at him. Lefty Bob was mad at him. Sweet Pea would be mad at him if he came home smelling of other dogs. And what had he done except try to do his job and look out for his partner?

This was going to be a long, hungry day. Good thing he'd accepted two of the melt-in-your-mouth chocolate chip cookies Tom offered him.

Yellow crime scene tape still marked the two graves, but on the first, one end of the tape had come loose and waved like the tail of a kite.

Noah watched as the afternoon breeze lifted and shook

it before dropping it in the dirt like the discarded body it represented.

What a depressing sight.

The only thing worse was the worry the two marked spots might soon have company.

"They're here," Conner muttered.

A dirty, beat-up van pulled in behind him and parked. Two people got out. Judging by her determined swagger as she trudged through the tall grass toward him, the woman was in charge.

She was short, five-three or five-four, and dumpy. More muscular than fat. Her skin was leathered from days spent in the sun. Salt-and-pepper hair puffed out around her face and hung down her back.

Add a slight tinge of green and a hat and she could be mistaken for the Wicked Witch of the West.

"You the men want to borrow my dogs?"

Noah held out his hand. "Detectives Noah Daugherty and Conner Crawford."

She gave Noah a quick glance and didn't smile.

Conner stepped past him and nodded her direction. "Thank you for coming, Ma'am."

Her eyes warmed as she shook his hand. "Gracie Hanks. This is my assistant, Haskel Rhoads. Good to meet you."

What the fuck? He'd been nothing but polite to the lady and she treated him like he wasn't there. Women always seemed at ease with Conner. They trusted him implicitly. They were right to, but that didn't make it any less annoying.

Haskel was about Gracie's height, early twenties, and appeared to have Downs Syndrome. He didn't speak to either man, but went to the back of the van and unloaded three of the ugliest dogs Noah had ever seen. They were healthy and well cared for, but a mish-mash of parts that didn't seem to belong together.

All were mid-sized, hefty dogs with thick fur coats. The first, Tag, was a reddish-blond and, except for stubby legs, looked to have some German Shepard in his ancestry. He held his head high, sniffed the air, wagged his tail, trotted past Noah and Conner without a glance, and sat beside Gracie.

The second dog, Elway, had one blue eye which made him look a bit creepy, but hinted at a husky somewhere in his distant past. He followed Tag to Gracie's side. His tail didn't exactly wag, but made circles in the air.

The third dog, Sierra, was slow to disembark. Not one thing about her resembled any breed Noah had ever seen. If her sire was a handsome stranger, he forgot the handsome part. She strolled through the high weeds beside the road as if trudging through deep snow. She ignored the passing traffic, any smells in the air, Noah, Conner, her two dog-mates and stood beside Gracie, yawning with indifference.

It might have been wishful thinking, but Noah thought he saw a small spark of intelligence in Tag's eyes. Elway, however, reminded him of the kid who ate snot in elementary school, and Sierra's eyes were cloudy with cataracts.

If this was the best Jansen could come up with, they were in trouble.

Gracie turned her attention on Noah as if he were the enemy. "Let me go over the rules."

He didn't know there were any rules, but he was willing to listen.

"Nobody touches the dogs but Haskel and me."

Fine with him. Tag looked like he might bite. Elway was already slobbering. And he wasn't sure if Sierra was a dog or a pig with hair.

"I'll work one dog at a time. Haskel will stay here with the other two. You." She pointed at Noah. "Come with me. While you." Her eyes stopped on Conner. "Will bring us anything we need."

Noah was prepared. He'd changed into jeans, a polo shirt, and knee-high waders, then liberally doused himself with bug spray.

Haskel handed him a fistful of five foot long sticks painted yellow. "Tag's markers," he said. The only words he'd uttered since they arrived.

Gracie glanced over her shoulder as she and Tag started for the field. "Each dog has its own color. When a dog alerts to a spot, we stick a marker in the ground."

She gave Tag ten feet of lead and the dog raced down the ditch and up the other side into the field, dragging Gracie behind him.

After four days of sun, the ground had dried, leaving only pockets of mud in low or shady spots. Mosquitoes buzzed around Noah's face but didn't bite. That expensive spray was worth the extra money if it kept working.

Tag yanked Gracie to the left and made a beeline for the nearest open grave. He gave one sniff and started howling like a wolf that had lost his pack. Noah was sure he saw tears in the dog's eyes.

Gracie ran up to the dog and threw her arms around him. He buried his face in her chest and whined. "That's what I was afraid of. These dogs are trained to find survivors. They know the difference when the subject has died and it makes them sad, like they failed and the death is their fault."

Why hadn't she said so when he called her? What goddamn use were they going to be to him now?

"Let's take him back to the van and I'll get Elway. He's not as sensitive."

Noah planted a yellow stick near the grave out of spite. He wasn't going to let this day pass with the field as barren as when they arrived. The crime scene techs weren't due to come unless they had a hit and he wasn't sure that would happen.

Elway had blue sticks and a weaker nose. It took him five minutes to find the open grave. He sat beside it and whined, but didn't carry on the way Tag did. After Gracie gave him a treat, he left the grave and spent twenty minutes searching the field.

In three spots he sniffed and circled and sat and stood and sniffed again and sat and got back up. Noah marked the spots with a blue stick but didn't hold out much hope.

Sierra was asleep when they returned Elway. She wrinkled her nose in disapproval at being awakened. Noah grabbed a handful of red sticks from Haskel and followed across the ditch for the third time.

She wasn't in any hurry, strolling through the field as if smelling daises. She hit on the two open graves, whined but moved on after a head scratch and a treat. She made an unmistakable hit on one of Elway's marks but ignored the other two.

After forty-five minutes, she'd given a firm hit on eleven sites. They ran out of red sticks and Conner had to bring them the leftover yellow and blue markers.

Noah's heart couldn't decide if it wanted to speed up or slow down, so it alternated, jumping from one rate to the other. Logically, he expected to find other graves, but deep down, he didn't *believe* so much destruction was possible.

CHAPTER FIVE

ONNER STOOD BESIDE the road and watched as Noah, Gracie, and Sierra worked the field. Every time Noah drove another pole into the ground, it felt like a stake in his heart.

He'd been skeptical at the start, and the sight of that bedraggled van and its misfit occupants did nothing to change his mind.

Tag's reaction to the open grave, while sad, didn't instill confidence. After Elway's indecisive is-it-or-isn't-it signals, he was ready to give up. Call it a day. Admit Noah's hunch was just that. A wild goose chase based on nothing but gut feelings.

After Gracie and Noah started off for the third time, Haskel had turned to him and nodded. "That Sierra'll do you right. She's like me, don't let nothing fluster her. Does her job and ignores everything else." His eyes gleamed with admiration for the homely dog.

Still, Conner had been skeptical.

When Sierra sniffed for several seconds in one spot, then sat determinedly as if saying, "This is it," Conner secretly suspected she was pulling Gracie's leg in order to gain extra treats. He was sure of it when she hit on one of Elway's spots.

Then she ignored the other two of Elway's marks, which was interesting. She went forward ten more feet, and signaled another find. After two more hits, Conner had to admit, Sierra was one smart dog.

She was either hitting on spots the other two dogs missed, or she was playing them all for fools. After three more hits he didn't have a choice, it was time to notify the big brass, let them decide.

Lt. Jansen was as skeptical as Conner. "Are you sure those dogs know what they're doing?"

Might as well be honest. "No, sir, I'm not, but the handlers are confident." He glanced at Haskel, who'd staked Tag and Elway in a shady spot and given them water. He was busy checking their paws for thorns or cuts.

"It'll take Crime Scene an hour to get there and set up. This time of year, the sun'll be down by then. I'll send a squad car to guard the field tonight and tell the techs to start first thing in the morning. You realize we'll be the laughing stock of the department if that field's empty."

"I know, sir. But I kind of hope the dogs are wrong." The alternative was too grim to contemplate.

Counting the two, no, make that three, bodies they'd found yesterday and the one from two weeks ago in the abandoned apartment building, if someone was buried under each colored marker, twelve dead bodies were waiting to be identified.

If Sierra was as capable as Haskel believed, they were chasing a monster.

Noah took off his knee-high boots and slipped on his tennis shoes. The top edge of the right boot had rubbed a raw spot on his calf. He wanted nothing more than to get home and hug Sweet Pea but it didn't seem right to send Gracie and her crew off without showing his appreciation.

They'd done a lot to help the department and all on their own dime. "It's been a long, hard day. Let me buy y'all some dinner."

Gracie picked sticker burrs from the leg of her jeans. "Thanks, but we'll have to pass. The dogs are still jittery and I don't want to leave them alone. I've booked a pet friendly hotel. Tag and Elway will stay with me and Haskel gets Sierra. After we give them all a bath, I'll order us a pizza."

Send them off to work some more and eat a pizza in their motel room? No way. "I have a better idea. Follow me."

Conner looked a little jittery himself and begged off, saying Jeannie needed him. Noah didn't blame him. Having someone soft and warm to go home to would do a lot to erase the horrors of this day—even if that someone did mess her diaper and throw up on your shoulder.

Noah drove to the nearest Five Guys Hamburgers and Gracie followed in her decrepit van. The dogs were dirty and disheveled—Noah, Gracie, and Haskel weren't much better—so they sat on the outside patio and let a gentle breeze cool them. The setting sun painted the clouds a rosy-pink.

At first the other diners avoided them until a little girl tugged on Gracie's sleeve and asked if she could pet her dog.

Gracie's face softened for the first time since Noah met her. Soon, all three dogs had been loved on and exclaimed over.

Gracie never mentioned what the dogs had been doing all day, but explained what she and Haskel had been training them for. After that, strangers came up to shake their hands and thank them for their work.

Noah bought Gracie and Haskel a hamburger, fries, and a milkshake. He also bought a hamburger, plain and dry, for each dog, although Gracie nixed the idea of fries.

The interlude was exactly what they all needed. A soft autumn evening, the sound of children laughing, the aroma of meat on the grill, and the mouthwatering taste of hamburgers done just right.

Noah took a last pull on his milkshake and emptied it with a loud *slurp*. They all laughed and pushed back from the table. Time to call it a night.

Haskel loaded the dogs into the van while Gracie stopped to shake Noah's hand. "We'll head out first thing in the morning. It's a long trip because I won't drive more than two hours without letting the dogs out to stretch their legs. I'm not looking forward to it, but I expect you to call me and let me know what you find. I have to mark it on their training sheets."

She dropped her head for a moment, then looked at him with sad eyes. "Good luck to you. Catch the bastard."

Yeah, you can bet I'll give it my best.

Noah got home before nine, played with Sweet Pea, and watched the last quarter of a football game. Today was bad, but tomorrow would be ten times worse.

That's when they'd open the graves and exhume the bodies.

Conner had never been so glad to get home in his life. It

wasn't the work they had done today. It was the knowledge of what tomorrow would bring. It felt like his soul had sprung a leak.

Deflated.

Caused him to lose his faith in humanity.

Jeannie met him at the door with a smile. He gave her a quick peck on the cheek, but stepped back when she tried to hug him. He wasn't ready yet. He needed time to transition between his day's work and his home. "I have to grab a shower before I can touch anyone."

Whether it was the smell or the look in his eye, Jeannie didn't argue. After four years of marriage, she understood him. How had he ever gotten so lucky?

"Did you eat supper?"

"Couldn't."

"Let me warm a plate for you. Betsy and I have eaten, but we'll keep you company."

Fifteen minutes later, he was clean, wearing fresh clothes, and hungry. A new man, ready to rejoin his family. The aroma of Jeannie's meatloaf drifted through the house and he followed his nose to the kitchen.

Betsy was swaddled in a cream knit blanket, sucking contentedly on her pacifier, swaying back and forth in her wind-up swing. Biding her time before her evening meltdown or giving him a much needed break from colic-filled nights?

Jeannie sipped on a glass of tea. She had on jeans and a T-shirt. Her hair was in a ponytail. And she was the most beautiful thing he'd ever seen.

His place at the table was set with a plate of meatloaf, roasted potatoes, and fresh, steamed broccoli such a bright green it didn't seem real. He felt like he was walking into a Norman Rockwell painting.

Only this was live and all his.

If you looked close enough, in a far corner of old maps, was the notation, *Here be Dragons.* Tonight, he wasn't looking any farther.

Whatever happened tomorrow was for tomorrow. It already was what it was and no amount of worrying on his part could change it.

For now, he planned to kiss his baby, make love to his wife, and shut out the rest of the world.

CHAPTER SIX

THE SKY WAS a clear blue, broken only by a few white, cotton candy clouds. The temperature hovered at sixty-eight, but was expected to inch up ten degrees before the day was over. All in all, a perfect autumn day.

And that wasn't how it should be.

Right or wrong, a day like this deserved gray clouds and a biting wind.

Noah hoped like hell Sierra and Elway were wrong. Four dead women were more than he wanted to face. Twelve was inconceivable.

He waited on the edge of the field while the forensic team worked on uncovering the first grave. They picked the one both dogs hit on as the most likely.

Conner stood next to him in a show of solidarity. Lt. Jansen paced on the other side.

The Chief of Detectives had sent an aide to let him know the minute the first body was discovered. He'd show up then and not a minute sooner.

Wouldn't do for him to be spotted at the site of a disaster. And in this case—after arranging for Forensics, and Crime Scene, and the M.E., and morgue vans—not finding a body would qualify as a disaster.

Enough bodies and the Chief of Police would show up.

No bodies, he, Conner, and Jansen might as well use the graves for their careers. The only thing worse would be not finding the killer.

Why hadn't he handed this whole mess off to Lefty Bob? Or ignored that nagging feeling the vacant lot was a killing field?

Because he'd made a vow to himself, to Betsy, to the city of Houston, to every person whose life was snatched away at another's hands. He would be their voice. He would never quit.

Benny Schroeder, the Bozo look-a-like Crime Scene tech, removed the first layer of dirt. And then a second.

How deep were the graves? Hard to judge by the two they had already found—not after last week's torrential rains. And exactly where were they located?

Did the dogs sit directly on top? What if Benny dug two feet to the left or right?

If they found anything, Mandy from the County Forensic Laboratory would photograph it from every angle. Nothing got by her. Four years in the army and a degree in Criminal Justice meant they didn't have to worry about some defense attorney claiming the evidence had been manipulated.

If they found anything.

His stomach felt like a volcano in an elementary school science project. Ready to erupt and overflow at any moment. He couldn't just stand there. He had to do something.

He yanked out his cell phone and keyed in a number.

"Who are you calling?" Conner leaned close and kept his voice low.

"Earl. He can start tracing the ownership of this field and the vacant apartment building." Since a blow to the head last spring grave Earl Sparks a concussion, he'd been working desk duty, relieving Noah and Conner and the other detectives the hassle of paperwork.

"He's already on it. I sent him a text this morning."

Was it possible to be both thankful for such an efficient partner and aggravated that he was almost *too* efficient at the same time?

Apparently, yes.

Benny cleared off another layer of dirt and leaned forward, peering into the deepening hole.

The inside of Noah's chest had turned into a teeming fire ant mound with the little buggers crawling every direction and stinging at will. He needed to know if the one older skeleton was a fluke or were others from the past waiting to be discovered.

He fought the urge to push Benny aside and start digging himself. But it wasn't easy. His hands clenched and unclenched. He tried to swallow but his mouth was too dry.

So far, the news media hadn't descended on them. That wouldn't last.

Benny dug a little deeper. He studied the grave and motioned Dr. Mackie closer. Doc M kneeled down, his white hair waving in the breeze. He took the trowel from his assistant and brushed at the dirt.

Mandy lifted her camera and stepped closer. Her brown hair fell forward as she leaned in.

Noah's chest ached from holding his breath.

Minutes seemed like eons until the doc glanced his direction and nodded.

He trudged through the ditch and across the field, Conner beside him. Jansen followed two steps behind. By the time they reached the grave, Doc M had removed two more shovelfuls.

Despite the sunlight, the bottom of the hole was dark. Benny flicked on his flashlight and pointed the beam toward a partially uncovered head.

Only a quarter of the face showed. The rest was planted downward, into the dirt. One ear was visible and Noah counted three holes in the lobe, but no earrings. Dark hair streamed past a pale white shoulder.

Fuck. The one time he honestly didn't want to be right.

He stared back toward the street where he'd been standing, mostly because he hated to invade the young woman's privacy any more than necessary. What he saw scared him more than anything he'd yet encountered.

The Chief's aide was on the phone.

This place was about to become a zoo.

An oppressive weight hung over Conner like a wet wool blanket. Drawing air into his lungs felt like breathing hot soup.

He should have transferred to Internal Affairs when he had the chance. He first thought of it the day after Betsy was born when he realized how caught up he'd become in the Beneficial Products case.

He'd considered the possibility of a transfer off and on during his Family Leave time, but put off making a decision. Jeannie kept saying it was up to him. She'd back him either way.

Noah returned to the job three days before him and called after his first day back at work. The excitement in his voice was contagious.

Conner loved Homicide. The cases could be complex and mentally taxing. Even the easy ones were intriguing.

Noah had taught him how to read people and evidence. They often came at a problem from different directions but reached the same conclusions. In the process, they'd become best friends.

When Noah's wife died, his heart ached for his partner. The last year had been tough on both of them, but Noah had come through and was stronger at last.

That had been his opportunity to get out. Take a job that was less involved, less stressful.

A quick prayer for the woman half-buried in front of him was all he could manage. He glanced around the field at the red, yellow, and blue poles. Too many bodies. He didn't have the strength to pray over each grave.

Tonight, when he went to bed, no matter how late, he'd pray for each of their souls. Pray that they found eternal rest. That their loved ones found peace. That their killer was brought to justice.

He'd also pray for himself. That he kept a clear head and didn't let his emotions get in the way. Something in him had changed the day he shot Aldo Rogers. Sure, it was a clean shooting. The man had already abducted a woman with nefarious intent, bashed Earl Sparks over the head, shot a young cop, and was aiming at Noah.

It was the only thing he could do. He had to shoot. Still, he'd taken a life. He never wanted to do that again.

He should have transferred when he could, but he hadn't, and now he'd missed his chance. This case was too big.

He was stuck.

So far, Noah had watched as Benny uncovered two recent bodies and one skeleton. The only dry holes were the two where Elway couldn't make up his mind and one spot where Sierra had hit on both the head and the foot of the same body. That meant ten dead women instead of eleven. Plus one left in the apartment building.

Like that made a difference.

All three bodies had been placed on gurneys where Doc M could give them a cursory examination. A fresh tech had taken over the digging, and Benny was resting in the M.E.'s van.

The stench of decomposition increased with each new discovery.

Noah pulled three cigars from his pocket, gave one to Conner and one to Jansen and lit one for himself. The Chief of Detectives was standing well back with a blob of Vicks under his nose. Amateur. Gordon Hines had only been with the department a few months, coming from a small town in Indiana. What could you expect?

Cigars worked much better. By the time you'd smoked one to the nub, you couldn't smell a thing.

It was almost noon and the temperature was inching up. Every grave had to be examined thoroughly for trace evidence. At this rate, they wouldn't finish tonight.

The Chief of Ds edged closer, getting weeds and sticker burrs on his expensive suit. "I've called Galveston for help. Luckily, their citizens are enjoying the autumn weather and not killing each other today. They're sending a Crime Scene crew and an ambulance."

Doc M glanced at Hines. "Good. I don't have room to store this many bodies."

"I've made another decision you may not like, but the Chief made a suggestion I think is right." Hines watched Jansen and Noah as if expecting a fight. "I've called the FBI for assistance."

What the fuck? That asshole only stayed long enough to be seen on TV. He doesn't have any idea what's best.

Hines was right. Noah didn't like it. But he understood. "I don't mind working with the Feebies, but other than profiling, I don't know how much they can do. They don't have the manpower for boots-on-the-ground type work."

"You're correct about that. They had a bombing in Seattle and a terrorist cell in New York, but one of their local agents says he can help organize and enter information into national data bases."

Conner nodded. "Tell him we appreciate that. We can use all the help we can get." That was the first thing he'd said in the last hour.

Noah didn't argue. The Feds were good at some things and if calling them in got the paperwork off his back, great.

Ten minutes later, a shiny black Chevy SUV with government plates wove its way past the news vans and their obstacle course of microphones and antennas. After a brief stop at the police barricade, the SUV drove through and parked behind Lola. The driver was in his early forties, tall, slender, with good hair and a charcoal gray suit. His shoes were as highly polished as his car.

The guy might as well have *FBI* emblazoned on his chest.

Noah glanced from the SUV to Lola and back. How did they get those black beauties to gleam that way? Did the government have access to a brand of automobile polish they designated top secret?

Would he have to sign a confidentially agreement to learn the name? Because joining the Feebies was out of the question.

The man shook hands with Jansen, Conner, and the Chief of Ds before heading for Noah.

"Special Agent Lincoln Montgomery. You must be Detective Daugherty."

How did he know that? Did the FBI have a dossier on him? He sucked in a lungful of air. *Don't be paranoid. The Chief probably told him.*

Noah crossed his arms over his chest, trying to hold back the resentment that filled his belly. What brought that on? Was it the shiny car? The good hair? The two last names?

Maybe. A little. But mainly the fact that Montgomery had the power of the government behind him if he wanted to swoop in and grab the case for himself. Sure, he needed an invitation, but that was easy enough to finagle with the right connections.

"That's right. Noah Daugherty. Lead Detective." There. It was out in the open. Let him argue with that.

Montgomery didn't bat an eye. "Excellent. I wanted to let you know—"

That you're taking over.

"—that I'm here to help in any way I can."

No. What?

"I've already spoken to your boss—Hines, isn't it?—and told

him I'll set up a phone line. You're going to start getting calls about missing girls as soon as this hits the evening news. I can also organize any fingerprints or DNA and list them on CODIS and IAFIS. Anything else you want, just tell me. I'll do my best to take care of it for you."

Fuck. This guy was better than having two Earls. Plus, the case was still his.

The question was; did he really want it?

Noah made it home at nine. Fifteen hours after he left.

For once, Sweet Pea didn't want anything to do with him. Not attention, not a walk, not food or a treat.

Between the stench that hung to his clothing and the bad attitude he could feel himself projecting, he didn't blame the little dog.

He'd stopped at a drive-thru for some chicken fried rice, but he set it on the counter and headed for the shower. The hot water pouring over his head helped wash the day away. When he came out, Sweet Pea was ready for her dinner and a game of tug.

His own dinner was cold by the time he got around to it, but he ate it without tasting a thing.

By ten thirty, he and Sweet Pea were curled up in bed. He'd watched enough of the news to realize Lincoln Montgomery was a master bullshitter. He sidestepped every question like an intricate tango, giving answers but no real information.

He was working with the HPD in an advisory capacity only.

This was an extremely complex case. Don't expect any quick answers.

It could be months before the victims were identified, if ever.

The HPD was working diligently to find the monster who committed these heinous acts.

The resources of the FBI were at the disposal of the investigating detectives.

It might be some time before they knew if these cases were connected.

Everyone should be patient and let HPD do its work.

Wow, if he'd told the news media to wait for answers, they'd have boiled him alive, yet they loved Montgomery and ate up every word he said.

Noah didn't care. It got the vultures off his back for a while, anyway. Only one thing worried him. In one shot, he saw an old red Sentra, faded to pink, parked among the news vans. Its owner stood apart from the Botoxed, fake-tanned, hair-sprayed news lightweights.

R. J. Perry from the *Houston Chronicle*. Gray Don King hair and more wrinkles than a shirt left in the dryer overnight. He wouldn't take hot air for an answer. He'd keep after the story when everyone else had moved on to the latest Hollywood divorce.

Noah set him on the trail of a good story once, then stepped back and let the veteran newsman do his work. In return, Perry kept his name out of the paper. That didn't mean they were friends. Or that he trusted the man.

If Perry thought that one encounter entitled him to special treatment, he was dead wrong.

Noah shifted restlessly, waking Sweet Pea. Thoughts of that damn dogged reporter pricked at his conscious. Perry might be a pain in the ass, but he never quit until he had his answers.

Could Noah say the same for himself? Had he once let go of a case without putting up enough of a fight?

Was it too late now to make it right?

God knows, he'd carried the weight of it for the last ten years.

CHAPTER SEVEN

NOAH HAD WORKED with Doc M often enough to know he'd be at the morgue early, no matter how late he worked the night before.

At 7:00 a.m., the office wouldn't be open yet, and the front door locked tight. He drove Lola around back to a door he knew the M.E. used. The sight of Doc's Carroll Shelby Cobra parked near the inconspicuous entry made Noah smile.

How could someone who dealt in death every day be a daredevil in his personal life?

The cherry-red car with the white racing stripe screamed speed. The guy was going to end up on his own table one of these days, but damn, he'd have fun until then.

One thing didn't make Noah smile. Parked next to the Cobra was a canary yellow VW bug he'd noticed at the crime scene which probably belonged to Doc's lab tech. Next to that was the now not-so-shiny black SUV with government plates.

Damn. How early did a guy have to get up to beat that Feebie into the office?

Inside, Montgomery stood with his back to the door. He wore a disposable paper lab coat over wrinkled slacks and held a clipboard in one hand. When he turned, Noah spotted a heavy beard-shadow.

The Fed hadn't beaten him into the office. He'd been here all night.

Doc M glanced up. His bloodshot eyes had bags big enough to store a week's worth of laundry. "Ah, Detective. Perfect timing. We were wrapping up here. Lincoln has agreed to type up his notes and send them to you. Isn't that right?"

Lincoln? Were they BFFs now?

The agent tapped his pen on the clipboard. "Absolutely, Milo. I'll try to get these over to Noah's office in the next hour or so."

What the fuck? Milo? He'd worked with the doc for several years now and he didn't even know the man *had* a first name.

Montgomery immediately started listing the salient points. "As a quick recap, we found a total of eleven bodies in the vacant field plus one in the empty building. Six are recent and six have been in the ground perhaps as long as ten years, although it could take months to narrow that down. Using visual examination of the fresher bodies and bone structure for the older ones, we know one woman was of Asian descent and three were black. Of the eight that are left, we know one was Hispanic and two were white. That leaves five unknown."

Yeah, yeah. I can do the math. Get on with it.

"Bone structure alone can't distinguish between white and Hispanic."

Another fact I already knew.

"But we believe at least two of those were white due to hair color. I've managed what I consider a fairly accurate estimate of each woman's age, height, weight, and any distinguishing marks still visible. I've assigned an approximate date of death to the fresher bodies. They range from one year to one month."

"He's killing one every other month." Now they were getting somewhere. A pattern always helped.

Doc M peeled off his gloves and nodded to his assistant to take away the body he'd just finished. "Not necessarily. A couple of the dates were close together and there were large gaps between others."

There went his first solid lead. "Is there anything you can tell me that might help?"

The doc's tired eyes lit up in anger. "My job is to give you facts. Your job is to interpret them."

Noah forced out a calming breath. The doc was exhausted or he wouldn't have snapped that way.

"If I may," Lincoln Montgomery spoke up. "All of the women were young, between seventeen and twenty-six, and of slight stature."

Less weight to lug across a vacant field in the dead of night.

"They were all manually strangled with great force."

An indication all were killed by the same hand, but not proof.

"Impossible to tell on the earlier victims, but the later ones show signs of forced sexual intercourse. However, no hair, semen, or trace evidence can be found."

Like Jansen said, lack of evidence is not evidence.

"Most had broken wrists or displayed signs of restraints."

Most, but not all.

"They all had shoulder length or longer hair."

Easier to grab hold of. Still nothing definitive he could take to the chief.

"None had food in their stomachs."

Whoa. There was something he could latch onto. Was the guy keeping them alive for at least a day?

"I've got something for you, Doc." Noah laid a folder on the counter. He'd been carrying it around since the first body was uncovered, but it had weighed on his mind much longer than that. "The dental records of a young female who went missing ten years ago."

Doc looked surprised, and not much caught the old goat unaware. "You've already been into the office?"

"No, this is a copy. I had it at home." He held his breath, waiting, but Doc didn't ask any questions.

Montgomery glanced up from his clipboard. "Leave that here and once we've made impressions and given them time to set, I'll send them off to a forensic dentist. Don't expect results anytime soon."

The delay would be hell for those sitting at home waiting, hoping.

He chose to go with his first lie of the day. "I understand. After all these years, what difference does a few more days make?"

Traffic between the morgue on OST and headquarters downtown on Travis Street was still morning rush-hour heavy. Noah considered cursing at the idiots who blocked intersections, causing gridlock, but really, what was the use?

It would raise his blood pressure, but fail to get him to work any quicker.

He turned up the radio, ready to sing along, when Paige Reimer's new single came on. For a moment, he pictured her naked, laughing and eating his share of the jelly beans. Then he pictured Conner's face as he stood over her stalker's dead body. The man she'd failed to mention had sent her threatening letters until it was too late.

Much as he missed Betsy, he'd rather be alone than with someone he couldn't trust.

Conner was already at his desk when he reached the squad room. How early did he have to come in to beat that guy?

"How was the morgue this bright and shiny morning?" Conner slid a cardboard cup of Starbucks finest his direction.

Was that a coincidence or had his partner learned his secret? He never ate or drank anything before a trip to the morgue. Throw up one time and the doc never let you forget it.

Hell, it was more than that, but that was a good enough reason.

"Doc M and our friendly, neighborhood Fed stayed up all night organizing, comparing, assigning numbers to the victims. Montgomery promised to email me the results within the hour. So far, the information is sketchy. Only what he could learn with a quick glance. Most of what they found, we already knew. They fall into two time periods. Ten years ago and within the last year. The doc promised to work over the weekend and have more detailed information for us by early next week."

Maybe the file I gave him will help. Maybe it won't. Either way, no need to mention it. That would only cause questions he didn't want to answer.

"Anything to show they were done by the same perp?" Conner had his memo pad out, ready to take notes.

Yep, if he'd told his partner about the file, it would be there in writing for anyone to read. He ticked off items on his fingers. "They were all manually strangled, young, slight build, long hair, but different ethnicities. Some in each group showed signs of sexual assault and the use of some type of restraint."

Conner sucked on his upper lip and put on what Noah called his *thinking face*. "Nothing to prove or disprove they're related."

Wait till he heard the next item. "Only enough left of the most recent ones to know for sure, but they had empty stomachs."

Sparks of interest showed in Conner's eyes. He knew that would get his partner's attention. "Hard to keep someone around even for a couple of hours in a suburban neighborhood. He liked that area near the ship channel for disposal. Maybe he likes it for other reasons, also. Did we ever find out who owned that land?"

They both twisted their heads toward the other side of the aisle and yelled in unison. "Earl?"

A smooth, mellow voice floated from behind them. "Back here, Hoss. You don't have to yell. What do you need now?"

Noah swung his chair around. That damn Earl walked on cat's feet. He could sneak up on you anytime. "You ever figure out who owned that lot where the bodies were found?"

"Yes and no. A corporation that's owned by another corporation that sold part of it to a different corporation. Check your email. It's in there."

Conner scrolled down his messages and until he found the right one and sent it to the printer. Meanwhile, Noah kept up the questions, trying to get a foothold, find a starting place on the case.

"And the abandoned apartment building?"

"Harris County. Foreclosed on by a bank that let it go for

back taxes."

He knew better than to expect the perp would actually own the land he used as a killing field. But that didn't mean he hadn't held out hope. "Any names match up on the two properties?"

"No names at all. Not a human to be found. Only corporations. Like three octopi in a deep sea *ménage a trois.* An untraceable tangle of tentacles. "

Oh lord. That blow to the noggin had turned level-headed Earl into a poet.

"Who writes the checks? Pays the taxes?" At least Conner hadn't gone goofy on him. Still down to earth.

"Well, no one on the apartment building, that's why the county inherited it. A property management company for the empty lot."

Noah pulled a quarter from his pocket. "Flip to see who drives out to the management company and who stays here and works the computer?"

Conner retrieved the print-out with the company name and address. "You've already been to the morgue. I'll visit," he glanced at the paper in his hand, "Trusty Property Management, Inc. Although any business with *Trusty* in its name sends my Spidey senses tingling."

"Somewhat better than *Honest,* but worse than *Mother's.*" Noah put his feet up on his desk. If Conner wanted to face an uncooperative business owner, he was welcome to it.

Earl parked a hip on Conner's desk. "Yep, never stop at anyplace called *Mom's* or *Mother's* or *Aunt Anybody's.* Got so sick at one I was throwing up meals I hadn't eaten yet. They all ought to be named *Tricky's* or *Shifty's.* Give us a little truth in advertising."

Noah bit back a laugh. *When had Earl gotten so cynical?* "What if it's named after some guy: Bob or Mel or Dickie?"

"Then you can put money there's no one by that name even eating in the joint."

This time he didn't even try to hold back his chuckle. Why should he? When was the last time he'd had a full-out belly laugh?

That's what was wrong with him these days. He was too uptight, humorless. A smile or a joke wasn't a sign you didn't take a case seriously. It meant you were dealing with death and devastation the best way you knew how.

And this case would take every ounce of coping skills he'd learned in twelve years on the force.

Conner looked over Earl's head and rolled his eyes Noah's direction. "You guys can discuss naming rights the rest of the day. I'm going to see if Mr. Trusty, Inc. will untangle your octopus for me. Other than this, there's not a thing we can do until Doc M sends us some DNA or fingerprint analysis or forensics finds us some type of clue we can work with. Once we have that, we won't have time to eat, sleep, or pick our nose until this thing is solved. It's already Friday. I suggest we take the weekend off. Hit the ground running on Monday. What do you say?"

Noah's backbone stiffened at the idea of relaxing while some creep was out there killing women. What if the scumbag worked during the week and cruised around on weekends looking for his next victim while he sat home watching a football game? What if he picked tomorrow to strike again?

They didn't know.

That's right. They didn't. Conner had a point. They could sit in the office all day Saturday and Sunday, and what good would it do them? They had nowhere to look and nothing constructive to do. Not until Crime Scene or the doc gave them some data to analyze.

Meanwhile, he could spend a couple of hours on the computer and see what he could dig up on Tom Meyers' past cases.

Then he could put the white-haired lawyer's problems out of his mind and concentrate on capturing the guy running around town strangling young women.

He tipped his head toward his partner. "I say you're right. Spend the weekend with Jeannie and Betsy. Forget this case for a couple of days. Until then, I'll call the county. Find out which bank foreclosed on the apartment. You work on the vacant lot and Earl's dancing octopi. If the management company is uncooperative, turn 'em into sushi."

CHAPTER EIGHT

THE SLIGHT GLIMPSE he'd caught of the old Noah put Conner in a better mood than he should have been considering where he was going. What was the likelihood he'd even find this company, much less they'd be cooperative?

Earl had dug up an address but couldn't come up with a phone number. Siri could find the street, but the block number confused her. This was going to be a fun day.

He took his own car instead of checking one out at the motor pool. In addition to a working air conditioner, his smelled better—part baby power, part upholstery shampoo. Betsy had thrown up on the back seat last week.

Investigating homicides with a car seat in the back felt wrong, but those things were too hard to get in and out to bother removing it.

He took the Gulf Freeway toward Galveston until Siri instructed him to follow a back road several miles past Pearland. The farther he drove, the less confident he felt about finding a professional management company hidden among welding shops, boat storage facilities, and the occasional field of cattle.

His heart gave an extra skip and jump at the sight of the field. Would he ever be able to pass an expanse of open land without wondering what lay hidden a few feet below the soil?

The road narrowed and a one-car bridge crossed a stream the size of his driveway with barely enough water to wet his ankles. The street numbers, which had been getting bigger, now grew smaller and East appeared before the name.

Now what?

Siri didn't say anything about turning around so he continued for another three miles when the street numbers jumped a thousand, skipping the number he was looking for.

He stopped in the middle of the road and looked around. On the left, behind a gas station he might need to use if he planned to drive much longer, a dirt road wound behind a patch of pecan trees.

Siri was unhelpfully silent.

The station owner shot him a look that would burn through steel when he made a big U-turn around the gas pumps without stopping to buy anything. Conner plastered on a don't-mind-me-I'm-just-lost smile and waved to the man before easing onto the dirt road.

Maybe he'd stop on the way back and buy ten gallons of gas and a bag of pig skins. He hadn't had any of those since Jeannie got pregnant. She claimed the smell made her nauseous.

Behind the grove of trees, a two-story frame house with a sagging veranda sat half a mile off the road. A hand-lettered sign in front read: Bed and Breakfast, Notary, Pecans, Fresh eggs.

The pecans were the only thing Conner considered a viable

option from the dilapidated building.

He stepped out of the car in time to be assaulted by an attack rooster.

The fowl squawked and pecked at his shin. He tried hopping from one foot to the other, but the feathery beast was too fast for him, ripping his pants and drawing blood.

"You leave George Clooney alone." The screen door slammed and a heavy-set woman in shorts and a tank top shook her finger at him. Smoke from the cigarette dangling between her lips obscured her face. "Don't you even think about kicking him. He'll take your foot off."

Well, he might have *thought* about it, but he wouldn't have done it. His Glock bumped against his hip as he danced away from the obnoxious fowl. However, a bullet though that tiny head and they could all have dinner and live happily ever after.

Conner made it up the steps with his foot intact, but not his pride.

"I'm looking for Trusty Property Management, Inc." Earl was right. This place should be named *Use-At-Your-Own-Risk*.

The middle-aged woman smoothed down her wrinkled tank top, flipped her half-smoked cigarette off the porch, and stood two inches taller. "That's me. Can I hep ya?"

Conner flashed his gold badge and his best smile. "I'd like to ask you a few questions about one of your clients."

The woman's face fell when she realized he didn't represent a fresh source of income. She swung around and disappeared inside.

George Clooney gave a warning screech and Conner rushed after her.

The inside of the house was dark and musty. It smelled of

last night's liver and onions. She turned to face him. Her gray hair hung past her waist and was held off her face with a clip painted to look like a chicken.

In fact, everything in the kitchen looked like a chicken or a rooster or baby chicks or Easter eggs.

His Aunt Jessie had a thing for cows—when he spent the night with his cousins, the milk for their breakfast cereal came from a cow-shaped pitcher—but nothing like this explosion of chicken-themed knick-knacks and decorations.

If he spent any time in this room, he might start to crow.

Chicken-lady pulled out a kitchen chair and plopped down. "Don't know that I can give you any information without a warrant. You got one of them things?"

"No, Ma'am. But I'm not looking for banking information, just a name."

"I'd have to think about that. You need any eggs?"

"Thanks, but I'm going to be in my car all day. They'd spoil."

"No, they wouldn't. These is fresh today. They'll last you good. Not like them store bought ones. They's old when you buy 'em."

"In that case, I could use a dozen. When I finish with my questions." He'd had more direct bribe demands, but not often.

He fished the slip of paper Earl have given him out of his pocket and set it in front of her. "Who owns this property? Where does the money come from to pay the taxes?"

The dry rot, the dust, last night's onions, the exasperation, the feeling of being watched by hundreds of chickens, all combined to churn in Conner's stomach. He wanted out of this place but Noah would never let him live it down if he left without the information.

Besides, he needed to take a mental note of everything about this encounter. Since Jeannie stopped working, her first question every evening was, "Did anything interesting happen today?"

This definitely qualified as interesting.

The woman pulled an old-fashioned ledger off a shelf. "Only some corporation. Every few years I get a money order to cover expenses."

"Who signs it?"

Heaving out an exaggerated sigh, she pushed back from the table and disappeared into another room. When she returned, she held a tattered file folder. "See for yourself."

The folder held a letter with a computer-generated letterhead saying "Medina Properties," and a date ten years earlier along with photo copies of two money orders, each covering five years' worth of expenses.

"What does managing this property consist of?"

"Anytime my husband and I have to go into downtown Houston, we drive by and make sure the fence isn't down and nobody's squatting on the land."

"How often is that?"

"Two, three times a year."

So she hadn't been there the last few days. Or recognized the lot from the news footage. Odds were, she shouldn't count on another year's payment. No point in him being the bearer of bad news. He might have more questions for her.

He leaned forward and used his phone to take photos of the papers while she scrutinized his every move. Probably worried he'd steal something. Like the hen and rooster salt and peppers shakers.

"You need me to notarize that?" Her cigarette breath was

inches from his ear.

Notarize what? His phone?

He flipped his memo pad to a fresh page. "Put down your name, your company name and your contact information."

The tip of her tongue appeared between her teeth as she concentrated on listing everything he asked. Then she pulled out her notary seal, signed the page, and stamped it.

Conner slapped down two fives—one for the eggs and one for the unnecessary notary seal—grabbed his phone, the paper, the eggs, and ran before George Clooney had time to attack.

CHAPTER NINE

EVERY FIBER OF his being screamed throw *something, break something. smash something...*

He grabbed the remote off the coffee table and reared back, ready to hurl it through the TV. He could almost hear the satisfying crash as the screen exploded.

But the reason he could still hear the glass shatter was because that's exactly what he'd done two weeks ago. And it hadn't made him feel any better.

Well, maybe. For a minute or two. Until he realized he'd have to buy a new TV.

He didn't mind buying yet another one, but he didn't want to deal with that nosy service man-installer and his incessant questions about what happened.

In order to control himself, he'd had to leave the room. The only way to keep from bashing his fist into the man's face and saying, *That's what happened to the TV. Any more questions?*

Plenty of other stores sold TVs. He could buy one there, but that didn't solve the problem of who the cable provider might send if he had as much trouble as he had with the last one.

He could kick something, but he was barefooted and unless it was a pillow—he'd tried that before, completely unsatisfying—he might break a toe.

Or, like the year he was ten, three toes and two bones in his foot. Plus a couple of ribs and an arm of another kid. (That would teach the maid to allow her kid to play with his toys when she thought he was at school.)

Once that happened, every step, every movement, for six weeks would be a reminder of the disgust in his father's eyes at his lack of self-control. A reminder of his stepmother crying, not for him, but in embarrassment at what the neighbor's might think.

A reminder of his trip to see a physiologist who diagnosed him as a sociopath. He was marched home double-time before the appointment was over. The social stigma of that pronouncement more than his stepmother would allow.

He never saw that doctor again, but several years later he Googled the symptoms. At first, he worried the doc might have been right.

Not restricted by normal social mores.

Impervious to feelings of shame or guilt.

A determination to prevail no matter the cost.

Invent outrageous lies.

Then he came upon two additional symptoms and realized with relief they didn't describe him.

Incapable of love. He had loved his mother. Or probably would have if she'd lived long enough.

Never apologize. As a kid, he'd had many apologizes beaten out of him.

Instead, the article described someone he knew all too well. His father.

The second time he got into serious trouble, at age fourteen, he was sent to a different doctor—a con artist in his opinion—who claimed his only problem was learning to deal with anger issues. A situation common in active, highly intelligent early-teen males.

The faux-doctor then prescribed more love and attention at home, and twice weekly visits to his office all summer for group therapy. He didn't mind the group therapy—twelve boys his age sitting in a circle lying about their feelings.

Only two kids actually tried to improve themselves. The rest, like him, were marking time until they could escape.

One boy kept his hands in his pockets during every session, enabling him to masturbate through the entire hour. He would have been disgusted if he wasn't impressed with the kid's *chutzpa*.

Instead, he waited, planning his next adventure, until his summer sentence was served.

The additional attention was something else. His father and stepmother watched over him like drill sergeants in case he got into any more mischief. What a joke.

All he had to do was outlast them and they soon lost interest.

After a week, his stepmother reverted to walking past while he watched TV and tousling his hair as if in affection when she knew how much he hated disarray. His father would follow her into the room five minutes later and yell at him for looking slovenly.

But even today, long after his father's death, the old man

still controlled the purse strings via a complicated trust that evaporated if he got into serious trouble. At least until his stepmother died. The witch.

He could make it without the money if he scrimped, but he'd have to give up his hobby. And that wasn't happening.

Sure, he'd managed to save a little over the years. Put it aside for a rainy day.

He just hadn't anticipated a *deluge*.

None of that helped him now. Now was when he needed to blow off steam.

He hurled his half-empty glass into the fireplace where it smashed into a hundred tiny shards. The impact was so satisfying he got another glass and flung it in to join its companion.

The idea of gathering every glass in the cupboard and continuing his tirade crossed his mind, but drinking high-dollar single malt from a plastic tumbler was a waste.

Besides, he already felt better.

He tossed a throw rug in front of the fireplace to cover any errant shards of glass and the smell of wasted scotch. Order was restored in his world.

Isabelle would come tomorrow. She could clean it up. He certainly paid her enough to keep her mouth shut. And lucky for her, she was old and fat and ugly. Not the least bit tempting.

He could put the time to good use scouting vacant fields. Because he didn't plan to move—again.

Hell, he'd always considered preparation part of the game, and searching for the ideal playground was almost as much fun as filling it.

That day he'd known he wasn't set up for another sacrifice, but what was a man to do when a delectable raven-haired princess pranced her tight little ass in front of him seductively?

Wait?

Hell no.

Ask her to come back next week?

Ha!

Follow his father's famous words of advice? *When you first see an opportunity, act. Don't delay.*

Absolutely.

And he didn't regret it for an instant.

Rush hour traffic had been a nightmare—a stalled pickup on I-45 and cars backed up for a mile or more. Noah had changed into shorts the moment he got home. Now he sat with his feet propped up on his desk and Sweet Pea snuggled in his lap. At the slightest movement, the dog looked up to see if there was any chance of another Cheetos nub, but she'd had her limit. Noah wasn't willing to clean bright orange diarrhea off the kitchen floor. And a trip to the emergency room vet was out of the question. That man still suspected Noah had tried to kill the little Yorkie last winter.

Phone to his ear, he leaned back in the Henry Miller chair Betsy had given him for a housewarming gift when they moved in eighteen months ago. "What did you get from the property management company?" he asked Conner.

"More than likely, bird flu, but I washed my hands so I should be safe."

What the hell was his partner talking about?

"The management company is a joke. They might drive past the property once a year but never get out of the car. The taxes are paid through a shell corporation using money orders."

He'd suspected that much. "Can you trace the money orders?"

"I doubt it. There were only two, sent five years apart and from opposite ends of the state. I have a feeling they were either purchased with cash or from a store that's no longer in business."

"I didn't do much better." That slipped out without thinking, but so what? For several years, he and Conner had an easy, uncomplicated partnership, not to mention friendship.

This last year had been different, difficult. He sometimes suspected that Conner was watching him. Waiting for him to screw up. To do something that showed he was no longer capable of handling the job.

He kept striving to prove his worth, like a first-year rookie.

What if it wasn't Conner worrying about his ability? What if he'd been the one who put a strain on their friendship by doubting himself?

Whatever it was, he missed the old relationship. Wanted it back. And lately, he'd felt hints of its return. An easy, comfortable feeling, like loosening your belt after a holiday meal.

Nice as that was, it didn't solve this case. And that had to be his top priority now.

"It took me forty-five minutes on the phone, but I traced the ownership of the apartment building to the bank that foreclosed, but the trail ended there. The title had transferred back and forth between corporations that no longer exist. Not one personal name to be found in any of their records. The last corporation declared bankruptcy six years ago and left a mile-long trail of unpaid debts."

"So another brick wall?"

"Probably. I did pressure the bank loan officer for a list of creditors. Most had gone out of business, but Earl found me a couple of promising leads. By that time, it was late-afternoon and too late to find anyone sitting in an office, working. I figured we could try tracking them down first thing Monday. See if anybody working there remembers dealing with a live human. Not too promising, but it'll keep us busy until Doc finishes the autopsies."

"Sounds like a good idea. One of the property management money orders was purchased in Katy and the company appears to still be in business. While we're out running around, I'd like to head over there on the off chance they kept any records for that long. We'll have better luck standing in front of them than over the phone."

"I agree. I don't like waiting on Doc and the forensics team. Maybe they'll come up with the key to unlock this whole thing, but maybe they won't. Until then, we do things the old-fashioned way; face-to-face. Pulling every thread, untangling every knot or octopi or anything we can find until we've traced it to the bitter end. Even if it means calling in the Feebies." Noah never thought he'd say that, but there wasn't any shame in admitting you needed help.

Montgomery seemed like an alright guy, but sometimes the Feebies could be jerks. Still, they were jerks with connections.

Valuable connections.

CHAPTER
TEN

SATURDAY MORNING AND Noah was in the exact same position he'd been in for hours Friday night. He shoved his chair back, startling Sweet Pea. He reached down and stroked the Yorkie's silky fur, a move that always calmed them both. Two wasted hours on the computer last night and another this morning tracking down Tom Meyers' hidden agenda.

He'd hoped to crack the tight-lipped lawyer's cryptic clues before Monday and all its madness set in. If he couldn't, he might not get back to it for weeks.

All the corporation names he and Conner had collected had been turned over to his least- disliked FBI agent Lincoln Montgomery in hopes the Feds could untangle the threads. If he had any answers by the start of the week, he'd dive in. If not, he and Conner would work the pavement, tracking down leads.

Either way, Meyers' problems would drop off his personal radar until this killer was caught. Or was it killers?

That was part of the problem; he still didn't know. And

wouldn't until Doc M finished the autopsies.

For now, he had two days to solve a riddle, get rid of Tom Meyers, and erase Conner's debt.

A good plan, except it wasn't working.

Tracking down Tom's cases was much like finding the one person who remembered the name of someone—anyone—connected with the multitude of corporations that owned or had owned or once owned or drove past and waved at the killing field or abandoned apartment.

It required a boots-on-the-ground approach.

Rachelle's mother-in-law was visiting this weekend so he wouldn't be seeing his sister or nieces. Danielle Hokpins son had a soccer tournament so his band of singing detectives wouldn't be performing at the children's hospital.

With the shorter autumn days, the grass wasn't growing as fast. He'd mowed his lawn and Mrs. Powell's next door last weekend and didn't need to again so soon.

Austin was only a two and a half hour drive away. His computer search had given him the names of five people he was certain were clients of Tom Meyers yet whose records were nowhere to be found. Someone at the Travis County Courthouse would be able to help him and do it in less time than he'd already wasted on a project of questionable importance.

He could be there and back by dark. Or he could spend the night and ask Mrs. Powell to feed Sweet Pea.

Why not? U of H wasn't playing this weekend so he had nothing to watch on TV, and UT had an away game so Austin would be empty. What did he have to lose except a lonely weekend and a sore rump?

Besides, if he stayed, he could have dinner at Scholz Garten.

How many years had it been since he'd been there? The thought of the German Burger—Swiss cheese and sauerkraut on a pretzel bun—had his mouth watering.

Plus, if he stayed overnight, he might hit Sixth Street. Listen to some music.

Tomorrow, without Sweet Pea to wake him, he'd sleep late and stop in Elgin on the way home for bar-b-que, then again at the Burton Café to pick up a lemon meringue pie for Mrs. Powell.

Okay, maybe one for himself, also.

He swung his chair around and deposited Sweet Pea on the floor. Why bother packing? He didn't need anything but a toothbrush. Hell, he wasn't going to see anyone he knew. He could brush his teeth when he got home.

Austin parking was always a bitch, but Noah found a spot a block from the Travis County Courthouse. The short walk gave him a chance to stretch and enjoy the cool air after the drive from Houston.

The 1930s style building with its oatmeal-colored limestone and bold geometric carvings loomed ahead of him, but Noah wasn't impressed. He'd been to dozens of courthouses in his career and they all served the same purpose: to make getting justice as difficult and complicated as humanly possible.

He trotted up the steps of the east entrance, under the frieze of a robed magistrate handing out judgments to shackled prisoners, and through the metal detector without a hitch. He felt naked without his weapon, but experience had taught him to leave it locked in a safety box bolted under Lola's seat.

Only four people were in line ahead of him in the County Clerk's office. With two clerks working, the wait time was bearable.

His turn came and he slid the paper with the list of names across the countertop. "I'd like to see the criminal files on these individuals."

The clerk took the paper without looking at him and entered the names into her computer. With each name she stopped to make a notation. "Records more than ten years old are kept offsite, in the warehouse. It's not far. Here are the file numbers and the address."

So that's why I couldn't find the information.

The clerk gave him back his list, flashed a pleasant if insincere smile and looked over his shoulder. "Next," she called.

The county warehouse required twenty minutes of winding his way through Austin's convoluted traffic plus another ten minutes to score a parking space.

This time, the two block walk didn't feel as welcome. But the air conditioning inside the building did.

Noah had expected something musty and dusty, with overflowing file cabinets and stacks of cardboard boxes, unused and unopened for decades. A mish-mash of an older Walmart, the library in a haunted mansion, and the cramped office of an overworked assistant DA.

Instead, while the building itself wasn't new, the insides were sparkling clean, smelled faintly of fresh paint, and was manned by a clerk with a new computer.

A woman wearing a navy blue business suit, sensible heels, and carrying her still shiny law-school-graduation-gift briefcase was exiting as he entered. Other than that, the lobby was deserted.

"Take a number, please." The clerk indicated a number dispensing machine standing like a lone soldier in the right hand corner.

What the fuck? I'm the only one here.

The clerk leaned back and drummed his fingers on his desk.

Noah stared at him for a full five seconds. Neither moved.

"Take a number, please." Exasperation coated the clerk's voice.

Noah glanced around the empty lobby in time to see a businessman trotting up the steps toward the glass front doors. He grabbed a number before the man got there ahead of him. "I'd like to see copies of these files, please."

The clerk didn't say a word but entered the numbers into his computer. After he finished, he reached under the counter and pulled out a blank form. "Copies are $35 each, cash only. Due now. Fill this out with your name, driver's license number, and cell phone. We'll text you when they're ready. Probably about two hours."

Behind him, the businessman took his number from the machine with a determined *snap.*

Noah pulled out his wallet and peeled off the cash. Good thing he'd stopped at the ATM near his house. But with the limit for withdrawal at $200, and counting the two twenties he started with, he was now down to $65.

Enough for lunch, and two pies, but not much else.

The clerk stamped an official looking receipt and handed it to Noah, the red ink so pale it hardly made a mark. "When you come back, you don't have to wait in the line. Step directly up to the counter."

Yeah, right. I need to avoid this line at all costs.

Two hours was plenty of time to go to Scholz Garten, have a burger and a beer. He was already out a hundred and seventy-five bucks. Add the cost of a room, and that little favor came with a pretty steep price tag.

Maybe he wouldn't spend the night after all.

Besides, hitting Sixth Street by himself wasn't that much fun and he was too used to getting up early to sleep in, even without Sweet Pea as an alarm clock.

He'd relax, enjoy a great meal, drive back to the warehouse to pick up the files, and be home by dark. If he hurried, he could still get those meringue pies.

That left all day Sunday to browse through the files. With the information hidden in there, it shouldn't take long to solve Tom Meyers' secret.

Then he'd be free and so would Conner.

CHAPTER ELEVEN

THE AROMA OF grilled hamburgers and sauerkraut sent Noah's mouth into waves of ecstasy before he reached the door of Scholz's. He placed his order and headed for a picnic table outside.

Why didn't he do this kind of thing more often? There had to be more to life than work, walking Sweet Pea, and occasionally playing with his nieces.

He was savoring his first juicy bite when he noticed a woman, two tables over. Her burger basket was shoved to the side and her head bent over some type of thick notebook.

Blond hair fell in a curtain, obscuring her face, but something about her posture, her deep concentration, seemed familiar. She made a notation on a legal pad beside her and he noticed she was left-handed.

His body made the connection before his mind caught up.

Laurel Bledsoe. The woman who'd helped solve her friend's murder by pointing him in the right direction.

Of course that wasn't her. Why would she be in Austin?

How bad a shape was he in if the mere sight of a woman sent electricity zig-zagging through his body like an old-time pinball machine?

He took a long pull on his beer and waited. Eventually, she had to move and he'd see that she was a college student preparing for an exam. Or worse, a state legislator figuring a new way to screw the populace.

But she didn't.

She read. She made notes. She drummed her pen on the table. But she didn't turn around.

Okay. What could he tell from this angle? Her body was nice and trim, but he wouldn't have compared her to Laurel if it wasn't. She was short. Her feet barely reached the ground from the bench seat of the picnic table. Once she twisted a strand of hair around her finger and he saw that she didn't wear a wedding ring.

Laurel had, the last time he saw her. But that was eight months ago and she was in the middle of a contentious divorce.

So that was it? From now on, every time he saw a short, left-handed blonde with a good figure and no wedding ring he'd light up like a Fourth of July sparkler? Cherry bomb the hell out of his brain?

He took another bite out of his burger then pushed it aside. Even the pretzel bun couldn't hold his interest. One deep swallow of beer for courage and he wiped his hands and face, checking for errant sauerkraut juice.

He needed an Altoid or a Certs or a peppermint or a toothbrush. Maybe all four.

What the hell. If he made an ass of himself, he didn't know

anyone here. Shit, he'd made a fool of himself in fancier places than this.

Four steps closer and he still didn't know. Three more steps and her profile emerged. Not clear enough to know for sure, but nothing to send him back to his seat, half-embarrassed, half-relieved.

Her pen rolled off the table and she bent to pick it up, coming face-to-face with his shoes, then his knees, and finally his face. Azure blue eyes landed on his own and stopped, widening in surprise.

"Noah?"

"Hi, Laurel." Lord help him. Was that the best he could come up with? He'd been better at this as a teenager. But he'd had practice in those days.

"What are you doing here?"

"I was about to ask you the same thing. You didn't move to Austin, did you?"

"Goodness, no. I'm taking a class." She tapped the notebook she'd been studying. "Working on my MCE."

"Your MCE?"

"Mandatory Continuing Education. I kept my Real Estate license current while I was married to Peter but he never wanted me to work so I fell behind in some of the required classes. I'm trying to get caught up in one long, hard weekend so I'll be ready to start working toward my Broker's license next year."

The words entered his head, but the only ones that registered were, *while I was married to Peter.*

Did that mean she wasn't married anymore? That her divorce had come through?

He searched his memory for the phrase his father always

used when he hadn't been paying attention and didn't know what to say. "Is that so?"

"Two more years as an agent and I'll be eligible to become a Broker. An old friend of Peter's offered to be my mentor. That way he'll be able to semi-retire and leave all the hard work to me."

"Wow. I'm impressed. I can see it now, a billboard with your picture and *The Laurel Bledsoe Real Estate Agency* in six-foot letters. Makes me want to sell my house and buy a new one."

Her laugh, when it came, wrapped around him like a warm blanket. "Your house is safe for now and it won't be Laurel Bledsoe. I changed my name the instant my divorce was final."

I knew it! She dumped the bastard.

"My maiden name was Newcomb, and that means old-time Houston money to people who care about that sort of thing. Peter did. It's why he married me. To give his underhanded schemes legitimacy. And it's why Royce Elkins hired me. Because that name opens doors to mansions in Memorial, River Oaks, Tanglewood, and every hidden enclave of wealth in town. My dad may have lost his fortune, but never his reputation. Kind of the opposite of Peter."

"So your name helped you land a job?"

"That and the fact Royce hates Peter with a pure passion. Peter scammed him out of some money, which he took with good graces, but then he caught my scumbag ex cheating at golf and that's unforgivable. Hiring me was his way of getting back at Peter. Of course getting a job is one thing, being offered a chance at a partnership is something else entirely. I had to earn that."

Damn. He always managed to open his mouth and insert his foot. This time it went all the way up to his knee. "I didn't mean to imply that. My last name probably still means something to those who heard my mother sing or my father play the violin. At best, it might get me an audition, but I'd have to prove myself to get a job."

"Is that how you got the gig in Paige Reimer's band?"

Yep. She'd seen him with Paige and wasn't going to let him get by with it. The chime of a text saved him.

He held up his phone, showing the message banner. "I have twenty minutes to pick up some legal papers or I'll lose my place in line. Why don't I tell you the story of my brief music career over dinner?"

She glanced at the time and jumped to her feet. "Shoot, I'm going to be late. I'm staying at the Omni on San Jacinto. See you at seven?"

He had four hours to retrieve Tom Meyers' files, check into a hotel, buy a clean shirt and find a toothbrush.

CHAPTER TWELVE

NOAH REACHED LAUREL'S hotel with twenty minutes to spare, so he browsed in the gift shop. Buying a box of breath mints seemed presumptuous so he settled on a pack of gum.

The elevator *dinged* and Laurel stepped into the lobby. She wasn't dressed up, exactly. Jeans, a blouse the color of his mom's azaleas, not high heels, but boots. She carried a sweater over one arm.

Her blonde hair was down and looked soft as Sweet Pea's fur. It swung slightly as she strode toward him, catching the light and changing shades with each step. His hand itched with desire to touch it.

"Hi, Noah. Aren't you proud of me? I'm right on time. Don't get too used to that."

All he could do was swallow and smile.

She stood on tiptoes and brushed a whisper-soft kiss across his cheek. "Did you think of a place for us to eat?"

His throat closed up and he had to clear it a couple of times before he could speak. "There's a seafood place down the block. I thought we could eat there and walk down to Sixth Street and listen to some music. Unless you have something else in mind." *Damn.* He didn't mean that the way it sounded.

"That sounds great. I'm tired of eating in this hotel and I've been sitting for two days. The walk sounds heavenly."

Outside, city lights blocked out the stars, but the air held the first hints of autumn. They walked companionably to the restaurant, ordered, and relaxed with a glass of wine while waiting to be served.

Noah searched for his missing backbone. He had some explaining to do. "I wanted to apologize for ignoring you at that Mexican restaurant last spring. I was working undercover as Paige Reimer's bodyguard. Trying to protect her from a stalker who'd been harassing her."

Laurel's laugh was like flipping on a light switch in a room that had been dark for too long. "I figured that out the minute I saw your earring. Although, I didn't know about the stalker until the news reports the morning after the concert. I'm so sorry you had to go through that. And Conner! I sent him a note, but what can you say? *Sorry you had to shoot that bastard and the media's accusing you of murder.* Conner thanked me for my support. How's he doing these days?"

She wrote to Conner but not to him?

"He's fine now, but you're right about the media. They don't let the facts stand in the way of a good story. He hired an expensive lawyer who made it all go away."

He shouldn't have had to. If I hadn't screwed up, I could have taken out the bastard before he pulled a gun and started shooting.

I'm making up for it now, but a little late to spare him and Jeannie the anxiety.

"Yeah. I saw him musty TV last week. He's so distinguished-looking."

"Conner?" Okay, some women might consider him nice-looking, but not distinguished. And what was he doing on TV?

"No, not Conner. The other guy. The lawyer. I can't remember his name but he has that beautiful premature white hair and always looks so elegant."

Fuck it. Tom Meyers. The guy's white hair wasn't all that premature and he looked more pompous that dignified. Nothing like a little old-fashioned jealously to get the blood pumping.

Wait, wait, *wait.* Tom Meyers was on TV last week? A couple of days before he called asking for Noah's help solving a problem?

Lately, he'd gone out of his way to avoid the news. Had he missed something important?

He didn't want to blow this by sounding too excited. "What was Tom Meyers doing on TV, drumming up business? Promoting a political candidate?"

"Some big case here in Austin. I'm not sure what. They had to let a guy out of prison after ten years due to DNA evidence. It raised a big stink because the murder was so brutal. Strangled? Dumped? I don't remember exactly. Some people were mad because they believe he did it. Others because the murderer is still out there loose."

A young, black-clad waiter slipped a plate of trout almandine in front of Noah, and deep-fried catfish in front of Laurel. Without a word, they traded dishes.

"Is there anything else I can bring you? Another glass of wine?"

Noah glanced at his glass of Zinfandel. It was still half full. Laurel hadn't drunk more than a couple of sips from hers. "We're okay for now. Thank you."

"How about a refill on your water. More bread?"

"We're fine, thanks."

"Do you have enough tartar sauce?"

What the hell? You couldn't get a waiter when you needed one or get rid of one when you didn't.

"We have everything we need for now. We'll let you know if something changes."

The waiter didn't move. "It's that… I'm going off shift in a few minutes and if you need anything, I'll be gone and it's too late."

Too late? Was he the only waiter in the joint?

Laurel kicked him under the table, a knowing smile playing at the corners of her mouth. "I think he needs his tip," she whispered.

The kid didn't answer. He just stood there.

Noah pulled a twenty from his wallet. "Thanks for your help."

The bill disappeared. "Thank you, sir, ma'am. It was a pleasure serving you. Have a nice rest of your evening."

Laurel bit her lip, holding in a laugh until the waiter had gone.

Noah looked at his empty hand, where a twenty had been moments before. Now he was down to $15 cash.

If this place didn't take credit cards, he was in big trouble.

The walk to Sixth Street took less than ten minutes and

would have been pleasant if Laurel's left boot hadn't pinched her little toe. The air outside was cool, but she didn't need the sweater she was carrying, especially after they reached a dive bar with live music spilling onto the street.

She hadn't remembered it being so loud and so crowded when she came here on weekends away from college. They sat on cracked-plastic stools and Noah ordered a dark ale.

"Do you have any specialty beers?" she asked.

The bartender had Paul Newman eyes, Orlando Bloom hair, and a body straight out of Men's Fitness magazine. If she didn't have the real thing sitting next to her, she might be interested.

"I've got a wheat beer a lot of women like. It's light but full-bodied."

"Sounds great. I'll take one."

They leaned back with their drinks and listened to the band. They sounded amateurish to Laurel, but Noah was the musician. "What d'ya think?" she asked.

"The back-up guitarist is carrying them. The drummer is okay but a little over the top and the keyboardist might be decent with a couple more years practice, but they need to ditch the lead singer and the bass player."

Oh. She just thought they were loud and mediocre.

"How'd you like playing a concert with Paige Reimer? That must have been fun."

He looked away. Took a long pull on his beer and she knew. Knew exactly what he was hiding.

He'd been more than a bodyguard for the country/western singer.

"It was okay. A lot of hard work. Hot, tiring, boring at times. Enough to assure me I made the right choice of professions."

"You're not tempted?"

"Nah. Once a week I play for sick kids at the children's hospital with a couple of my cop buddies. That's enough for me. The good thing about sick kids is they're so happy to see anybody, they don't even care if we're any good or miss a line." He used his thumb to peel the label off his beer.

Why is he suddenly nervous? Can't be me. We've been talking easily enough all evening. "You never told me what you're doing in Austin. Is it business or pleasure? Are you working while you're here?"

"I'm working, but not on a case. I'm helping out a friend. Is there any chance you would recognize the name of the defendant in the Tom Meyers case you saw on the news last week?"

A friend of Noah's? Did this involve Conner? No way had that man done anything illegal or immoral. She trusted him as much as she trusted Noah. Which was a boxcar's worth even though they hadn't spent that much time together.

"The name didn't register with me. Maybe if I saw a list of suspects." Curiosity was about to eat her alive, but Noah would have told her if he could.

Noah fumbled with his beer. Discomfort evident on his face. "I have the case files in my room. I can bring them to your hotel and we can go over them in the lobby."

Ahh, that's why he was fidgeting. "Seems like a lot of extra work. Why don't we go to your place and you won't have to drive back and forth?"

Shoot. Had she just suggested going to a man's motel room? And on a first date?

"I only have one requirement," she added.

If he'd looked uncomfortable before, now he was downright

antsy. "What's that?"

"You have to get the car and pick me up. My feet are killing me."

CHAPTER THIRTEEN

NOAH UNLOCKED HIS motel room door and flipped on the light. Laurel had already followed him inside when he realized the room wasn't anything to brag about. It was cramped, the carpet was worn, the curtain sagged, and the air conditioner gave off a faint, moldy smell.

He hadn't helped any by leaving his dirty shirt on the bed, a wet towel in the bathroom, and a vending machine snack of soda and half-eaten cheese crackers on the bedside table.

Maybe she wouldn't notice.

"Why don't you sit here?" he asked, pulling the only chair in front of a desk that held seven square inches of work space.

One by one he dragged over the five cardboard boxes. He took the top off the closest one and rummaged through a stack of loose papers, pulling out a copy of a booking sheet, along with a photo and arrest record. "Can you glance over this and see if the name or anything else looks familiar?"

Twenty minutes later, she pushed the chair back and

massaged her forehead. "I'm not positive, because I wasn't paying that much attention, but I don't think it was any of these guys."

Well damn. There went most of his cash and two days' worth of wasted work. He glanced at Laurel. Maybe not totally wasted.

"The guy the news was talking about got *out* of jail last week, but the news clip they showed was old, and had him going *into* jail. And I don't think Tom Meyers was his lawyer because another guy was standing in front, talking about a *travesty of justice.* Tom Meyers was standing off to the side, smirking."

Yep, that would be Tom Meyers. The one smirking.

Laurel twisted in her chair until she was facing him. "Do you have your computer? I'll bet if we did a Google search we could find out why he was in the news."

"No, but I can probably pull it up on my phone." If the case on TV wasn't about one of Meyer's clients, were they on the wrong track? Wasting their time? He'd check anyway, but more because he gave his word than because he believed it would lead anywhere.

"Reading anything longer than a paragraph on a phone is tough. Let's go back to my place. I've got my laptop and we can be more comfortable." She jerked her head around, allowing her hair to swing forward, hiding her face, but not before a slight blush crept onto her cheeks.

Yeah, she'd noticed. An hour to kill and he'd spent it fretting when five minutes work would have made the place presentable. On the other hand, no amount of cleaning would turn this dump into a five star resort.

But it had been cheap, available, and on the correct side of town for a quick get-away in the morning.

The big question was: Why did he care? He wasn't in the

business of trying to impress people. Paige Reimer had spent two days at his house and all he'd done was rinse out their coffee cups.

On the other hand, the first time Betsy had come to his apartment he'd scrubbed the bathroom and bought a vase of flowers.

He returned the papers to the file boxes, shoved $175 worth of trash into the corner, and grabbed his keys. He didn't have time to psychoanalyze himself. He had a mystery to solve and a serial killer to find.

He'd better get busy and forget about chasing a life he was never meant to realize.

Laurel's hotel had everything Noah's didn't. Valet parking. A bright, shiny lobby with a smiling desk clerk. Signs with directions to the pool, the workout room, two different restaurants.

Noah hadn't noticed when he picked her up. He'd been too busy worrying about the time, and his clothes, and his breath. And rather this was a date or something less.

Seeing her room, with its thick carpet, pristine white spread, and desk you could actually work on didn't ease his insecurities. Only a quick glance at make-up strewed across the bathroom counter helped with that.

"This hotel is where the classes are being taught and my boss was anxious for me to come so he made the reservations and picked up the tab. He can write it off as business related. He got a pacemaker in July and I think he's ready for me to take over some of the work of running the office. Nothing like a health scare to make you reevaluate your priorities."

He'd agree, but it had taken him the better part of a year after Betsy's death to begin looking past the end of his nose. He still couldn't plan more than a day or two ahead.

Laurel pulled a second chair in front of the desk, straightened her workbooks and papers, and opened her laptop.

A giant fist slapped Noah in the chest, knocking the wind out of him.

Laurel's screensaver was a photo of Crystal Hudson. Her best friend and neighbor. A woman whose death Noah was investigating when they met. A woman cut down in her prime because her husband would rather pay a hit man than pay for a divorce.

A woman whose brother Laurel worked to help place in a year-long drug rehab facility instead of prison.

"Have you heard anything from Crystal's brother? How are things working out for him in Arizona?" He believed rehab was the only hope for most addicts, really he did, but the cop part of him was skeptical. He'd seen too many relapse the minute they hit the streets.

"I've gotten a couple of notes from him. The last one had a drawing of Crystal that was so good I would have hung it on my wall if it weren't on notebook paper. The facility keeps me apprised of his situation. It's been eight months so he can start leaving the center with supervision. He's going to get those awful rotten teeth fixed while he's there and someone can drive him and pick him up and take care of him after. Ice packs and chicken broth, I guess. I suspect he's shit-out-of-luck on pain meds."

"What happens after that?"

"A half-way house for nine months to a year. They operate a training program that turns strays into service dogs. Supposed to be good for the patients and the dogs."

Crystal dead. Her husband dead. The hit man locked away for life. Wouldn't it be nice if something good came of it all?

If so, it was due to Laurel and her hard work for someone she barely knew. Contrast that with Paige who'd used him. Used Conner. Used everyone she'd ever met to promote her career.

And now Laurel was helping him chase down a maybe-criminal without even asking why.

The *da-ding da-ding* of the laptop coming online sounded and Laurel put the cursor on the info bar and started typing. In an instant, she had a page full of Tom Meyers hits.

She scrolled down, tried an entry, backed up, tried another, narrowed her search parameters and tried again.

In less than two minutes, they were head-to-head, reading an article from the Austin American-Statesman. The newspaper had two photos. One of Jeffery Landers being released from prison, into the arms of his family.

The older photo showed Landers—orange jumpsuit, handcuffs, armed guards—being led away from court, his elderly lawyer by his side. Tom Meyers stood in the background, wearing the smirk Laurel had mentioned earlier.

He put his arm around Laurel's shoulders and squeezed. "You're better than ten of Earl Sparks."

Laurel's laugh was liquid light, shining into his deep, dark corners. "I guess I'm flattered. Who's Earl Sparks?"

"Cop I work with who got conked on the head at that concert last spring. He's been on desk duty ever since. He's a great help—filling out forms, typing up warrants, researching—but he can't spell, uses the hunt-and-peck method of typing, and isn't exactly tech-savvy. He's one of the guys in my band. Has this great Barry

White voice you wouldn't believe could come out of someone so skinny."

"Well, don't tell anybody. I wouldn't want to steal his job."

"That's going away, one way or another. He has until the end of the year to get an all clear from his doc, or take early retirement."

Noah glanced around the room, suddenly uncomfortable. "How about we go downstairs to the bar and I'll buy you a nightcap? I owe you for finding this for me. It'll save me hours of work."

"I accept on two conditions."

Always with the conditions. "What's that?"

"One, I don't have to report it on my income tax. And two, instead of a drink you make it one of this hotel's famous double fudge brownies."

Laurel eyed her plate of double fudge brownie topped with vanilla ice cream doused in chocolate syrup. She scooped up a spoonful and promptly dripped chocolate on her coral blouse. Well damn, that would leave a stain. You couldn't take her anywhere.

Only one bite was left.

It looked tempting, but there was no way. She was too full. Not to mention the calories. She and Noah had walked several blocks, first to the restaurant for dinner and then to Sixth Street for music. That should count for something.

Who was she kidding? An hour on the stair-stepper wouldn't erase this evening from her hips.

She pushed the dish away and glanced at Noah. He had done

everything but lick his plate clean. She watched as he examined her remaining dessert.

Men. They could eat anything without disastrous results. It wasn't fair.

Nothing about this was fair. He'd approached her. He'd asked her out to dinner, where they'd had a lovely time. He'd even asked for her help with a case.

Sure, she'd given him a slight peck when they met, but he definitely seemed to enjoy it. Then *bam!* Nothing.

He'd turned cold when she suggested going to her room. Did he think she was offering more than the use of her laptop?

Maybe he was involved with a certain country/western singer.

Maybe he wasn't ready to move on to the next step.

Maybe he was as confused, unsure, ill-at-ease as she was. In that case, she was in trouble.

She was a nervous eater. If she kept spending time around Noah, she'd weigh four hundred pounds in no time.

"You finished with that?" His voice startled her.

"What? Yes. You want it?"

"I don't actually *want* it. I'm just trying to help you out."

"How do you figure that? Are you worried the chef will be insulted?"

"Well, it's never good to make the chef mad, but I was more worried about your problems with the IRS. If I force myself to eat this, they can't claim you were paid for helping me."

"An ingenious plan, I must admit, but I thought all you public servants stuck together."

"Ha! I do my best to stay away from those alphabet soup folks." He forked the last remaining crumbs of the brownie. "IRS,

CIA, FBI, NASA, SETA, Triple A, the DMV. You can't trust any of them."

"All of them?"

"I will admit to knowing one FBI agent who is helping with the case we're working on. So far, he's been okay, but give him time. He'll show his true colors eventually."

"It's good to know you're not disillusioned. That you always keep an open mind. Is it the case with Tom Meyers and Jeffery Landers?"

"No, that one's personal. Something I'm trying to clear up on the side. That Fed is helping identify the bodies in the Killing Field Murders. You may have seen it on the news last week."

Oh, no. Was Noah involved in that case? No wonder he was uptight. How did he handle something so horrible? And here she was worrying about a stain on her blouse.

Noah paid the check and walked her to the elevator. "What time are you leaving tomorrow?"

"My class ends at four, then I'm heading straight back to Houston."

"I wish I could stick around, take you to lunch. Or even breakfast. But I need to get home and hit my computer. See if I can finish with Tom Meyers' problem this weekend. Once I get to the office Monday, I won't have a spare minute until somebody is locked up."

"You'll let me know what you find out about Landers?"

He used his thumb to wipe something—chocolate?—off the corner of her mouth. "You'll be the first one I call. You did more to solve it than I did. This is the second time you've set me on the right track on a case. I already knew you were a lot nicer than me, and funnier, and better looking. Now I know you're smarter.

If I have any sense at all, I won't let you get too far away."

"You best remember that." Maybe he wasn't a lost cause after all.

CHAPTER
FOURTEEN

Sunday didn't go exactly as Noah planned.

He did stop in Elgin and picked up some bar-b-que to go, wrapped in butcher paper and oozing grease. Good thing they put the finished package in a plastic bag. Even then, the aroma almost drove him crazy on the way home.

His stop in Burton was brief. Just long enough to grab two pies. The cafe only had one lemon meringue, so he settled on apple pie for himself.

The problem started when he got home. Sweet Pea was fine. She had clean piddle-pads and a few bites of fresh-looking dog food in her bowl so he knew she'd been well taken care of.

When he knocked on Mrs. Powell's door, carrying her pie, her voice drifted through the thick wood, "Come in, Noah. It's open."

His heart did a hop, skip, jump. That woman had never left a door unlocked in her life.

She was leaned back with her feet up in a recliner that had

belonged to her late husband, not her usual chair with its sewing basket, crossword puzzle, mystery novel, newspaper, laptop, telephone, and TV remote close at hand.

"Oh, Noah. You'll have to pardon me. I think I got a little overheated. That wind last night made a mess of the pansies I planted yesterday. I was outside cleaning up and got a bit dizzy. That'll teach me to garden in the middle of the day."

The day was overcast, a pewter gray, possibly seventy-four, seventy-five degrees, with a slight breeze. He'd seen her working outside in July.

Her face was ashen. If she'd gotten overheated, shouldn't it be red? "How long ago was this?"

She glanced at the clock on the TV. "Oh, my. It's been an hour. I must have dozed off for a while."

Dozed off? The queen of get-up-and-at-'em had taken a nap? "Do you want me to drive you to the hospital?"

"Heavens no. I'll stay here and rest a while. At seventy-eight, I think I've earned a day off." She patted the arm of the faded blue chair. "This is pretty comfortable. Don't know why I never use it."

Because she called it a death trap. Said her husband retired, dropped down into it, and stayed there for the next two years. Vehemently declared she had no plans to sit around and rot.

"How about the Redi Clinic? Let them check your blood pressure."

"How about you go home, play with Sweet Pea. She misses you. If you want to be a help, you can pull my garbage can out to the curb."

Holy crap. She'd never asked him to do anything except to move furniture or get something down from the attic. He'd helped her plant some new roses once, but only because he'd seen her struggling with the shovel.

He occasionally carried her trash cans out to the curb or back, but only if he beat her to it. Come to think of it, starting last August, that was most weeks.

His only grandmother had died when he was nine, his mother had been gone for sixteen years. His dad, a foster kid with no family, for seventeen.

He did have an elderly aunt in a nursing home he'd visited last summer. The first time he'd seen her in several years.

Even Betsy's mother had disappeared into her own world of Alzheimer's.

He'd sort of adopted Mrs. Powell—or maybe it was the other way around—but he couldn't afford to lose her. There weren't that many people in his life.

There had to be something he could do to help her. "Want me to bring over some lunch?" That way he could keep an eye on her.

"Rachelle's tofu casserole?" Horror coated her voice.

"Yes, but a different recipe. She and the girls took a cooking class last summer and this one's actually edible."

When he returned fifteen minutes later, Mrs. Powell had set her kitchen table with a placemat, silverware, and a water glass. She reached into the cabinet for a cloth napkin and swayed, grabbing the counter for support.

"That's it," Noah said, his voice cracking. "I'm taking you to the hospital."

Few stars were visible in the cloudy sky when Noah got

home. Sweet Pea gave him a dirty look. Her dinner could be an hour late and she understood. Three hours and she was an unhappy dog.

He lowered himself into a kitchen chair and scooped the tiny dog into his lap. "Sorry, Pea, your favorite babysitter, Mrs. Powell, is in the hospital."

The dog cocked her head to one side.

"Don't worry. The doctor says she's going to be fine. It's her tachycardia. She'll be home tomorrow."

Sweet Pea wiggled down and stood by her food bowl. So much for her concern over their friend.

Noah fed his dog, then pulled the butcher-paper-wrapped bar-b-que from the fridge. It was cold, and the grease congealed, but he ate it straight from the package, standing over the sink.

Was eight thirty too late to call Laurel? He'd like to let her know what happened. Explain why he hadn't had time to work on Tom Meyers' mystery after all the help she'd been.

Especially since it was likely to be several weeks before he could get back to it. Monday morning the answers would start dribbling in on the Killing Field Murders.

If that FBI agent was worth his salt.

A positive ID on even one of the victims would be nice. How long did it take to check dental records? And how would he explain having a copy of that file at home if it came back positive?

Info on the owner of the apartment complex or the vacant lot would give him another direction to look. Meanwhile, he and Conner would start searching out the money order in Katy and then any business that had ever owned any part of the apartment complex.

He stared at Laurel's number on his phone and tapped it

before he could change his mind.

"Hi, Noah." Her voice held an upbeat tone. Did that mean she was glad to hear from him?

"Hi. I wanted to make sure you got home from Austin okay." *Geez.* That sounded lame even to him. He'd always checked on Betsy or Rachelle when they were out, but that didn't give him a right to check on Laurel.

"Thanks. Traffic was a pain, but that's to be expected on a Sunday night. I've been home long enough to unpack and start a load of laundry. You?"

"I got home about eleven, but I wasn't able to work on that information you were so helpful with. My neighbor got sick and I had to take her to the hospital."

"Oh no. What happened?"

"Her heart decided to do the River Dance. Apparently that's happened before. The doc increased her pills and wants to put in a pacemaker, but with her husband gone, one son dead in Afghanistan, and the other working on a ranch in Wyoming, that will have to wait until Christmas break when her daughter-in-law can come down."

"She's lucky to have you."

Not as lucky as I am to have her. Noah toed off his shoes and leaned back, the first time he'd relaxed since he woke up. "Anyway, it may be a few weeks before I can start trying to trace down that information you gave me. I didn't want you to think I didn't care."

"My boss is going out of town for the week. Monday I'll be busy, catching up for missing Friday. After that, I have to answer the phone, set up appointments and stuff, but I won't be overly busy. I had planned to take a book to keep myself occupied. Why don't I see what I can find out about the relationship between Jeffery Landers and Tom Meyers? I'll email you anything interesting."

She'd do that for me without even knowing why? Well, she knew it was for a friend, and she knew Tom Meyers was Conner's lawyer, so she probably figured out part of his problem.

He had to be careful. He'd seen she was smart, but every time he was around her, he became more aware how sharp, how quick she was.

Not that he planned to lie to her, but parts of his work were confidential. And then there were his secrets.

He had a couple of doozies that no one left alive knew. Rachelle *thought* she knew, but she was only half right.

Betsy had known. He never considered asking her to marry him until he made sure she realized exactly what type of man she was getting.

CHAPTER
FIFTEEN

CONNER STROLLED INTO the office, set a coffee on the edge of his desk and one on Noah's, then pulled out his chair. "How was your weekend? Do anything interesting?"

"Same old, same old. You?" Noah kept his head turned toward his computer, never looking at his partner.

Uh oh. Not again. Something was wrong. After Betsy died, Noah had avoided him, kept secrets. The main one, Conner felt certain, was his plan to join Betsy on his own time schedule. Not until someone tried to do the job for him had Noah lightened up.

The last few months he'd caught glimpses of the old Noah. He'd thought that foolishness was past, so he'd let his guard down.

Did he need to start worrying again?

They were hip deep in the biggest case of their careers, the biggest case the city of Houston had ever faced. They wouldn't see daylight for weeks, months. He couldn't work that way and deal with Noah's moods.

If he couldn't trust his partner, maybe it was time to step away. Now. Before he was sucked in any deeper. So a new partner could start at the beginning.

Noah closed his computer screen before Conner could get a look at it and swung his chair around. His smile wasn't the best Conner had seen, but it didn't scream *fake*. "I hate to admit this, but you actually look pretty good. What'd you do, ditch Jeannie and the baby and go to a hotel for a decent night's rest?"

"My mother-in-law came for the weekend. She slept in the room with Betsy and I…slept. That's not all. I don't want to jinx this by saying it out loud." He knocked on the fake wood of his desk. "But I think Betsy might be outgrowing her colic. She only cried half as long last night."

"Wow. That is good news. I hate to see my Goddaughter suffer."

Conner eyed Noah over the rim of his coffee cup. "What about your partner? Doesn't he count?"

"He can take care of himself, although I do worry about his wife. She has to live with him *and* a sick baby."

Maybe he'd jumped to conclusions. Noah's smile was genuine and his eyes bright. But then any discussion about his late wife's tiny namesake made him smile.

"Ready to get to work?" Noah's voice brought him back to the crowded squad room. "I printed off the address on the money order and a list of the businesses involved with the condemned apartment. Want to work together or split up?"

"Have we heard anything back from the Feds?"

"Not a solitary fucking word. So much for Special Agent Lincoln Montgomery, the FBI's wonder boy and our supposed white knight."

"Then we might as well work together. You tell the Lieu where we're going and I'll call down for a motor pool car. If we're going to spend the day together, you might as well tell me what you did this weekend. You know I'll get it out of you."

"Drove my next-door neighbor to the hospital and ran into Laurel Bledsoe at a restaurant. Only she's Laurel Newcomb now that her divorce is final."

Conner didn't answer. His voice would have given away his excitement. Glory Hallelujah. No wonder Noah looked sheepish.

"Did the two of you…?"

"No!"

"Did you at least…think about it?"

Noah groaned. "Obsessively."

Conner let out a laugh. There was some hope his partner might develop an actual life.

The October temperature was mild, so the air conditioner on the motor pool car was able to keep up while blocking the worst of the exhaust smells and traffic noises from the ever-busy Katy freeway.

Conner drove and Noah used his phone to find the address printed on the first money order. He leaned back and let Siri give the directions. For grins, he set her to an Australian accent because he knew it would dive Conner crazy.

In 500 feet exit right onto Fry Road, then turn left onto Fry Road.

Conner shot him a dirty look but kept driving.

From Fry, they wound around onto Park Row Drive where they found a strip center that had seen better days.

So had the owner of Assad's Jiffy Stop.

The man was fifty-seven according to the fact sheet Conner had printed out. But they must have been fifty-seven hard years.

He was missing half a leg, three fingers, and part of an ear. His nose wasn't looking any too healthy.

Noah and Conner hung back while a biker-type paid for his cigarettes and lottery ticket.

As they approached the counter, Noah eyed a glass dome of hot dogs, rotating slowly like a Ferris Wheel containing strips of leather cut from an old boot and smelling like yesterday's underwear. "Mr. Assad?" he asked.

The owner nodded and his face lit up, but fell just as quickly when he saw Noah's badge.

Conner placed a photo copy of the document he'd taken from the Chicken Lady on the counter. "Did you sell this money order?"

Assad pulled on a pair of quarter-inch thick glasses and peered at the photo. "This isn't very clear."

"You can see the check number and the date right here." Noah tapped the upper right corner.

"This is from ten years ago. We don't even use this form anymore. I can't issue a refund on something this old."

"We're not asking for a refund. We're looking for information on the person who purchased it." If Noah had to stand next to those hot dogs much longer, he was going to lose his appetite for lunch, dinner, and tomorrow's breakfast.

"I wouldn't keep records that old in the store. I'm not sure I have it at all."

"If you do have it, where would it be?" Why was digging information out of people always so hard?

"I used to keep old papers and receipts and stuff, some in boxes in the store room and some in my garage. A few years ago, when I had this surgery," he leaned on one crutch and pointed to his missing leg, "my son came home from college and spent the summer helping out around here. He cleaned up and "organized" things. He threw out a lot of stuff and put the rest in the attic. If I've got it, that's where it would be, but I'm not in any shape to get it down."

"Do you have any neighbors or friends who'd help you?" He didn't look like a real friendly guy.

Assad shot him a yeah-right-my-neighbors-would-love-to-climb-around-in-my attic look. "If I bribe my son with a home-cooked meal he might come over, but we'd have to wait until it was convenient for him. Then he'd bring his girlfriend. My wife would *looove* that. She calls her 'That little tramp,' because she dyes her hair. Of course, my wife's at the beauty salon dying her hair, but that's to cover the gray, not turn it pink."

Noah handed Assad a card with his cell number and the photo of the money order. They had another copy back at the office in the murder book—the detailed file they kept on every case. They could make more copies if they needed to. "Call me as soon as you're able. We need this information yesterday."

He started for the door, but glanced back in surprise as conservative Conner pulled out a five and bought a mega-bucks lottery ticket.

"What? Babies are expensive. By the time Betsy's ready for college, it'll take this million to send her."

Shit. He knew the combination of legal and medical bills were taking a toll on Conner. He needed to get on the Tom Meyers problem ASAP and get that much off Conner's plate.

The pool car started on the first try, something Conner considered a minor miracle, and he let it idle as he turned toward Noah. "Where to next, Oh Mighty Navigator?"

"Siri says Jumbo Trucking is only three miles from here."

They drove in silence until Conner's irritation got the better of him. "We had to buy something at that store or he'd never bother to look through his records. Everything in that place was covered in a layer of dust. I wasn't about to buy anything edible, even something in an air-tight package." The lie sat heavy on his conscience.

"Those hot dogs were left over from the Regan administration. I was afraid I'd get food poisoning just from standing next to them."

He couldn't blame Noah for being shocked at his actions. He'd never bought a lottery ticket in his life and knew well the price of one ticket wasn't going to change the man's mind about cooperating.

But he had bills, both now and in the future, and the investment of five dollars was a small price to pay. One day he'd turn around and Betsy would need braces, and a dress for the prom, and she'd want to go off to college, and maybe, when she was thirty-five or forty, a wedding.

And he needed to start saving for those things. As soon as he got today's bills paid off.

Your destination is on the left in 200 feet.

That was Jumbo Trucking? Looked more like a salvage yard to him.

A corrugated fence sagged between posts and a gravel

driveway led to a dilapidated trailer. The hand-lettered sign over the door was faded, but he could make out *Jumbo's* in what was once red paint.

A *click* sounded as Noah unfastened his seatbelt. "What'd ya' think, partner? You have a good feeling about this place?"

"I think we'd have had better odds going to Assad's house and climbing around in his attic."

"Me too, but his wife was at the beauty parlor, getting her hair dyed."

Conner stepped out of the car cautiously, keeping one eye out for a junkyard dog. He and Noah hadn't gone more than five feet when the trailer door slammed open.

"We're not open," a voice boomed out. A mountain of a man stood in the doorway, blocking any ray of light that might have tried to seep past him.

And if they were open, what did they sell? Wrecked cars? Broken down trucks? Something more sinister?

"Is this Jumbo Trucking?" he called out, keeping his distance.

"Not anymore. Now scram. We're closed."

Conner held out his badge, but kept one hand loose, near his weapon. Beside him, Noah did the same.

"I'm Detective Crawford. This is my partner, Detective Daugherty. Are you the owner?"

"Yep. I'm Jumbo."

You certainly are.

"We'd like to ask you a few questions regarding a company you did business with about ten years ago."

"Hell, I don't keep records that long."

He and Noah took a few steps closer when barking erupted from inside the trailer. The sound was more of a *yip* than the *woof* of a large dog. A ball of matted fur that might contain a Shih Tzu squeezed between the man's legs and he bent to scoop it up, revealing a bowling ball-sized head devoid of hair in the front and sporting a long, graying ponytail in the back.

Had he rubbed half his hair off on the top of the doorframe?

"This here's Princess. She don't like strangers coming around."

No wonder he didn't have any business if customers weren't allowed on the property.

Noah edged closer. "I know you're busy—"

Doing what? Conner could hear the strains of a soap opera coming from inside.

"—and we don't want to take up any more of your time than necessary, but we're looking for information on a contractor who built an apartment complex near the ship channel. You were listed as one of the suppliers that didn't get paid."

Jumbo barreled out of the trailer and down a set of wooden stairs. The trailer rose several inches and the stairs sagged into the dirt. "Those fucking sons-of-bitches. You find 'em for me and I'll squeeze the money out of their useless hides. I didn't get enough from them to pay for gas, much less pay my drivers. You know what happens when you don't pay your drivers? Word gets around and you can't *hire* any drivers. Then you're up shit creek and the bank repossesses your trucks. "

His voice was loud enough to rattle window glass and Conner's heart did a back flip. If the guy came after them, he and Noah together couldn't stop him.

Conner held up both hands, palms out. "I understand, sir. That's why we're trying to find these guys. Any information you have would help. The records we've uncovered go back seven or eight years, when the lawsuits were filed. Can you give us a more precise date?"

The guy had slowed down some, but was still agitated, hopping from one gigantic bare foot to the other. "Hell, I don't remember today's date, much less more'n a year ago. I do know it was back when I had a full head of hair and could still see my toes."

"Do you remember any names? Anyone specific you dealt with?"

"Nah. I never had any names. Just different corporations that disappeared along with the money they owed me."

"What about your drivers? If you could give us their names, maybe they could help."

"Well…the thing is…. I didn't hire the type of guys you kept track of or paid with checks. That's one of the reasons I dropped the lawsuit. I didn't have any records."

Another dead end.

Back in the car Noah twisted toward him. "We learned one useful thing from Mr. Jumbo."

He had no idea what Noah was thinking, but he'd bite. "What's that?"

"If we find the scumbag who killed all those women but we don't have enough evidence to convict him, we can give his name to Jumbo and let him take care of it for us."

No doubt his partner was blowing smoke, but Conner had to admit, the idea did have some merit.

CHAPTER SIXTEEN

NOAH AND CONNER stopped at the next business on their list only to find it was now Fuji Massage and Spa. Soft music and the smell of incense greeted them as they opened the door.

The woman who stepped out to meet them was the polar opposite of Jumbo. All of four foot eight, she had jet black hair pulled into a neat bun on top of her head. She wore a blue silk, form-fitting dress with a high collar, gold embroidery, and a side slit about three inches higher than was decent. Long, red-lacquered nails completed her outfit.

When she saw Noah's badge, her face twisted. Twin laser beams of hate filled her eyes. The first words out of her mouth were, "Do you have a warrant?"

Why the hell would they need a warrant to ask if she knew what happened to the previous business? "We're looking for Sabine Accounting. They used to be located at this address. Do you know what happened to them?"

"No one here when we moved in five years ago."

A *bing-bong* sounded as the front door was thrown open. Noah swung around with his coat still hooked back, showing his badge. A heavy-set middle-aged man, his smile frozen as he glanced from Noah to the petite dragon of an owner and back, began to stutter. "Uh. Um. I think I have the wrong address." He was outside and in his car before the door had time to close.

Dragon lady moved behind the counter and flipped a switch, turning off the *Open* sign over the door. She turned toward Noah. "Sorry. We all booked today. Come back another time. Best to call first. Make an appointment." She turned her back, letting them know they were dismissed.

Conner jotted down the name and address of the business before starting the car. "Hard to see how they can be booked up if they're not even open."

Noah looked up to see the woman watching them through the window. "If we did score an appointment, do you think we'd be offered a *Happy Ending*?"

The air conditioning gave a *burp* and sputtered to life as Conner pulled out of the parking lot. "All I know is tonight when Jeannie asked me what we did today, I'm not mentioning this place."

"Want to drive around the block and see if she has the *Open* sign back on?"

"Nah. When we get back to the office, I'll drop by Vice and give them this address. For now, let's hit one more business before we break for lunch. I guess you're going to want bar-b-que again."

"No. I still have some I picked up on my way home from Austin last weekend."

Shit. Shit. Shit. Had he said that? Conner didn't seem to notice. He was busy driving. "How about we stop at that Vietnamese place for some *pho*?"

Conner flipped the air conditioning up a notch. "Sounds good to me. I'll be hungry by then."

Noah found the next closest business on his list and gave Siri the address. Maybe they'd have better luck with Sleeman Cement.

In one mile, exit right onto North Eldridge Parkway then take an immediate left.

Conner flipped on his blinker and changed lanes. "I looked this place up online. At least they seem to still be in business."

"Surely someone there talked to a real live person. How else would they have known where to pour the cement?"

Your destination is on the right. You have reached your destination, mate.

God, he loved Siri. She could irritate Conner for him while he enjoyed the show.

Conner was right. Sleeman Cement Company was a thriving business. The office had several cars parked in front and a cement truck, its big barrel-shaped container turning, waited for them to pass before exiting. He pulled into a visitor's parking spot near the door.

A film of cement dust rose with each step as they approached the building.

"May I help you?" A perky young receptionist greeted them from the front desk, her pink hair bouncing with every word. Maybe she was Mr. Assad's future daughter-in-law.

"We'd like to speak to the manager, please." Noah pulled back his coat, showing his badge.

The girl's happy face fell faster than an overdone soufflé. She lifted the phone and punched a button. "Mr. Sleeman? There are two...officers here to see you." She paused, keeping her eyes on her desk and her head lowered, as if they couldn't hear the conversation if she wasn't looking at them. "No, sir. I don't."

Her boss must have given the okay, because she ushered them to an office at the rear of the building.

A kid not long out of grade school stood behind a desk older than he was. "I'm Joel Sleeman. May I help you?"

While Conner explained what they were interested in learning, Noah wandered around the room, studying the photos.

Other than one portrait that must have been of the kid's father—same pasty complexion, widow's peak, and prominent ears—the photos were all of completed buildings. One notable exception was the building where the first victim was found.

Young Joel Sleeman scowled when Conner mentioned the address of the apartment. "I remember that place. If it hadn't been for my bullheaded father, that job would have been the end of us. He had a hard-and-fast rule. Half the money up front and the rest before the next load was poured. If we showed up and they didn't have the money ready, we left."

The kid rubbed his chin, memories dancing behind his eyes. "I argued my head off. Told him we were losing customers. He said they knew the conditions before they hired us. Stubborn old coot. Collecting on that building was a fight every load, but because of him, it ended up costing us only half a load. A heavy hit, but one we could survive."

Noah's mood lifted. Now they were getting somewhere. "Do

you remember who you dealt with on the project?"

"I didn't deal with anyone. I had just graduated from college, a business degree clutched in my hot little hands. So of course he had me working outside, in the yard. Directing the loading."

"What about your dad? Would he remember anything?"

"He had a stroke last year. He doesn't talk, just sits on the sofa watching *Wheel of Fortune*."

"Any paperwork? Records?"

"He didn't bother with that. He knew the second time the owner changed names, the whole project was a lost cause."

Frustration crept into Noah's voice, but he bit it back. They couldn't afford to give up too easily. "Is there anyone here who might remember the name of a person? Someone actually on the job site?"

"Luis has been here forever. He might remember. You lucked out. He's yard manager now so he'll be on site. I'll call outside and get him."

While they waited for Luis, Conner passed the time asking Joel about the different buildings pictured on the walls and where he went to college.

Sure, his partner was a nice guy and talked easily to strangers, a talent Noah lacked, but this was part of his method of dealing with witnesses. Ensuring they felt like part of the investigation and would be eager to help, while sizing them up in case they were hiding information.

Noah simply paced, trying to keep his expectations under control.

When Luis appeared, he could have passed for a ghost. Everything about him was gray—his skin, his hair, his clothes— all covered in a thin layer of cement dust.

"Sure, yeah. I know the place you're talking about," he said, his voice accented but easy to understand. "There were workers on the building, but we didn't talk to them. There was one guy—the foreman, the owner, the architect—I don't remember, but he was in charge. He had a simple name. Bill, Bob, Tim, Tom, I don't know."

"What'd he look like?"

"Like a guy. Hard hat, work boots, yellow safety vest. It was a long time ago."

"Was he white? Black? Hispanic? Asian?"

Luis didn't answer.

"North Korean? Maori?"

That earned him a fuck-you stare.

"I had to translate, so not Hispanic. I'm thinking white, clean cut, management looking, so probably no facial hair."

A warm sense of triumph spread through Noah's chest. Sometimes Conner's 'Let's be friends' method worked. Sometimes his 'I'm not your friend' method worked. That's why they made good partners.

He had the guy cooperating. Now wasn't the time to stop. "Tall, short, fat, thin?"

"I'll check with my guys when they get in this evening. Maybe one of them will know."

"Can either of you give me a date? Exactly how long ago was this?"

Joel rubbed his baby-face. "I was straight out of college, so I'd have been twenty-two? I'm thirty-two now so I'm guessing ten years."

That kid is four years younger than I am? What'd he have hidden in that desk drawer, the key to the fountain of youth?

Maybe that's what happened when you spent your days sitting behind a desk in a business your father built instead of tramping around vacant fields, stepping on dead bodies.

Luis shrugged, sending up a puff of cement particles that settled on Noah, making his nose itch. "My Gracia started kindergarten that year. I dropped her at school on my way to work every day. She had her Quinceanera last summer. So, yeah, about ten years."

Noah handed both Luis and Joel his card with instructions to call if they had anything to add, but didn't expect them to.

Didn't matter if they called him, he'd call them. Assad, Jumbo, Sleeman, Luis, and anyone else they talked to would receive a reminder call, tonight, tomorrow, and the day after until they had something useful to tell him, some nugget of information, anything that gave them a starting point.

Conner pulled out of the parking lot in a cloud of dust. "I'm worried we're wasting our time asking about the derelict apartment building. We should be concentrating on the vacant lot and the victims."

"You're right. They're more important. But we have learned one thing of value today. The apartment construction was going on at the same time as the first set of murders. That's quite a coincidence."

Conner was silent for a few minutes. Concentrating on his driving or thinking? When he spoke, his voice barely covered the sound of the engine, but held a certain strength. "I don't believe in coincidence."

"I tend to agree with you. That's why I say we keep the lot and victims on the front burner, but don't forget about the building."

"You haven't heard anything from Doc or the Feebies? I'm

beginning to lose faith in our federal friends."

Noah checked his phone for the hundredth time. Maybe he hadn't heard it over Siri's directions. "Nope. No text. No email. No phone call. Nothing from Montgomery, Doc M, or Earl who promised to let me know if anything showed up at the office. My faith's a little shaky right now too, but chasing down these businesses is all we have to go on for the moment."

"It's frustrating, knowing that lowlife is out there laughing at us."

Noah bit the inside of his lip. That kind of thinking would get them nowhere. "I prefer thinking of him as quaking in his boots, knowing who's coming after him."

Less than a week, and due to a major apartment fire, a terrorist attack in a foreign city he'd never heard of, and a complete lack of progress made by the two idiots who were in charge of the investigation, the story was already relegated to a back page.

Was that good or bad?

Didn't people realize they were under attack right here? On their own streets? That he was their only hope?

Did they think he was doing this for himself? No. He wasn't a monster, attacking innocents. He was working for them.

Not that he didn't *enjoy* his work, that's what made him so good at it, but he was the garbage man, taking out the trash. The cleaner, sanitizing their neighborhoods.

Making the streets safer for their impressionable children and easily-tempted husbands.

Maybe it was time he stepped forward. Reaped the rewards

for his efforts. Let them know who they were dealing with.

The media. Not those two bumbling *Inspector Clouseaus*. They couldn't find their shoes on their own feet.

He'd have to be careful. Keep his identity hidden. He liked Houston. He'd made friends here. Or at least they *thought* he was their friend. He had a good job supervising other men while they did the heavy lifting. And he had his own money. No longer completely hobbled to the threats and whims of his father's purse strings and his stepmother's vengeance. Only using it as a backup, a cushion, a safety net in case of emergency.

His life here was arranged, orderly. He didn't want to move on. He'd done that too many times already.

He smoothed down his hair, and with that familiar movement a sense of calm washed over him.

He'd send a letter to the newspaper explaining everything. All he needed was a name to call himself. That fool reporter wrote about The Killing Field Murders. That referred to the vacant lot, not him.

He needed a signature that was powerful. Like The Son of Sam, or The Zodiac Killer.

A name that struck fear in the soul of the depraved and raised hope in the hearts of the righteous.

He'd think of something. And when he did, he'd strike up a one-way correspondence with that *Chronicle* reporter he'd seen hanging around the crime scene, R. J. Perry.

When people realized the service he performed, he'd get the respect he deserved.

CHAPTER
SEVENTEEN

SWEET PEA MET **Noah** at the door, doing her happy dance. She wagged her tail, leapt into the air, twirled around, and jumped from foot to foot in a miniature version of twerking.

"Well, hello to you, too, Pea. Are you glad to see me or do you just need to go outside?"

When the Yorkie didn't answer, he scooped her up in one hand and scratched the silky fur behind her ears and on top of her head.

He opened the door and sat on the stoop while she made her rounds of the backyard, checking for intruders. A spot in the corner where a neighbor's cat liked to visit got special attention.

Noah slumped forward: elbows on his knees, chin in his hands. The day certainly hadn't earned a spot in the win column.

The next three businesses he and Conner had visited yielded no new information. Doc M called, but they already knew the fingerprints on victim number one—the one found in the abandoned apartment—didn't match any known person, so discovering her DNA couldn't be matched came as no surprise.

The fingerprints on victim number two, the one whose grave Noah had stumbled into, should be available by tomorrow. Fingerprints and DNA on the remaining women would probably dribble in, one or two at a time.

On the plus side, Mr. Assad had called. His son promised to come over on Wednesday and get the box of papers down from the attic.

Luis hadn't called yet, but that was a case of no news is good news. As long as he hadn't stated no one in his crew remembered the foreman guy, there was still hope.

As for Lincoln Montgomery, the FBI agent had let him down. Sure, he'd been pulled off the case to help with a terrorist attack in France that had killed two American college students and he'd emailed a shit ton of papers listing corporations involved in the bankruptcy of the apartment building, but now what?

Earl was off for the week, getting checked out by his doctor, the department doctor, the insurance company doctor, the union doctor, and a barber in a white coat who happened to be walking past.

He and Conner had three choices. They could waste a day driving around town asking questions no one remembered the answers to. They could stay in the office and waste a day on the computer. Or they could split up and waste a day doing both. No matter what they did, tomorrow was likely to be a wasted day.

If only he had something, anything, to sink his teeth into.

Surprisingly, the thought didn't depress him the way it would have only a few months ago. Sooner or later, they'd find the douchebag. If not this week then next, or the week after or the year after.

He'd never let this case go no matter how long it took. And he was too stubborn to die before it was solved.

Something else nagged at the back of his mind. As much as he wanted this guy, would move mountains to find him, he finally understood. This was his job, not his life.

Seeing Laurel again had sparked something deep inside him. A hope for the future. He wasn't a fool. He realized he barely knew her. She might not be *the* one.

But she was definitely worth trying for.

Noah stood and whistled Sweet Pea inside for dinner. After he fed the dog, maybe he'd call Laurel.

Would calling two nights in a row be pushing things?

Laurel had just finished painting her toenails—a sparkly blue because the color made her smile—and was fanning them with a magazine when her cell rang. She hobbled on her heels to the kitchen table and swiped *answer* without looking.

She'd avoided her mother's calls all day and she might as well get the conversation over with even though she knew exactly how it would go.

Yes, she was still working for Royce Elkins even though he was a *nouveaux riches,* who only hired her for her name and to get even with Peter. Yes, he paid her well, but no, she couldn't loan her mother any money. Yes, her sister's—new car was beautiful, kid was a genius, husband was brilliant, home was gorgeous, vacation photos were to die for. Yes, she was sure she couldn't loan her mother any money.

She didn't bother with pleasantries, simply muttered,

"Yeah?"

"Laurel?"

At the sound of the deep male voice she fumbled the phone, dropping it on her cat, causing the black and white tom to let out a *screech* and run under the sofa.

"Are you okay? Is this a good time to talk?"

"Hi, Noah. I'm fine. Just dropped the phone on Harvey."

"If you have company I can call another time."

"My cat. Harvey. I named him after the invisible rabbit in that movie because you never see him until you step on him."

"The Jimmy Stewart movie. I saw it on TMC a couple of months ago."

"I saw it too, and that's when I got him. He's a rescue that allows me to feed him and clean his litter box. I think he's warming up to me. He gets close enough for me to hand him a treat and occasionally scratch behind his ears. He wouldn't do that when I brought him home."

"Sounds like my relationship with Sweet Pea. My dog. It took her three months to do more than walk past me after Betsy died." He stopped abruptly.

Now what? Should she ask about his wife or keep talking about the dog? The dog was a safer subject. "But she got past it, right?"

"Oh yeah. She's in my lap right now. I'll bet Harvey will in time, too."

"I'm counting on that, but if nothing else, I saved his life and gave him a warm home and plenty of food."

"That's worth remembering. How was your day? You said you'd be busy."

"I was. No good fairy came in did my job for me while I was

gone. Plus my boss left me a list of busy-work tasks to keep me occupied while he's gone."

"Don't worry about checking out that news story. Your job comes first."

"Are you kidding? I'd been planning to bring a book, maybe do my Christmas shopping online. This might be the only interesting thing I do all week." Was he brushing her off or being considerate? Decoding, over the phone, with someone you didn't know well yet was tough. She needed a Rosetta Stone for the newly divorced. A *Dummies Guide to Dating for the Over Thirty Set*.

This stuff hadn't been as hard when she was in her twenties. Guys came around like the proverbial bus, one every fifteen minutes. She'd pick one and pass on another for no more reason than the mood she was in.

When Paul showed up, her father not-so-subtly pushed her in his direction. Her mother invited him to spend Christmas day with them. Her sister *oohed* and *aahed* over her great catch. They couldn't all be wrong, could they?

Hopefully she was smarter now. Knew how easy it was to make a horrendous mistake.

She hit the speaker key and let Noah's voice fill the room. "Only if you're sure it won't interfere with your day job, because there's no rush on this. Say, did you meet Lefty Bob while we were working on Crystal's case?"

"No, I don't think so."

"As another lefty, you'll get a kick out of what that idiot did at work today. He's too cheap to buy business cards, so he designs his own on the computer and prints off a page worth at a time. Then he cuts them up to fit in his wallet. Except the station only has right handed scissors. I didn't even know there was a difference."

"Oh, yes. There's a big difference. If you use your left hand, your fingers don't fit through the holes in the handle. If you use your right hand, you usually manage to crumple up whatever you're cutting and turn it into a wadded mess."

"I got that idea. Lefty's fingers were stuck in the handle and he flicked his hand, trying to get them out, when the scissors came loose, flew across the room right in front of the Lieu and stuck into the wall. Another inch and they would have trimmed the boss's eyebrows, which would have been a blessing for all of us."

"Am I correct in guessing somewhere in your office, there's a Righty Bob?"

"Naw. There used to be a Bob, but he retired years ago. You know how it is. Once you have a nickname, you're stuck with it."

"So what's your nickname?" This should be interesting. What would his friends call him?

"I've been called plenty of names, but usually by someone I'm arresting. I occasionally call Conner Choirboy, but I'll do that to his face. He seems to think it's a compliment. In a way, I guess it is. What about you? Did you ever have a nickname?"

"A friend in high school used to call me Klutz. If it could be stubbed, bruised, or broken, I'm your gal. I swear inanimate objects spring to life just to jump out and trip me."

"I'll have to remember to be careful around you."

"Oh, yes. I've been known to stomp on toes or splash coffee on anyone close by. Do you have more *how cheap is he* Lefty Bob stories?"

"Enough to fill a bookstore."

They talked for fifteen more minutes, and each word was easier than the last. In no time they were laughing and interrupting each other.

Maybe she could learn to do this dating thing—if that's what this was—without feeling like a total fool.

Conner carried the running stroller into the house as gently as humanly possible and lifted the sleeping baby.

Jeannie stepped out of the kitchen, her eyes wide. A tinge of fear coated her whisper. "She's not crying. Is she alright?"

He mouthed, *fine,* and inclined his head toward the nursery where he practically tiptoed to the crib and laid Betsy next to the velveteen rabbit that had been Noah's gift to his Godchild.

Jeannie hovered over the sleeping baby. Checking her breathing? He tugged on her arm, pulling her out of the room before she woke Betsy. The baby monitor was on but unnecessary. If she woke, people in Pasadena would hear her crying.

"She simply…went to sleep?" The wonder in Jeannie's voice made him smile. Tough to manage in his exhausted state.

"Do you think maybe that doctor actually knew what he was talking about?"

Jeannie swatted his arm. "I feel like a terrible mother, putting a timer on her feedings and taking her off while she's still nursing."

"How do you think I felt? Jogging down the block with her screaming. You wouldn't believe the looks I got from strangers. But she stopped after five minutes. Even the books say don't overfeed. Use rhythmic motions and sounds to sooth."

"Promise me you didn't sing to her."

He wasn't an idiot. He didn't want the neighbors *and* Betsy crying. "Nope. Only the sound of the tires on the sidewalk and a breeze through the trees. Another few weeks and it'll be too dark to run after supper. I'll have to take her to the park where they have lighted paths."

"She's coming up on three months. Maybe she'll have outgrown the colic by then."

If only. He wasn't sure which was harder, listening to his daughter cry and being unable to calm her or watching his wife ache for the same reason.

Conner stood at the window, staring into space, but Jeannie turned toward the bedroom. "Whatever the reason, Betsy's not crying now and she could be in ten minutes. I'm going to bed while I can. You coming?"

"In a minute. I was just thinking." Something he hadn't had a chance to do lately. Not with this case and Betsy's colic and money worries and life in general.

Jeannie slipped behind him, putting her arms around his waist and nuzzling her head between his shoulder blades. "What has you so worried you don't want to come to bed with me?"

Whoa. Where did she get that idea? And how fast could he correct it? He swung around and planted a kiss on the top of her head. "Nothing is that important. I'm right behind you."

She held up her hand. "No. Tell me. I want to know what's on your mind. Is it the Killing Field case?"

"I can't lie. It's the worst case I've ever worked. Ever will work, I hope. And it will probably keep me up nights before it's solved. But I was thinking about Noah. He's started being secretive again. He slipped out of the office during the middle of the day without telling me where he was going. He went to

Austin last weekend and lied to me about it."

"He got past the anniversary of Betsy's death without any problems I could see. That's the date I was worried about. And he's seemed fine the last few times he came over. Does he act depressed like he did last year?"

"No. He actually looked happy Monday morning. That's why I asked about his weekend."

"Then he's earned some privacy. We've watched his every move for too long. He's a big boy. Let him be. He saved my life and he saved Betsy. You know I love him like a brother, but I don't want him in my bedroom."

He could live with that. There was plenty of time to worry about Noah another day. Right now, Jeannie's hair looked like it hadn't been washed or brushed in days. She had on stretched-out yoga pants. And she smelled like a cross between baby puke and breast milk.

And she'd never looked sexier since the day he first met her.

CHAPTER EIGHTEEN

*D*AMN. CONNER MUST *have gotten laid last night.*

Noah watched as Conner, goofy grin plastered across his face, loped into the office carrying a cardboard container with four Starbucks coffees.

He set one on his own desk, handed one to Noah, one to Lefty Bob, and hesitated at Earl's empty desk before shrugging and giving the last one to Lieutenant Jansen, who was standing in the door of his office, his wooly eyebrows knitted in a frown.

The Lieu took a sip and nodded toward his office. "Daugherty. Crawford. May I have a word with you, please?"

Shit. Not good when Jansen was polite. When the Lieu was brusque, almost rude, it meant he was in a rush. Give him the facts and move on. When he said "Please" he was in a bad mood. Probably getting grief from up above. Or from his wife. Which would be better for him and Connor in this instance.

"I came in to find a memo from the Chief on my desk. What the fuck the man was doing wandering around the station that late I have no idea. Probably had a fight with his wife." Jansen stuck his lower lip out like a petulant teenager.

Holy Shit! The Lieu was in trouble at the office *and* at home. It would take more than a free coffee to improve his mood. He shot Conner a get-ready-for-a-long-day look, but the idiot was still smiling.

Jansen placed his coffee on the corner of his desk, untouched except for the first sip. "Seems he checked the murder book for the Killing Fields last night and didn't find it to his liking. You two got a break with that terrorist attack in France, but that was two days ago and the media's forgotten about it. Now they're back to focusing on us. We gave you the cadaver dogs. What more do you want? Do I need to turn this over to Lefty Bob Hernandez?"

Oh. Hell. No. This was his case now and he didn't plan to let it go. It wouldn't *be* a case without him. He found the third body and insisted there were more. No one took a case away from him.

"We've been making progress, sir." Conner finally spoke up. About time, too. The paper-jockey was in charge of the murder book. "We've found the store that sold the money order paying taxes on the land and should have a copy of that by Thursday. We're following up on leads to a man who worked for the owners of the apartment building and hope to have his name later today. Give me an hour and the book will be up-to-date. As soon as Doc M sends us more information on the victims, our progress will pick up speed."

Actually, Doc had sent a text claiming to have some additional information on one of the bodies, but Noah didn't see any reason to mention that now. No point making Conner look bad because he came in late looking like a frat boy on Sunday morning. He'd stood up and taken the hit on the murder book.

Jansen crossed behind his desk and settled himself in the ergo-dynamically designed chair Noah coveted. "Get to it, then. I've got enough work to do without riding herd on you two dickheads."

Aaand the boss was back to his grouchy self. Maybe the day wouldn't be too bad after all.

Noah left Conner at the office, working on the murder book, while he headed for the morgue. Lola knew the way by now.

When he pushed open the door to room three, Doc M was up to his elbows in what had once been a woman. Lefty Bob stood to the side, taking notes.

"That's not another one of my victims, is it?" Could the boss have gone behind his back and pulled in Lefty?

"No. I believe this is what you and Detective Hernandez call an open and shut case." The old ghoul had the nerve to laugh as he sewed up the body.

Noah couldn't tell if Lefty Bob was laughing behind his mask—as if a piece of white paper could block the smell—but there was definitely a hint of a chuckle in his voice. "We already have the husband in custody. They were playing for the club couples championship when she had the nerve to question his backswing, his choice of club, and his parentage. When SWAT broke down the door, he was cleaning the blood off his putter and her body was still warm."

Noah took another look at the divot missing from the side of her head and knew it wasn't one of his strangler cases. "What'd ya call me over here for then, Doc? To help Lefty Bob fill out the paperwork?"

"Due to my years of experience, dedication to hard work, and the promise of overtime pay, I have information on two of your victims."

Now he was talking. "Spit it out. Don't make me come after you."

Doc offered him a steely glare. He'd been a fighter in his younger days and had the broken nose to prove it. "I have managed to acquire fingerprints on Kathy—"

"You've identified her?" Wow. That was quick work. Even for the doc.

"Out of respect for the women, I've assigned them names instead of numbers. Remember, they go from longest dead to most recent. I've named them Anna, Bertha, Cloe, Danni, Elsa, Fran, Grace, Hattie, Inez, Joyce, Kathy, and Lucy."

Damn. He should have thought of that.

"We already had fingerprints and DNA for Lucy. Now I have the prints for Kathy and Joyce. I've sent the prints and DNA samples to Lincoln to put on the FBI data base."

Good. The FBI had better contacts than HPD.

"I discovered one thing I overlooked in Joyce. She had a spiral fracture of her left humerus."

Noah blinked, running through the names of bones until the doc pointed to his upper arm.

Shouldn't Doc have noticed that sooner? "You told me her right wrist was broken, but her left arm also? Did he do that on purpose to keep her from escaping?"

"No, it was broken before, when she was a kid. Not your usual slip-and-fall fracture. Caused by more of a twisting motion. Along with a couple of ribs. I didn't see it until the x-rays came back. Either she was an incompetent athlete, which I don't believe due to her musculature, or she was abused as a child."

Noah's heart dropped. The poor kid never had a chance.

Hard to see how that was any help in solving the case, but it was more than they had yesterday.

"That's not the reason I asked you to come by. I could have emailed you that information."

Exactly what Noah was thinking.

"I checked out the dental records you gave me before we sent the impressions to the forensic dentist. I'm no expert, and the x-rays you gave me were made when she was still a growing girl, but to me, they could be a match for the woman I named Cloe. There's a possibility she's Felicia Vickers. As you seemed to have an interest in the case, I wanted to notify you personally, although I would appreciate it if you didn't make this public until it's official. I could easily be wrong. After all this time, what difference will a week make?"

Noah opened his mouth, but didn't have enough air to speak. Doc M had no idea.

Noah's phone chirped as he waited outside Headquarters for Conner. The number was unfamiliar but that didn't matter considering how many of his business cards he'd passed out lately.

He hit *Accept.* "Daugherty."

"This is Luis, from Sleeman Cement."

"Yes, Luis. Did any of your workers remember the name of the guy from the apartment building?"

Conner opened the door and slid into Lola. He started to say something but Noah pointed to his phone.

"Everyone agrees his name was Dick. They called him Big Dick because he was, you know, big and a dick. It was summer, late summer like July or August, and we were dying in the heat. But every time we needed him, he was AWOL. We'd find him sleeping in his truck with the air conditioning running."

Now they were getting somewhere. Maybe. "Any other description?" Big didn't carry much weight with a jury.

"He was white. Caucasian. No facial hair. Always had on sunglasses. He wore work type clothes, but nicer than ours. Pants pressed with a crease, shirt starched. You knew he was basically a suit playing dress-up."

"What about his truck. If you had to find it to wake him up, maybe you could identify it."

"One of those panel vans everybody has. A light color. Jose needed something—a screwdriver maybe—and he opened the back. It was full of brand new tools and construction equipment."

The information was flying in. One girl had a shitty childhood and a big guy named Dick worked on a construction site. They should wrap it up any day now.

And oh yeah, the name of a victim he hadn't mentioned to Conner yet.

Noah switched off his phone and switched on his blinker.

"What was that?" Conner asked.

"Dick," Noah snapped. Somehow, he couldn't force himself to say more.

Conner sat in silence as he maneuvered into traffic. From the expression on his face, the wheels in his head were spinning faster than the ones on Lola. "The construction foreman," he finally answered.

"Yep. A big guy. Looked like management but drove a light-colored panel van full of tools. Plus one of the victims was likely abused as a kid."

"Okay then. We might as well turn around and go back to the office. This one's obviously solved."

Yep, my thoughts exactly.

The bank that had foreclosed on the apartment building was less than ten minutes from Headquarters and Noah would have suggested walking but the sky was an ominous gray and spit out occasional fat drops of rain, as if it couldn't make up its mind what it wanted to do.

Lola's wipers were set on automatic and would *shrrack, shrrack* each time they wiped across the too-dry windshield, sometimes once and pause, sometimes twice and a longer pause.

The combination of the irritating sound and the uneven rhythm had Noah ready to climb out the window and leave Lola with Conner no matter what the weather.

They made it inside the bank two seconds before the deluge. Rain poured down in a solid sheet. The day had turned into night in the time it took the door to close behind them. Flashes of lightening lit the sky and thunder sent out shock waves that rattled glass.

An air of nervous energy filled the lobby as customers tried to decide whether to run for their cars or wait out the storm. Free coffee and cookies won, and patrons rushed for the few available seats like a game of musical chairs.

Noah approached an elegantly dressed black woman with a name tag that read *Abby.* "We'd like to speak to the manager, please."

Abby looked puzzled. "Are you applying for a loan or

opening a new account?"

"Neither. Hopefully talking to the person in charge."

"I can do a better job of steering you to the right person if I know what you need." She was pleasant, smiling, but unable to fit them into one of her little boxes.

Noah pushed his coat back far enough to let his badge peek out before allowing it drop back again. "I'm investigating a murder, twelve murders, and I'd like to speak to the person who has the power to give me the information I need."

Abby's pupils doubled in size, becoming brown circles with a slight rim of white. She held up one finger before pirouetting and disappearing around the corner.

Two minutes later, she reappeared and beckoned them closer. "Mr. Sheffield will see you now."

Inside the postage-stamp office, the rain drummed on the roof and splattered against the window, causing a reverberating echo.

A teenager sat behind an almost wall-to-wall desk.

What was with kids running the world these days? Had everyone over forty been put out to pasture?

The kid held out a manicured hand. "Eric Sheffield."

Noah shook his hand harder than necessary. "Detectives Daugherty and Conner. We're looking for any information you can give us on the original owners of an apartment building located on Varner Road, near the ship channel bridge. The property was foreclosed on six years ago."

"I know the property you're talking about. The FBI contacted me yesterday. I sent them the name of the corporation earlier this morning."

"That company is out of business with no forwarding

information. We're looking for the original owners and some personal data. Names of the officers."

"I gave that nice FBI agent everything I had. Sorry."

Sheffield didn't look sorry. He looked annoyed at the interruption. And if Lincoln Montgomery was coming across as "nice," he wasn't doing his job.

"Do you have any old files or records, anything that might date that far back? They foreclosed six years ago, but started construction four years earlier."

"Like I told you, I wouldn't have anything more than I already sent the FBI. You'll have to talk to them." Sheffield leaned back in his chair and steepled his hands, like a grade school principal finished with his lecture.

Noah wanted to slap the snot out of him, but Conner stepped forward, handing the kid his spiral notepad. "If you could write down the number for your supervisor and whoever in the corporation is in charge of this type of recordkeeping, we'll be out of your way."

"I've told you twice. We don't have that information," Sheffield whined.

The reason Noah knew he whined was because the rain had lightened and he could hear the pleading in the kid's voice.

Noah could also hear a growing disturbance outside the office. The sound of raised voices penetrated the closed door.

He turned his back on Conner and Sheffield and opened the door three inches. From his position, he couldn't see into the lobby, but he could hear a man's voice.

"Everybody down on the floor. Now!"

Noah eased through the door, edging closer until he could see the lobby reflected in the glass of an office. A man wearing camouflage shirt, pants, and ski mask had a gun pointed toward the ceiling.

Why the hell did those stupid numb-nuts wear camo? Did they think no one could see them? That they'd blend into the woodwork?

A *crack* split the air as lightening flashed. The lights flickered and went out. During the pause before the generator kicked on, a long, slow roll of thunder filled the room.

Noah inched forward on cat's feet. He slid his weapon from its holster. A customer screamed when she saw him and the rest of the patrons looked his direction.

The man in the mask began to turn around as Noah smashed him in the head with the handle of his Glock. The knitted fabric of the mask blunted the blow and the man paused, but didn't go down.

Noah tuned out the sound of screaming that bounced around the lobby. He pulled his arm back as far as it would go and swung at the only part of the man's face uncovered by the mask.

His nose.

This time the man went down on his knees. Blood spurted from his nose like someone had turned on a water tap. He dropped his gun and sagged to the floor.

Noah stepped forward and stomped on the man's hand as he groped for his lost gun.

A black dress shoe appeared from behind him and kicked the weapon, causing it to skid, spinning, across the floor.

Conner.

His partner dropped to his knees and slapped cuffs on the prone robber, being careful not to get blood on his clean slacks.

"If you'd just shot the fucker I'd be out of here in time for dinner and my nightly jog. Now we'll have to take him to the hospital and I won't get home until after dark."

Noah scooped the can of dog food into Sweet Pea's dish. She lapped it up immediately, surprisingly accepting of dinner at ten thirty.

He reached down and stroked her back. "You've certainly turned Zen on me lately. There was a time when you refused to eat except at your regularly scheduled time of six thirty in the morning and six thirty at night. Have you learned to forgive me for working crazy hours or did you get tired of being hungry?"

The Yorkie didn't look up until the dish was licked clean.

Conner, on the other hand, seemed to be heading the opposite direction. Sure, nobody likes to come home in the dark, when everyone in the house is asleep but that's part of being a cop.

Shit happens.

Especially if you stumble into a bank robbery.

The fact that Conner used the term "fucker," was the equivalent of the Pope shooting the finger to TV cameras.

Noah used that term and worse several times a day. But not Conner. The choirboy didn't approve of cursing and didn't do it himself.

So missing dinner and his nightly jog had to be a big deal.

What did that mean? Was his partner regretting his decision to stay in Homicide? Longing for the regular hours of Internal Affairs? Considering a transfer to Media Relations?

Or had Conner picked up on the fact that Noah was keeping

secrets?

Noah dropped the empty dog food can into the trash and slammed the lid. He was supposed to be a detective, dammit. He couldn't even decipher clues from someone he was around every day. How was he supposed to solve a case with no clues whatsoever?

Only one good thing had come from this day. Well, two. He'd taken down a hopped-up drug head waving a broken gun and no one got hurt.

Thank God he didn't have to shoot the kid.

After the robber had been hauled away in handcuffs, Sheffield had refused a second request for more information. But Abby, the bank's assistant manager, had hugged him tight, thanking him loudly and profusely for saving her life.

Meanwhile, she'd slipped a note in his hand and whispered, "This is the number of the guy who used to be in charge of loans here. He might be able to help you."

Tomorrow he'd have somewhere to start. A toehold.

CHAPTER NINETEEN

NOAH BEAT CONNER into the office by a whole three minutes. Would wonders never cease? He'd already opened his email when his partner set a coffee-shop cup of dark roast goodness in front of him.

"Sorry I was an ass yesterday. Evenings are when Betsy's colic kicks up. If I can take her out for a jog, she calms down and we can get her to bed with only minimal fuss."

Hell. Maybe I was the ass. Had he cut Conner any slack for daddy duties? "Why don't I come over this weekend and let you guys go out for dinner? I prefer lifting weights, but I can jog if necessary."

Conner's eyes lit up like he'd won the lottery. "Are you sure? It's not easy. She's been known to scream for two, three hours."

Really? He had no idea it was that bad. Why hadn't Conner let on? "I can handle it. I've babysat Emma and Iris since they were born."

But they never had colic. They'd cry for a few minutes, but he'd rock them and sing and they'd settle down. Maybe that was the problem. Maybe Conner sang to Betsy. That would make anyone cry.

Time for a subject change. "I got an email from Doc M at the morgue. He sent the DNA results on the first two victims over to Lincoln Montgomery who posted them on CODIS. There's a chance we'll have something in a few hours." And a chance they wouldn't hear anything for days, maybe months. Even with the new rapid DNA techniques, suspects came before victims.

Conner's voice held a note of disbelief. "That was fast. Now we can find out if working with Montgomery and the FBI is worth the hassle. So far, I'm voting yes. You?"

Noah was torn. Unlike Conner, who had a slight case of hero worship for Feds, he had an ingrained distrust for the Feebies, their condescending agents, and the two-last-names Lincoln Montgomery with his perfect hair and shiny SUV in particular. But Montgomery had stayed all night to help Doc, kept him and Conner up on any information he'd uncovered, and made use of federal resources on their behalf. All while working other cases. "I'm going to hold off voting until I see what CODIS turns up."

"What about the message Abby at the bank slipped you last night?"

He'd seen that, had he? Conner didn't miss much, that's for sure. Maybe that's what his partner was pissed about last night. Maybe he didn't have any idea about the other secrets. "It's the phone number for the guy who handled loans during that time period. She said he might remember something. You want to call him or shall I?"

"She gave you the number."

But you're better with people than I am.

Conner flipped on his computer and began checking his messages. Noah gave up and started dialing. The number was the man's home phone and his wife answered. Noah identified himself as a Houston detective, but gave no other information.

Curiosity filled the wife's voice, but Noah declined to elaborate. The number she gave him reached a local bank in Kilgore. He waited while the operator transferred his call.

"Auto loans. Nick Travers." The voice was pleasant, not young or old, definitely southern.

"Mr. Travers, this is Detective Noah Daugherty with the Houston Police Department."

Travers gave a short laugh. "I didn't leave any unpaid parking tickets behind when I moved, did I?"

"Not that I know of, sir. I'm working on an old case. Can you remember any details about a loan you approved for an apartment building on Vernon Street that eventually went into foreclosure? That would have been about ten years ago."

What were the chances he could remember one loan out of hundreds, maybe thousands? Noah barely remembered his address ten years ago.

"I'm going to take a wild guess and say Abby Willis gave you my number."

"That's correct. The manager of that bank wasn't particularly cooperative and she thought you might remember something helpful."

"You didn't tell my wife Abby gave you my number, did you?"

Had he? He couldn't remember. "I don't believe I did. Just identified myself as a police officer."

"Doesn't matter. She'll have a fit anyway. Abby should have gotten that job when I left, but that snot-nose Sheffield was the CEO's son-in-law. I'm not surprised he wouldn't help you. That would mean he had to make a decision."

"Do you remember the loan I'm talking about?"

"Oh, yeah. Cost me my job. Although that might be the best thing that ever happened to me. I love it here. The bank's smaller. You get to know the people you're dealing with. No one looking over my shoulder all day. The kids have more freedom than in the big city. Gave me and my wife a chance to start over."

What'd they say? TMI. Too much information. Although he'd bet there was a story in there between Travers and Abby. "What can you tell me about the loan? I'm looking for the names of individuals." Noah held his breath. If Travers said he didn't remember or needed a warrant, he was dead in the water.

"Old man Dwyer pushed for the loan, even though it was too big for us to handle. One of the partners was his fraternity brother from college. The first corporation was named Frio or something like that. It had Dwyer's frat brother, Darius Mason, but also Bradly R. Bachman, Senior and Junior, and the Keillor brothers. I can't remember their names. Maybe a couple of more people. Mason's wife might have been listed as a secretary or something, but that was in name only because she was a recluse. Never left the house."

Noah made notes as fast as he could. Even asked for confirmation of spelling.

"Anyway, Mason died, he was the money man, and the corporation fell apart. Only to be put back together with a few new people under a new name. Llano, I think. That's the first time I asked Dwyer for permission to lay the loan off on a bigger entity. Then Bachman senior wanted out. He was going through a nasty divorce. He'd loaned Junior the cash for his share of the investment, which meant he was out, too. Not surprising. The kid was a loser. A college dropout playing with daddy's money. One of the Keillor brothers got into some tax trouble and moved to Costa Rica and a new corporation was formed. By this time, I knew we were in deep shit."

Interviewing over the phone was tough. You couldn't see the guy's face. Noah didn't want him to quit talking, so he threw in an "Uh huh."

"The construction costs kept climbing with all the delays. By that time, they owed everyone and their uncle plus a bucket-load of back taxes. All the money was gone because they paid themselves big salaries. I lobbied to take over and finish building but Dwyer wanted to retire so we washed our hands of it and let Harris County deal with the headache. The whole situation was a black mark on our loan department so I lost my job and reputation. The joke's on them. I'm much happier now."

Noah drilled him for more information and got a couple of tidbits, but nothing substantial. Now he had a few names. Not much to go on, but somewhere to start.

He put down the phone and glanced over to see Conner grinning like a kid with an ice cream cone and holding up a slip of paper.

The sky had cleared since yesterday's rain, leaving a few puffy white clouds against a robin's egg blue background. Noah glanced up and smiled. No wonder he loved autumn.

Any decent pool car—an oxymoron if ever there was one—

would be gone by this time of the morning, so he drove Lola and Conner navigated.

The duplex in Montrose was gray-painted brick with a black wrought-iron hand rail on both sides of the four steps up to the miniature porch. Noah rubbed the worry stone in his pocket as the doorbell *bing-bonged* inside.

"Think he's in?" Noah whispered.

"His website lists him as an interior designer at this address. If he wants business, hopefully he's working."

The man who opened the door had a shaved head, tattoos crawling up the side of his neck and a Metallica T-shirt. He was probably an inch shorter than Conner so about five-eleven without the steel-toed work boots. Not exactly how Noah would have pictured an interior designer.

"I'm sorry. I wasn't expecting anyone this morning. Did you have an appointment?" He had the door open, so Noah stepped through. That was an invitation as far as he was concerned.

"No. No appointment. I'm Detective Noah Daugherty and this is my partner, Conner Crawford. We're looking for Niles Biermann. Is that you?" It better be. The guy was in Niles Biermann's house.

"Yes. What can I help you with?" He seemed surprised, but didn't back away as if he had something to hide.

"We're looking for information on one of your missing relatives."

Hazel eyes didn't blink. "You'll have to be more specific. All my relatives are missing."

Conner held out a drawing of Kathy Doe made by the department forensic artist. "Do you recognize this woman?"

Biermann took the drawing and headed toward the back of

the house. "Let's go to my office. The light is better in there."

Noah tried to get a feel for the house as they traipsed through the living room and dining room but Biermann speed-walked to his office. All Noah managed was a quick glimpse of original artwork and a mirrored wall with a ballet barre.

The interior designer's office might once have been a patio, but now sported glass walls and ceiling, Moroccan tile floor, and a whiteboard covered with paint chips, fabric swatches, and floor plans.

Biermann reached for a pair of steel-rimmed glasses. He laid the drawing on his worktable and switched on a lamp. Taking his time, he scrutinizing every line. "You say she's my relative? What's her name?"

"That's what we came here to find out." Noah tried to keep the exasperation out of his voice, but from the look on Biermann's face, he failed.

"I was born in the women's restroom of the downtown Hilton Hotel and left there to be found by the cleaning crew. I have no idea who I might or might not be related to. That's why I had my DNA tested and posted on a site that promises to search for long lost relatives. In three months, this is the only hit I've had."

That's why the results came back so fast. One mystery solved. A dozen more to go.

"What is she, my sister?"

"They only give the results in percentages. She's most likely your half-sister, although first cousin is a possibility."

"So dear old mom kept it up and had more kids after me." He reached out a finger and traced the curve of her face. "I'm guessing she's dead, not missing. Otherwise you'd have real photos instead of a pen and ink sketch, even if it is well done. What the fuck, Mother. Why not mess up another life while you're at it?"

"We don't actually know if she's related to you on your mother's side or your father's side."

"Does it matter?"

Probably not. Damn this case. If there'd been anything unbreakable around, Noah would have kicked it. Pain and suffering every direction he looked.

He turned to study a stylistic drawing of a flower and let Conner handle the comforting words.

"Niles?" A beautiful—and pregnant—woman came into the room. "I didn't realize we had clients."

"Hi, honey. You feeling better?"

"Much better, thanks." Her head swiveled from Noah to Conner and back.

Biermann draped his arm around the woman's shoulders. "This is my wife, Aurora. The talent behind this business. I was a pretty messed-up kid, but I always liked to draw. She's the one who taught me how to channel that talent. Honey, these gentlemen are police detectives checking on a missing person who may be my half-sister."

"Really?" Her eyes lit up. "They found your family?"

"Only this one woman they can't identify." He showed her the sketch.

"Did something happen to her?" Tears filled her eyes and her lower lip quivered.

"For the moment, she's just missing. Why don't you go back upstairs and finish your nap. Doctor's orders. I'll come up later and bring you some tea."

After Aurora left, he turned toward Noah. "You'll have to pardon my wife. We've lost two babies already and she got it in her mind we needed to check for birth defects in our families. She knows every ancestor of hers on both sides back to the Civil War, so it must be my fault." He pointed to the drawing Conner was now holding. "What happened to her?"

"Did you see the news last week?" Noah hoped to Hell he didn't have to go into more detail.

"The Killing Field?"

"Yeah, sorry."

"On the bottom of this picture you wrote Kathy Doe."

"We gave them all names."

"Would you do me a favor? Since she's related to me, could you call her Kathy Biermann?"

Noah glanced at Conner. Why not? "We can do that."

"One more thing. Well, two. May I keep the picture?"

Conner took a last look at the sketch and handed it to Biermann. "Sure, we have more at the office."

"Also, when this is over, and you get ready to dispose of the bodies. I'd like to take care of her funeral."

Noah couldn't bring himself to speak so he gave a quick nod. Maybe people weren't so bad after all. "If it's any consolation, I read the autopsy report. Doc said she was in good health."

Biermann looked up the stairs where his wife had disappeared. "That does help. Thanks."

Yesterday's rain had left the night sky clear as a pane of glass. The stars stood out like diamonds on black velvet. Even the air smelled fresh, new.

He'd only wanted an evening drive. To enjoy the beauty of city lights reflected in the wet pavement. But that wasn't to be. A force beyond his control pulled him toward the meaner side of town.

To neighborhoods where darkness was a friend. Where dirty streets cried out, begging to be swept clean.

Where a snippy little tramp sashayed her tight ass in his face, daring him to call her bluff.

Perhaps he should have tried harder to resist. Said, "All in due time." But then what? Let filth overrun the city? Allow more families to be destroyed by depraved temptations?

The moon wasn't full, but did that matter?

Not when he had a calling.

Not when there was so much work to do.

Not when there was so little time left to do it.

He'd had his fun. He'd taught her a lesson, although she was stubborn. It had taken all night and most of the morning. Now what? Tonight he'd wash her clean. Send her on her way pure. But where? He hadn't prepared a place.

He *was* getting sloppy and that wasn't like him. He smoothed back a lock of errant hair, maybe it was time to move on after all. Find a new home. He'd never stayed in one place this long before. Now he understood why. Starting afresh on his mission would keep his mind sharp.

Houston was too big. If he cleaned one area, the filth popped up in a new spot. Like Whack-a-Mole but with harlots.

As soon as he disposed of his visitor, he'd start considering a move.

But if he moved, no one would know what he'd done. How he'd dedicated his life to providing a safe environment for mothers and children.

His name wouldn't be forgotten.

It would never be known.

The lull between lunchtime traffic and rush hour was short but vital. Noah didn't need Siri's advice to find Headquarters. He and Conner drove in silence until Conner sighed in frustration. "We've worked every lead we have for the last week and aren't one iota closer to knowing the identity of our local, neighborhood psychopath. Any suggestions?"

A panel van with a plumber's number on the side sped past. Noah briefly considered making an impromptu traffic stop. At least they would have accomplished something worthwhile today. Better not. He'd probably end up having to appear in traffic court. Best to concentrate on the case they were working.

"Want to drop by the lab and see if they have anything of interest to tell us? They've had several days to work on trace evidence. Then tomorrow, if we still don't have an identification on any of our victims, we can drive out toward the ship channel and case the area, see if we can find anyone to interview." Well, they'd identified one victim but he wasn't supposed to know that yet. Why hadn't he told Conner about taking Felicia Vickers's file to the M.E. that first day? Now it felt like a weight between them. All because he was embarrassed to admit a failure from ten years ago.

"That's likely to be a wasted day, but we have to do something, so lab today, location tomorrow. Unless something better turns up."

Noah had no sooner agreed than his cell rang. One glance at

the number and he took the phone off hands-free. Not something he usually did and Conner noticed immediately.

Too bad. His partner didn't have to know everything about his life.

"Hi." *Shit.* His usual greeting was a curt *Daugherty.* Way to advertise this was a personal call. Conner didn't say anything, but he noticed everything.

"Hi Noah, This is Laurel."

He knew who it was, but just repeated, "Hi."

"Did you get the email I sent you? I found the information you wanted on Tom Meyer's old client."

"My phone showed I got an email, but I've been out of the office all day. I was waiting till later to read it. That sounds great. Thanks. You saved me a lot of work."

"I'm sorry. I didn't mean to disturb you. I'd never sent you an email before and wanted to make sure I had the right address."

"You didn't disturb me. Conner and I are driving over to the lab to pick up some reports."

"Tell him I said hello."

Not gonna happen. Conner could sit there and wonder. It would do him good.

"That was the most fun I've had all week. Is there anything else I could look up for you? I'm going crazy sitting here with nothing to do, and my boss won't be back until Friday."

It didn't sound like fun to Noah. He'd rather walk on nails than search for information on the computer. But with Earl out, that's what was waiting for him. "I've got a couple of names you could check out for me. If you really want to. This would be finding their phone numbers and addresses only. I don't want you to call them or contact them in any way. Promise?"

"Sure. I feel like Mata Hari."

The thought scared him. "Well, you're not, so don't try to act like her." This was a mistake. He shouldn't have included her. She was a civilian.

Too late now. He rattled off the names he could remember from his phone conversation with Nick Travers in Kilgore.

"Got it. I'll get right on this and let you go back to work."

"Thanks, Laurel. I appreciate it."

Shoot. He'd used her name. No point in pretending now. "That was Laurel Bledsoe…uhmm Newcomb. She's going to look up some phone numbers for us."

Conner didn't blink. "That's nice."

And Noah had thought he was the one with a poker face.

CHAPTER
TWENTY

OR A PLACE that was supposed to be sterile, the crime lab
smelled distinctly dirty. Every time Conner visited, he
worried about cross-contamination.

He pushed through the door to Trace Evidence leaving Noah
to check in with Fingerprints.

Inside, Benny Schroeder looked up from his microscope.

"Have you found anything new for us?" Conner asked the
Bozo lookalike.

"Did I call you? Ask you to drop by? Because I don't
remember doing that. Yours isn't the only homicide in Houston."

"It's the majority of them. Come on. Give. I know you have
something I can use." The damn techies considered the lab their
personal fiefdom.

"Do you have any idea how much dirt I've had to comb
though, to catalogue, to identify? Eleven graves. Each with its
own case file. Each with a separate tag number. And you want me
to rush? What happens if I get on the stand and make a mistake?

Get confused? There goes your case. Is that what you want?"

Talk about a *prima donna*. Somebody didn't get enough attention as a kid.

"What I *want,* is to solve more murders than you can count on two hands and put away a deranged killer before he strikes again. Do you have any information that could help me with that?"

"I've processed the dirt from seven of the graves. So far I've discovered—just as Dr. Mackie said about the bodies—about half the graves are from approximately ten years ago. The rest are fairly recent. The killer left no hair, fibers, or semen, in or around the graves."

The first warning bites of heartburn chewed at his gut. No information wasn't an acceptable answer. The murdering creep must have left something somewhere. "This case is a priority. Don't push it aside to do a favor for a friend. We need to get this guy off the streets."

"If you're in such a God-awful hurry, you can help me identify something. I've collected a few of these seeds from three of the sites. They come from the common cattail which grows about anywhere there's water: a pond, a ditch, a low, marshy area. Trouble is, they don't show up in any of the photos of the area. And I have to explain how they got into the graves. There would only have to be one or two plants if your guy brushed against them."

Conner took the folder and headed for the door. He didn't want to *delay* Benny a minute longer than necessary. He was waiting in the lobby when his partner returned from Fingerprints. "You get anything?" Probably not, if he returned that fast.

"No, but they'll have two more sets of prints by this afternoon. The only way this many girls have disappeared unnoticed is if they were hookers. If that's true, maybe one of them will have a record. What about you? Was Benny helpful?"

"Not intentionally." Conner handed Noah photos of a cattail plant and the seeds that came off it. "Our guy apparently brushed up against one of these plants and Benny can't find any photo of them on the site. He wants proof they grow in the area. I'm thinking if we knew where they grow on the lot, we'll know the path he took with the bodies."

If he and Noah were going to check the neighborhood tomorrow, it might be helpful to know which direction to start.

His plan was wild. Insane.

So crazy it just might work.

He'd driven past the lot an hour ago—he hadn't planned to, his van seemed to go that way of its own accord—and found the place deserted. No cops. No guards. No media.

Unbelievable!

His heart sped up, racing along with his thoughts.

The crime scene tape was still there, flapping in the breeze. Mounds of fresh dirt littered the landscape. Colored marker poles remained planted beside each disposal site. He didn't like to think of them as graves. The occupants were trash. Good for nothing but compost.

For all practical purposes, the area was as useless as the day he spotted it. Forgotten. Abandoned.

Waiting.

He needed to switch to his car and go back. Drive around the scene a couple of times. Look for hidden surveillance. Cameras. Parked cars.

If he didn't find any, there was plenty of time to go back home. Take a long nap. Set his alarm for midnight. Spend a pleasant hour cleaning, sanitizing. Finishing his work.

Then he could reawaken the land. Put it to good use again.

He hated waste of any kind.

Noah leaned back in his Henry Miller chair and put his feet on his desk. How quickly this had become his new evening routine. Even Sweet Pea now padded to his office, waiting to be scooped into his lap and fed an occasional Cheetos nub, instead of heading for the den and a night of watching TV.

He pressed *call*. Talking to Laurel was the high point of his day.

Even if it didn't mean anything. They were just friends. He refused to read anything more into their relationship.

"I can't believe how fast you uncovered those phone numbers. Not one of those people is easy to find. It would have taken me all day. Especially Keillor, the guy in Costa Rica."

"I'm not sure most of them will do you any good. The home that old lady lives in doesn't specify on their website, but I got the impression it was for nutcases. Rich nutcases maybe, but still…"

"And the guy hiding out from the tax collector isn't going to be anxious to talk to any type of police. But hey, I'm willing to try. The problem is I don't know that they'll be able to tell me much even if they're willing to. The killer probably saw the empty building sitting there, abandoned, when he was in the field and decided to use it. What I wish I had was the owner of the land where the bodies were found, but that's so tied up in secrecy, I'd need to dig it out with a backhoe."

"Hey, are you underestimating my powers again? If its real estate related, I can find it. I know every backdoor, secret hideaway, slippery paperwork scheme known to mankind. Text me the address and I'll wave my magic wand at work tomorrow."

"You can do that?"

"Sure, but it'll cost you."

"I don't know. You sound pretty pricy to me and the department's famous for having arms too short to reach their pockets. What were you thinking?"

"Tacos al carbon and a Margarita should do the trick."

"I think I can swing that. I'm supposed to babysit for Conner and Jeannie Saturday night. How about Sunday?"

"Perfect. There's a hole-in-the-wall Mexican place a block from me. Afterwards, we can go to my place and watch the Texans play the Colts."

"You like football?" Betsy had tolerated it, curling up next to him and reading while he watched.

"To tell the truth, I prefer the college games. The pros are too...professional." She chuckled at her own joke and Noah joined in. "But you have to keep up with the home teams. The Texans, the 'Stros, U of H."

"You remember our deal." If she could lay down conditions, so could he.

"Our deal? I didn't know we had a deal."

"You find phone numbers and addresses only. You don't call the numbers or contact the people in any way."

"You don't trust me?" Her words were serious, but her voice held a playful note.

He wasn't taking any chances. "I trust you just fine. It's him I don't trust. I don't want you on his radar in any capacity. Plus there's the problem of testifying in court. You don't want to get tangled up in that mess."

"I'm fine with that. I'll stay well in the background. So, Sunday night. How about six-thirty? Want me to text you my address?"

He was a cop. He'd already found her address, but that sounded a bit on the creepy side. Best not to let her know. "Sure, that's a good idea."

Noah checked his computer. Costa Rica was an hour behind Houston, so that made it 7:20 local time. Not too late to call.

The woman who answered had a heavy accent. Keillor's maid? Local girlfriend? Nurse? Certainly not his wife who had stayed behind in Austin to divorce him.

Mr. Keillor was out on the dock, fishing. Was this important? She could go get him.

It was important.

The wait was long, but Noah wasn't paying by the minute. If he left a number, he'd never hear from the guy.

Jerome Keillor's footsteps sounded strong and his voice vigorous for an eighty-two-year-old man. "Yes? Who is this?"

"Good evening, Mr. Keillor. This is Noah Daugherty. I'm a detective with the Houston Police Department—"

"I have no desire to speak to you."

"I'm investigating several local murders and one of the bodies was found on a property you once owned a portion of. I'd be very grateful for any information you could give me about an apartment building on Vernon Street."

"That money pit? I got out of that venture years ago and good riddance."

"Do you know the names of anyone who actually worked on the site?"

"Of course not. I lived in Austin. I never saw the site. Darius Mason put together that deal and I went along for the ride. And it was a bumpy one."

"But you were paid a salary as an officer of the corporation."

"I thought you said you were a police detective, not an IRS agent. I don't know anything about that building, what happened to it, or where the money went. Or about some murder two thousand miles away from here. Now, if you'll excuse me, the bass are running."

Noah stared at his phone. Thank goodness cell phones didn't have receivers to slam, or his ears would have been ringing.

CHAPTER
TWENTY-ONE

THURSDAY MORNING THE temperature had cooled off to a reasonable seventy-four, with an expected high of eighty-two. The sun was out. The sky was clear. Despite being hung up on by Jerome Keillor last night, Noah was in a good mood.

Today was the day. Something good would happen. Something to move the case along.

Conner beat him into the station which was a sure sign life was returning to normal. Although …he did like it better when his partner was late and brought in coffee as a peace offering.

Luckily, he'd already had two cups before he left the house.

"I talked to Jerome Keillor last night." A dirty trick, but one way to see if Conner had been listening in to his phone call with Laurel.

Conner blinked a couple of times, going through the Rolodex of names in his mind. "One of the Frio Corporation directors?"

Damn that man had a memory.

"Yeah. He had tax problems, not exclusive to but exacerbated by, his part ownership of that building. He fled to Costa Rico and spends his time fishing."

"And what did he have to say that might help us?"

"Nothing. He knew nothing. He did nothing. He remembered nothing. The bass were running. Goodbye."

"Wow. Is there any way we can jam him up? Encourage him to be more helpful?"

"I doubt it. The IRS probably knows where he is. He's an old fart with enough money to spend the last few years of his life in Costa Rica, but nowhere else."

"You gonna call the rest of them?"

"I will because I don't have anything better to do, but I doubt I'll learn anything useful. One old lady is in a nursing home on her last legs. She probably never even knew she was listed as an officer. Just drooled and drew her salary."

"You remember in high school when they showed you the film about how colds or viruses spread? One person coughs and spreads it to another who touches something you touched, and so on. That's what this reminds me of. A virus that leaves everyone who comes in contact with that building or vacant lot contaminated."

Damn. Sometimes the things Connor came up with were positively profound.

If they didn't come up with a lead to work on soon, he'd have to tell Conner and the Lieu about the possibility that Felicia Vickers was one of their victims. Then he'd have to explain how he knew and why he'd kept that piece of information to himself. And he *really* didn't want to admit that.

Noah flipped on his computer and scrolled through five

mundane messages before hitting one from Lincoln Montgomery. They'd found a DNA match for another victim.

He swiveled his chair toward Conner. "Saddle up, partner. We're headed for Huntsville."

Once past The Woodlands and Conroe, Lola ate up the miles to Huntsville. Noah and Conner were parked and inside the prison by 10:30.

Getting permission to visit one of the inmates took a little longer.

God, Noah hated that place. If the Harris County Jail was bad, the prison was ten times worse.

Rancid food fought with body order for the worst smell. Filth seemed ground into the cement.

The constant noise was unbearable. Barred doors clanged shut while electric motors opened others. Unseen voices echoed from one end to the other.

Harsh lighting glared in spots and left others in shadow.

The only color was gray. Gray floors. Gray walls. Gray faces.

Even the air felt heavy with desperation and dashed hopes

If the place affected him so deeply, what must it do to those who spent decades inside? How could they ever hope to live a normal life when released?

Roscoe "Burning Man" Madison wasn't a big man. Maybe five seven or eight. An ugly scar down one arm. Face like a boxer who'd never won a round.

But one look at his eyes and Noah had no desire to meet him in a dark alley.

"I'm not supposed to talk to you without my lawyer."

"Then why did you agree to?" Noah found he really wanted to know the answer.

"Ahh. I'm not even sure I still have a lawyer. Haven't set eyes on one in probably five years. Nah. This here's a chance to get out of my cell. Talk to someone different. See a new face." He leaned closer. "A face I won't forget if you try to screw with me."

Conner cleared his throat and Madison sat back in his metal chair. "We didn't come about your case, Mr. Madison. This is a personal matter."

"What, a rich uncle died and left me money? Whoop-de-doo. Lotta good it'll do me in here."

Noah took a deep breath and wished he hadn't. He refused to cough in front of the prisoner. Any sign of weakness and the guy would clam up. "We're looking for information about a murder, but let me say right at the start. We don't suspect you or anyone you know. This murder took place within the last two months. You'd been incarcerated for twenty years by then."

Madison laughed and the sound went straight down Noah's spine. "How the fuck do you expect me to help you with a murder from two months ago? I think my alibi's pretty solid."

Conner opened the folder he'd been holding. "We need assistance identifying the victim. She's approximately eighteen years old, has brown hair, and green eyes. DNA tests tell us she's your daughter."

"The fuck you say." Madison slammed his hand on the table and the sound of the chains on his wrists rattled through the tiny room with an echo that bounced from wall to wall filling every corner. "Where's she been the last twenty years? She sure as hell never visited me."

Probably best to avoid that question.

"If she's eighteen, that means you had relations with her

mother shortly before you were arrested. Did you have a specific girlfriend at that time?" Conner's voice was smooth, calm, but listening to him ask this thug about his sex life left Noah biting back laughter.

"I wasn't much older than that myself. I liked to play the field. Try a little taste of this and that. Ya know what I mean?"

"I can certainly understand that." Conner didn't blink. Just kept going like this was the most natural thing in the world. "What about during your trial. Was there anyone special who came to court? Visited you in jail?"

Madison's eyes dropped. The first time he'd shown any hint of regret. "Didn't nobody come to my trial. Hell, my lawyer barely showed up and then he slept through half of it."

Noah'd had enough of this. Conner's gentlemanly manner wasn't getting them anywhere. Time to crawl down to the inmate's level. "If I was sent to this place and knew I wouldn't touch another woman for twenty or thirty years, I'd remember every minute of the times I had. I might lie in my cell at night and relive every second. Remember what she tasted like, smelled like. What her skin felt like under my hand. How she tossed her hair. The sounds she made. The things she did to me. Are you telling me you didn't do that? Don't still do that?"

Madison glared at him but didn't answer so Noah reached over, pulled out the drawing the forensic artist had made, and pushed it across the table. "Does she remind you of any of that multitude of women you slept with?"

"I maybe exaggerated a little." Madison glanced around as if making sure no one else could hear him. "I was only with a couple of girls. Thing is, I don't necessarily know their names."

Ah fuck. Why did I expect anything different?

Noah sagged against the uncomfortable chair. "Can you tell

us anything? What'd they look like? Where'd you meet them? Where'd they live? What'd you call them? Honey, Sweetie, a pet name?"

"Dancing Queen."

Now they were getting somewhere. Maybe.

"The one girl was black, so it wasn't her. The other, she liked to go to this joint on Shepherd. Called Night Magic or something like that. Had live music on weekends. She liked to dance. She had the moves, I'm telling you. She drove a dark blue Honda. We did it in the back seat two, three weekends in a row." He smiled at the memory and Noah's hands tingled with the urge to throttle him.

"One thing. She wore this necklace. Like a pair of pompoms." He crossed his wrists as best he could with the restraints. "Don't know if she was telling the truth, but she said she was a cheerleader. I mean, damn. A fucking cheerleader."

Madison studied his fingernails before looking at the picture again. "What happened to this girl? My daughter."

Noah let Conner answer. He was better at that sort of thing. "She was strangled."

"Raped?"

"Yes." Probably best not to tell him about the abuse she went through as a child.

Madison slid the drawing back across the table. "Do me a favor. If you catch the guy, make sure you put him in here with me."

Noah left Lola's windows down and the AC on as they flew down I-45. The air tasted sweet and he wasn't worried about messing his hair.

It took ten minutes to clear his lungs of the prison stink.

"Think we can find this alleged cheerleader?" Conner asked.

The street noise made talking difficult and Noah pushed a button to close the windows before answering. "I'd say chances are fifty-fifty. First let's find this Night Magic dance club. Then we can figure out which high school is nearest. After that, check their yearbooks for cheerleaders."

"That sounds like a good plan. Let's see if I can find an address."

Noah let Conner work on locating the twenty-year-old nightclub while he concentrated on driving. He didn't sympathize with Madison—the man was exactly where he deserved to be—but the thought of spending the majority of your life in a place like that gave Noah a claustrophobic chill.

He'd lost a lot in life, and he'd allowed his world to shrink smaller and smaller. If he wasn't careful, he'd be living in a prison of his own making.

"Got it."

Conner's exclamation snapped him away from the pull of depression.

"What'd you find?"

"The place burned down fifteen year ago. Looks like Lamar High School on Westheimer is our best bet."

The October sun felt warm but not hot, traffic was light, and despite her misadventures, Lola was pure power under his hands. He hadn't set foot in Lamar High School since a choir contest more years ago than he wanted to think about.

The assistant principal made noises about a warrant but Conner set her straight by mentioning that the yearbooks didn't contain any privileged information.

She led them to the library, showed them the yearbook for the correct date, and left them, but not before whispering instructions to the librarian. Those instructions must have included the phrase, "Watch them like a hawk. They're not to be trusted."

This must be how a bug under a microscope felt.

Two pages of the yearbook were devoted to the cheerleading squad. One page showed pictures of the girls in a pyramid, cheering a touchdown, and selling mums for homecoming. The other page featured individual photos.

Two of the cheerleaders were male, so Noah ignored them. That left six girls. One was blonde and wore a pompom necklace. Her name was Darlene Quinlen—Dancing Queen?—but he used his phone to snap pictures of each one, just to be thorough.

Fifteen minutes spent editing the photos so that only their faces showed—he didn't want an identification based on the necklace alone—and he emailed them to Huntsville.

The warden could show the pictures to Madison and get an ID. Noah wasn't going back to that prison unless dragged.

Conner clicked his seatbelt and settled against the leather seats, anxious to get away before the bell rang and waves of students enveloped them, trapping them in teenage hell.

Noah switched on his blinker and pulled out of the parking lot. "Let's get back to the office and see what we can find. We can start a search on this Darlene Quinlen and be ready when we get the ID."

"I'm all for it, but there's something I'd like to do first. Benny

Schroeder asked us to check the killing field for cattails. It's only a couple of miles out of the way and if we can figure out where he parked his vehicle, maybe we can find some store—even if it's a couple of blocks away—that has video surveillance. If we can identify the cheerleader's daughter, maybe we can come up with a date to check."

"That's a lot of *ifs*, but you're right. We can hardly complain about Trace not sending us anything when they asked for our help. Besides, every time we've been there, the place was crawling with personnel. I'd like to stand in the center of that field in silence. See if I can get a feel for it. I still have too many questions."

That might sound ridiculous to anyone else, but Conner knew exactly what he meant. If you stood perfectly still in the middle of a crime scene, you learned things. How far did sound carry? How much traffic passed? How much warning would you have if someone was coming? How fast could you hide? "We'd have to come back at night to answer some of the questions, but this would be a start."

Conner leaned his head back and relaxed, letting Noah take care of the driving. Betsy had been doing better the last few nights, but he wasn't fooled. The crying jags could start up again at any time. He'd learned to rest when he could.

What would happen if Jeannie went back to teaching in January? He'd told her over and over that she didn't need to, but she knew the money situation as well as he did. They had two choices: He could get a part time job, be exhausted and never see Jeannie or Betsy, or she could go back to teaching. Then they'd both be tired and never see Betsy.

Would things be better if he'd stayed in seminary? No.

Except for a few mega-churches, pastors didn't make any more than civil servants. He should have been a lawyer or a doctor. Then he'd have student loans to pay off. Lincoln Montgomery wore expensive looking suits. Did the FBI pay better than HPD?

"We're here."

"What?"

"The field. I hate to wake you, but we're here."

He hadn't fallen asleep, had he?

"This was all your idea. Where do you want to start?"

Not his idea. Benny Schroeder's. "How about that corner. If I were a murdering psychopath, that's where I'd want to be. Farthest from the freeway and feeder street. Hardest to see."

"Your wish is my command." Noah drove Lola around the corner and parked. Climbing onto the truck bed, he opened the lockbox and took out a pair of knee-high boots.

Well damn. Why hadn't he thought of that? There was one place he could save money. Start buying less expensive clothes. Maybe pants could be washed instead of dry-cleaned.

Conner held out his phone with a photo of a cattail. "This is what we're supposed to be looking for. It grows near water. I don't see any ditch, but some of the spots were low. Maybe that's enough for them."

Noah held out his arm, stopping Conner. "I don't see any ditches, but I see something else."

"What?' He glanced up from his phone.

"Look ahead of us. What do you see?"

At 3:00 the sun was low in the sky, casting its rays in a slant across the field. A faint but definite trail of bent grass led across the vacant lot. Conner used the camera on his phone to take a photo, but clouds drifted across the sun and he wasn't sure how well it showed up.

Noah put a hand on his shoulder. "Good call, partner. If I even need someone to slip into the mind of a psychopath, I'll call on you. I think we definitely found his path."

"Why didn't we see it before?"

"We were never here this time of day before, or from this angle. He must have driven down this street. I think I saw a few shops a couple of blocks to the west. Let's head that way. See if we can find any surveillance footage."

"Not so fast. We're here. I'm not facing Benny without spending at least fifteen minutes searching for cattails."

CHAPTER
TWENTY-TWO

NOAH FOLLOWED A few feet behind Conner as they wandered around the field, skirting the now empty graves, in their search for cattails. This was his partner's idea, let him take the lead.

Walking over the uneven ground covered in weeds and bushes was tough and Noah broke out in a sweat.

After five minutes, they split up to save time.

Conner scoured the east side of the field while Noah combed the west. Not a hint of a cattail anywhere. He'd call the whole thing a fool's errand if they hadn't spotted the trail indicating where the perp parked. And even that could have been made by an animal. Or one of their own investigators.

He was almost finished when his foot sunk into a patch of soft dirt.

Dammit. Good thing he'd put on the boots from his cargo box. That didn't help his pants, but it saved his shoes.

Last time he'd pulled his foot straight up. That hadn't worked out so well. In a number of ways.

No crime scene techs were around with their handy shovels and he'd be damned if he planned to stand there like a bear in a trap waiting for Conner to come rescue him. Maybe if he wiggled his foot from side to side.

Just when he was about to give up, his boot broke free with a solid *sluurpp*. But a section of dirt and several stalks of tall weeds came with it.

Something wasn't right.

He did a slow pivot. The lot contained all types of weeds, some tall, some short, some with flowers, but with the recent rains, they all looked strong, healthy.

The weeds by his foot were dry and droopy.

He lifted one sprig and it slid straight out of the dirt, its root long and clean. As if it had just been planted. He reached behind him and pulled on a healthy weed. It broke off at ground level.

Someone had been planting weeds. And there was only one reason to do that. He did a slow pivot to count the graves.

Ten.

"Conner," he called to his partner on the other end of the field.

"I hope you found some cattails," he said, tromping through the weeds Noah's direction. "I'm ready to ditch this place and get back to the office while we still have time to start searching for that cheerleader."

Noah's heart sagged in his chest, as if it weighted forty pounds. "I don't think we're going to make it back to the office any time soon."

It wasn't supposed to work this way.

His job was to solve the crime. He came in after and picked

up the pieces. Asked questions. Took notes.

He wasn't supposed to discover the bodies. But he had. Twice now. And he didn't like it.

Noah kicked at a clod of dirt while he waited for crime scene to uncover the grave. Or was it re-uncover? They'd dug this one up once before.

Whose was it originally? He ought to know out of respect to the dead woman. All the dead women. The ones already in the morgue and the one being unearthed now.

This was one screwed up case.

What did all the wisecrackers say? Be careful what you wish for? He'd started the day sure he'd find something to move the case forward.

He just hadn't planned on another body. How many more would there be before they locked this sucker away?

Dr. Mackie stood beside him as the last of the dirt was swept away from the woman's face. "I hate to be picky, but could you give me a couple of weeks before you find any more bodies. We're full up at the morgue these days."

"Fuck off." Had he really said that to Doc M? Out loud?

Doc put a hand on his shoulder and he shrugged it off. What was that, sympathy? To hell with it. Time to get off the pity train.

Conner was standing beside the grave, taking notes. Noah waved him over. "Want to get out of here and see if we can catch this guy?"

"About time we did something constructive. I've had it with twelve-year-old techies ordering me around. *Don't' stand in my light. Don't step there. Don't touch that.*

"I don't care if we have to search five blocks in every direction. We're still in the middle of Houston. There's got to be a security camera someplace he drove past. Now that we know a time frame, we can start searching."

Lola roared to life the instant he turned the key. She was as anxious to get started as he was. Two blocks later, Noah saw a bodega. Closed for the night.

A block after that was a bank. The ATM was inside the locked foyer, but visible through the glass. Conner made a note of the name and address of each place so they could start on a warrant for any surveillance footage first thing in the morning.

Circling back on the other side of the lot, they found a gas station/convenience store still open. On the off chance they had a video and were willing to share without a warrant, he and Conner went in.

The camera was mounted in plain sight as a deterrent, but according to the clerk had been broken since he started working there six months ago.

Conner snapped his memo book closed as they stood under the store overhang and watched a sudden shower spring up. "What'd ya say, partner? Go back and stand in the rain while they load the body into the bus or wait till tomorrow and see what the doc has to say?"

Noah glanced at his watch. "Everybody's gone by now. Let's head home. I'll start work on the warrants tonight and email the info to your computer at work. You can tweak it in the morning and run it past the Lieu. We'll take it to a judge and head for these stores as soon as the ink's dry."

"You don't want to go to the morgue first?"

He never *wanted* to go to the morgue. "Tired as Doc looked, he won't get to her autopsy before mid-afternoon. We'll have plenty of chance to serve the warrants first. Any spare time we'll spend looking for the cheerleader." Identifying one of the earlier victims didn't seem as urgent as it had that morning.

When he'd first gotten up, he'd bitched because they didn't have any leads to follow. Now they had more than they could manage.

Why didn't that make him feel any better?

Even Sweet Pea had fallen asleep by the time Noah switched off his computer. The warrant information was as detailed as he could make it.

If he was asking to search someone's house, a judge might balk. But for copies of surveillance videos? He didn't foresee any problems.

Not even if he had to go in front of Hard Ass Hargity.

The numerals on his phone flipped over to 11:14. Too late to call Laurel. This was the first time he'd missed since they reconnected last weekend.

Only a few days, but funny how he already missed hearing her voice before he turned in for the night.

She'd certainly understand. Especially since it was all over the evening news. He'd hoped for another day before the media vultures picked up on the story.

The pressure would start the minute the Chief got to the office, bellowing about how he was up half the night with irate phone calls.

Bullshit. Everyone knew he transferred all calls to his assistant after 7:30. He needed his beauty sleep to look good in front of the cameras. Oops, too late. He should have gone to bed about 1985.

Maybe their friendly FBI Agent, Lincoln Montgomery should take over the on-camera news conferences. Not only could he put together two sentences without tripping over his tongue, he had a face made for TV.

Not like his lieutenant. With those eyebrows, Jansen looked like a Cro-Magnon throwback. Who was he kidding? The Chief lived for the limelight. He'd never pass up an opportunity to have his picture taken.

Usually with his foot in his mouth.

While that might give Noah perverse personal pleasure, it didn't help the department. So now the pressure ramped up to solve this case. Not only to get some murdering bastard off the streets, but to save face for the department before the Chief made all cops everywhere look like imbeciles.

Way to add tension to a job that was already stressful.

Other than that, he'd had only one email all evening. Apparently Doc had stayed late to finish the autopsy. He'd hoped for something, anything, that would lead to her killer. But no such luck. Nothing in it was a surprise.

The girl was approximately eighteen. She had been strangled. Her wrists showed signs of restraints. And she'd been washed clean. There was only one slight difference. Her stomach contents showed the remains of a date.

Did that mean the killer didn't keep her as long for some reason? Or had she eaten the date immediately before her abduction?

No way to know. And did it make any difference?

Noah switched off his computer, let Sweet Pea out for a final run, and called it a night.

Maybe they'd catch a break tomorrow.

CHAPTER
TWENTY-THREE

"DAUGHERTY. CRAWFORD. MY office. Now." Lieutenant Jansen's voice was like a cup of cold water in Noah's face.

It had to be something bad. He hadn't had time to screw up this morning.

Conner glanced his way and shrugged. Whatever it was, his partner didn't know either.

The squad room grew deathly silent as the occupant of every desk turned their head to see what disaster was about to befall them.

Noah jumped up and banged his knee on an open desk drawer, driving a sharp pain into the bone. Tingles traveled up and down his leg. Several choice curse words found their way to the tip of his tongue, but he swallowed them down.

Things were about to get serious. He didn't need to make them worse.

The Lieu stepped back and opened his door wider to allow

Conner and him to enter. A visitor was sitting in the best guest chair—the one saved for VIPs. One glance and Noah's heart skipped several beats before slamming into his rib cage and trying to crawl up his throat.

And he thought facing the Chief was the worst thing that could happen.

A head of Don King hair and a face even a mother would have trouble loving turned toward him.

"Detectives." The Lieu nodded toward his guest. "You remember R. J. Perry from the *Houston Chronicle*."

Fuck. Noah remembered him. He'd just hoped never to see him again. And if the son-of-a-bitch made the slightest reference to the story he'd put him on the track of, he'd make the reporter's life so miserable he'd beg for an assignment covering polar bear hunting in the Arctic.

He'd never mentioned to Conner the report he'd slipped Perry, but the subsequent newspaper articles were hard to ignore, and his partner was anything but dumb.

"Nice to see you again, Mr. Perry." Conner's words were warm, but his tone was cold.

Noah simply nodded. He didn't trust himself to speak.

"Mr. Perry has been kind enough to bring us a copy of some interesting information he acquired on our recent murders." Jansen's face was a mask, allowing no hint of emotion to slip through.

Perry unclasped a manila envelope and a plastic baggie with a sheet of computer paper and its matching envelope fell onto the Lieu's desk. The slight *thump* was a hammer in Noah's chest.

That fucking strangler was writing letters to the paper?

"Unfortunately, several people touched this before it reached my desk and I realized what it was. I immediately took pains to see it was preserved. I didn't receive it in time to make the morning edition but it will appear in full on our website and tomorrow's paper. You may certainly keep this. I made copies."

Of course he made fucking copies. He's a lowlife newsman. Now he'll probably write a book and get rich off other people's misery.

Jansen cleared his throat and it sounded like an overloaded freight train heading up a hill. He didn't make it to lieutenant by being a wuss. "We would prefer that you kept this confidential while we complete our investigation. No point in giving this... *person*...the notoriety he obviously wants. Plus, we need time to study this communication. Pull every ounce of information from it possible."

Perry had the nerve to smile. "I'm sure you would prefer that. Not going to happen."

"I can take this to court. Get an injunction." Jansen's voice still had a low, threatening rumble.

"Good luck with that. No judge who hopes to be re-elected would ever stomp on freedom of the press. I'll tell you what I will do for you. I'll hold off until morning. That'll give you time to get started before the poop hits the propeller."

Mr. Big-Hearted. Acting so full of compassion, understanding. He'd never have made that offer without the prior approval of his boss. And that guy's boss. No, he needed the time to do the research necessary for a proper, award-worthy, feature. Not to mention, online articles didn't sell newspapers and opened the door for TV to be first on the air with the juicy scoop.

Jansen motioned for Noah and Conner to stay behind after

Perry left. A totally unnecessary move. Noah wasn't stirring until he'd studied that letter.

Without removing the protective baggie, he slid the note under the Lieu's desk lamp for a closer look. There was nothing extraordinary about the letter itself.

Printed on standard computer paper. The lab could probably tell them the brand of paper and printer.

Mailed in a four-by-nine white envelope with a peel and stick flap. No DNA there.

Addressed to R. J. Perry at the *Chronicle*, but no return address. Probably used the same computer.

One of those self-sticking Forever stamps. Again, no DNA.

The cancellation stamp read "South Houston," but that didn't mean a thing except that the perp probably lived anywhere *but* South Houston.

Noah smoothed the plastic and began to read.

My Dear Mr. Perry,

The cops can't be trusted. They neither do their job nor tell the truth. So I put my faith in you and a free press.

Our fair city, and many others in this great country, are overrun with filth. Harlots walk the streets in broad daylight, poisoning the minds of impressionable children and tempting husbands away from their faithful wives.

Loving homes are destroyed. Families are ripped apart. Children become pawns in a never ending game of pass the blame.

Young boys grow up with a twisted sense of

morality.

Innocent girls are tainted with sin.

Don't look to our police force for help. Greed and glory blind them.

The power of politics is all they know. Their leaders are corrupt so they are corrupt.

Who can you turn to in these trying times?

Who can you depend on to do what is right no matter the cost?

Who will clean your streets? Collect your garbage? Take out your trash? Who will teach a lesson to those who use their charms for evil purposes?

Who will protect those driven mad with temptation?

I will.

I have been anointed your defender.

Do not look for me for you will not find me. I am both invisible and invincible. I have walked through fire and come out unscathed.

I pass you on crowded streets, yet you do not see me.

But I am always there.

In case you doubt my sincerity, return to the place we first met. I have left you a gift.

The Sanitizer.

"Holy shit! Who does this guy think he is, Batman?" Noah slammed the letter onto the Lieu's desk. "We have to get Perry back in here. Ask him if anyone spoke to him at the first crime scene. See if he's being followed."

"Relax, I've already done that and the answer is a resounding *No*."

"How do we know he's telling the truth? He's a reporter. He can't be trusted."

Jansen sat for the first time since he'd called Noah and Conner into his office. "Of course he's lying. That's why I have Lefty Bob tailing him."

Conner was struggling to get a decent photograph of the letter inside its plastic baggie when he stopped and glowered at Jansen. "What about his fingerprints? We know he touched the letter."

"He claims we have them. He's in the system."

Noah's head popped up. "What? He has a record? Do we know for what? Is there any chance *he's* the Sanitizer?"

"Why do you think I have him under surveillance?"

"It'll take more than one person." Frustration was building in Noah's chest. He wanted to get out there and chase the reporter down.

"If you'll give me five minutes, I'll arrange that. Hard to do when he's standing in front of you."

Noah started to pace the room. Making a list of needed actions. "We've got to get copies of every newscast. Not only the film they showed on air, but every frame they shot. If Perry talked to anyone, I want to know about it. If he didn't, I want to know that, too."

"Again, give me five minutes to start making phone calls. Now, you two guys have a warrant waiting to be served."

The Lieu had to be kidding. Drop their first solid lead for some lame-ass videos? "We need to get on this. See what Perry's record says."

"Believe it or not, I still remember how to look up a rap sheet. Now, get out there and pick up those surveillance videos. While you're gone, Crime Scene can be analyzing the letter. See what they can learn. Lift all available fingerprints. By the time you get back, maybe we'll have something to work with."

Well, damn, they finally had a suspect. And it was R. J. Perry. Who would have believed it?

CHAPTER
TWENTY-FOUR

IT GALLED NOAH to admit the Lieu was right. When he and Conner got back from picking up the videos, Crime Scene still hadn't finished analyzing the letter.

The bodega owner had bent over backwards to be helpful. He pulled the surveillance video from its compartment without even asking for a warrant. "You let me know if you need anything else. I'm always happy to help *la policia*."

The man tried to push fresh fruit and vegetables on the partners, but Noah refused. Conner took two ears of sweet corn but insisted on paying for them.

The bank was a different story. The manager was friendly, polite, yet insisted on seeing the warrant. He then called his boss. He called the head office. He called the security company.

The result was a tie. No win. No loss. He was happy to turn over the video, but it was kept off premises. Come back on Monday and he'd have it for them.

The drive back to the office from the bank took fifteen

minutes. Noah wasn't sure what Conner was thinking about, but *he* spent the time plotting the perfect revenge for those who delayed releasing vital information while a serial killer roamed the city.

Slowly sinking in quicksand while your rescuer finished his lunch? Waiting on death row for the governor's pardon? Spending eternity in Hell running on a treadmill with a bottle of water barely out of reach?

He had finally decided on being caught in a riptide and swimming for shore while the current pulled you farther away when they reached Headquarters.

Once inside, Noah got two diet Cokes from the vending machine while Conner set up the bodega videos.

"This copy starts on Monday. He could have taken her then, but I'm guessing it was Tuesday evening or night. Kept her till the early morning hours on Thursday. She hadn't been in the ground more than a few hours when we found her." Conner fiddled with the control knobs and the screen lit up.

The bodega owner had positioned the camera to show the sidewalk in front of his store. The bins of fruits and vegetables he'd set out were clearly visible. A section of the street heading east was in view, but westbound traffic could only be seen in quick glimpses between cars.

Conner paused the video constantly, listing every car that passed, noting the time, and his best guess at color. Difficult from the grainy black and white film.

Noah was the car guy and offered his opinion on make and model when possible. Otherwise Conner wrote sedan, pickup, SUV, panel truck. In that neighborhood, there weren't any late model sports cars.

At 3:26 a.m. on Thursday morning, more than an hour since the last car passed, a white panel van drove past the bodega in the direction of the Killing Field.

Thirty-seven minutes later, it drove past again. Going the other direction.

"Let's start over from the beginning and see if he's been by before."

"I have almost two dozen light-colored vans listed as passing. Not sure how we're going to know if it's the same one." Conner tapped the list he'd been keeping.

"This one's got a different rim on the rear driver's side tire." The color was the same, but the shape was slightly different.

Conner peered at the paused video. "Dang. I never noticed that. Good eye."

"Put up the picture of the van leaving the scene. See if we can find any distinguishing marks on the passenger side."

Five minutes later, Conner had printed off two copies each of both sides of the van. "What's this mark here? Near the back. Is it rust?"

"Could be. Kind of small but if we can get a good angle we might be able to see it."

Noah rolled his head from side to side, stretching his neck. This was it. He could feel it. The trick now was to stay calm, not get excited and miss something.

The video started early Monday morning. The bodega owner set out his bins of produce, cars rolled by, customers shopped, the sun went down, and the owner brought his bins inside and closed for the night.

Seven panel vans passed, but they were the wrong model or lacked the correct markings.

Tuesday morning's video started the same way. The bins went up, people shopped, trucks passed but not the right one, and the sun began to set. Traffic and pedestrians thinned to almost nothing. The owner came out and began to close for the night.

"Stop right there," Noah shouted. "It's our victim."

"How do you know? You can barely see her. The owner's in the way. Sure, she's short and has long dark hair, but this is an Hispanic neighborhood. That description fits half the women who've shopped there."

"He tried to talk her into buying some dates. Look, he gives her one to taste."

"Son-of-a-bitch." Conner seldom cursed at all, and Noah had never heard him use that term. "Her last meal. Doc found the remains of a date in her stomach."

Noah reached across his partner and pressed the *play* button.

Seventeen seconds later, the white van drove past.

Where was the fucking bank video when you needed it? Two blocks down the street. Was she still walking? How long did it take the van to cover that distance?

Noah revised his revenge estimate. A riptide alone was too easy. Add sharks. No, then it would be over fast. Make that a swarm of stinging jellyfish.

And a lifeguard on shore smiling and waving while promising to help on Monday.

Noah dug for his wallet and pulled out Lincoln Montgomery's card. He punched in the number and waited until he heard the FBI agent answer.

"Montgomery."

"Daugherty here. I'm taking you up on your offer of help. There's a bank with surveillance video I need. I'll text you the address and phone number. They already have the warrant, but say they can't get me a copy before Monday."

"I'm in Nebraska."

"I don't give a fuck where you are. I want that video in an hour."

Noah, Conner, and Lefty Bob Hernandez crowded into Lt. Jansen's office. There were only two visitor chairs so Noah leaned against the wall.

He was too antsy to sit anyway. "You're sure Perry is covered?"

"We can't loiter inside his office at the *Chronicle*, but I left Kevin Gilmore watching his car."

"He's a rookie."

Jansen shot Noah a *fuck you* glare. "He's new to Homicide, but not to the force. I think he can handle watching a parked car. Especially one that ugly. Hernandez is more valuable here."

Lefty Bob broke in, "I'm already working on a warrant for a tracking device for his car."

"But he drove a van when he abducted that woman."

"He lives on the tenth floor of a high-rise apartment. As soon as Gilmore relieved me, I drove out there. No light-colored panel van in the parking garage or on a nearby street."

Conner rubbed his eyes. "Kind of hard to drag an unconscious woman up and down ten flights of stairs and using an elevator is out of the question."

"Could wrap her up and use the freight elevator." A growing sense of desperation gnawed at Noah. He wasn't going to give up. Not on something this important.

"Perry? He's got sixty-five in his rearview mirror and not in the best shape. If he's spent a day in the gym in the last twenty years, it was to do an expose. I watched him walk out of here and two blocks to his car. He was wheezing like an asthmatic in a house full of cats."

A ball of acid formed in Noah's gut and began climbing its way up. "He's our best suspect. We're not going to write him off because it would have been inconvenient for him to abduct all those women."

"Of course not." Conner snapped his head around to face Noah. "Trace Elements said three of the women had cattail residue on their bodies. There weren't any cattails in that field or anywhere around Perry's apartment. Odds are, he, or whoever did this, has a cabin—a hideout, if you will—where he takes them for privacy. A tracing device on his car will show us where."

They were right, dammit. "Yeah, and if it's not him. Maybe it can lead us to whoever he talks to. If he didn't write that letter himself, somebody else did and they picked him to contact."

Jansen sat up straight and put down the pen he'd been drumming on his desk. "Alright then. We're in agreement about the tracking device. What's next?"

Conner checked his memo pad for the questions he'd noted. "Did we find anything about Perry's record?"

"You'll love this." Jansen gave a half-laugh. "Protesting segregation at the Woolworth's lunch counter in downtown Houston, 1968. Protested segregation at University of Texas, Austin, 1969. Chained himself to a tree at River Oaks Country Club, 1973. Don't know why. Maybe the tree didn't want to integrate with the other trees. I've heard pines and oaks don't get along well. His last arrest was for Occupy Wall Street. That one was in New York, so he's an intra-state protester."

Fuck. That didn't sound like someone who abducted and raped women. Or someone with the bitterness expressed in that letter. But who knew what was true and what was a lie? Maybe he used activism to attract women.

"Okay." Noah pushed away from the wall and squared his shoulders. "If we can keep Lefty Bob for a while," he glanced at the Lieu for confirmation, "he can work on Perry. Find out if he owns any property. Does he have another car? Where was he on the night of the last abduction? And any other juicy tidbits you can find."

"Roger that." Lefty Bob gave a mock salute. "Can I search his apartment?"

Noah wanted to see inside that apartment so bad he could almost taste it. Something had to be in there. He held his breath and let it out in a long sigh. "I'm afraid we don't have enough for a warrant. You find *anything* you let me know and we'll go for it. Until then, we'd just piss off some judge we might need later."

Jansen cleared his throat and put on his serious face. Never a good sign. "There's another reason we can't mess with Perry without something more concrete, and it's political."

The three men turned on the Lieu as one, glaring and sputtering. Jansen held up his hand. "I know, I know. I don't like it either, but here you go. Perry will be seen as a newsperson who is refusing to reveal his sources. That's sacrosanct and every media outlet in the country will jump on us. Call us 'Jackbooted thugs.' It's not right, but that story will live longer than these murders."

"So we let him get by with it?" Noah could hear the horror

in his own voice.

"Absolutely not. For now, we tiptoe. The instant you bring me something substantial, I'll unleash the hounds."

The idea of politics sticking its polluted nose into a murder investigation chaffed at Noah big time, but maybe the Lieu was right. He'd been at this longer. "So, Lefty Bob stays with Perry. Conner, can you go over the news footage and see if anyone approached Perry at the crime scene?"

His partner groaned and put his hands over his eyes. Was he starting to need glasses or not getting enough sleep? Or simply tired of sitting in a darkened room watching videos? Either way, it had to be done and Conner was the most detail-orientated one of the squad.

"Lieutenant, do you think you could call whoever took that letter and see if they learned anything we couldn't figure out for ourselves?"

"Will do. What about you? What do you have in mind?"

"I'm heading back over to the bodega and see if the owner can identify our latest victim."

CHAPTER
TWENTY-FIVE

"THIS LITTLE ONE? She's the one with the lights and ambulances and helicopters?" The bodega owner nodded toward the field.

Noah handed him the best photo he had, but her face didn't show. "Yes, she's the one. Do you know who she is?"

"Ahh. No." He shook his head and heaved out a sigh. "I don't know her name. I call her *Princesita*. Little Princess. She comes by here twice a week on her way to school."

On her way to school? That didn't sound like the harlots the Sanitizer talked about.

"Is there anything else you can tell me? Where did she live? Go to school?"

"She walked up from that street." He pointed with his head, still holding the photo. "Every Tuesday and Thursday evening. I know she caught the bus on that corner because sometimes she had to run." He nodded the other direction.

"Mostly she had a backpack, but one time she had a notebook

with the letters HCC."

Houston Community College? He'd check the bus route.

"She was so tiny, thin. I don't think she got enough to eat. I always pretended to try to sell her some fruit. I would hold up an apple and say, 'Try it. See how good it is.' Tuesday she was a little late. I had most everything put way. I gave her a date because she said she'd never had one before. Then she ran off, laughing. Did she ever have a chance to eat it, I wonder?"

She did, but he couldn't tell the man that. Not yet, anyway. "What about her family? Do you know them?"

"I don't think she had any family. She worked a couple of jobs and went to school. All on her own. And so young."

"Two jobs? Where'd she work?"

"She went in before I got here in the mornings so before five a.m., but came home around noon. One time she had a bag of donuts and offered me one, so I think maybe a donut shop. The other job, I don't know. Maybe fast food on the weekends."

Not as much information as he'd hoped. He could check on the bus route. Try to figure out where she went, or he could scour the neighborhood. Knock on every door for three square blocks. Hope one of the neighbors recognized her.

Even if he found someone willing to talk to *la policia*, the photo didn't show her face. He needed the bank video. That would offer a better view.

Noah checked his phone. It had been an hour since he called Lincoln Montgomery.

Nothing.

Maybe the Fed sent the video straight to Jansen. He crossed his fingers and called his boss.

"Haven't heard a word. And don't bitch to me. You're the one who suggested working with the feebies."

"Does anybody know anything they didn't know before I left?"

"If so, they haven't told me. Lefty Bob is working the phones and computer. Conner is still watching videos. The lab hasn't gotten back to me on the letter."

Noah pinched the bridge of his nose. "It's the same old story. Hurry up and wait. Just so long as nobody else turns up dead while we sit around and twiddle our thumbs."

"What about the bodega owner? Did he have anything that would help us?"

"She walks past his shop often, rides the city bus on Tuesday and Thursday evenings—might be taking a class at HCC—and possibly works at a donut shop early in the mornings. But he doesn't know her name or where she lives. I might as well come back to the office and waste my time there."

"Nothing you can do here for now. Why don't you start a canvas of the neighborhood? Find out if anyone knows her. Meanwhile, I'll see if HCC can tell me where she was headed on Tuesdays and Thursdays. I'll call you the instant we get any kind of news. Then we'll meet back in my office and discuss what to do next."

The Lieu didn't get where he was on his good looks. If that counted, he'd still be walking a beat. He was sharp and had seen it all once, maybe twice. He could look at a problem and tell you your next best step.

He also knew when to give encouragement, when to offer a calming hand, and when to deliver a swift kick in the ass.

So which was it the Lieu thought he needed today? Probably all three.

"Buenos dias, Senora." Noah tipped his head to the woman with an arm full of groceries. He held out the photo of *Princesita*. Damn, he needed a better picture. "Do you know this woman? She lives somewhere in this neighborhood."

"No habla ingles." The woman shook her head and tried to brush past Noah, something that wasn't easy to do even when he was in a good mood.

And he hadn't been in a good mood for the last hour.

Maybe it was time to be blunt. "She was brutally raped and murdered a few blocks from here. I hate to think of someone as violent as her killer roaming the streets, looking for his next victim."

The woman's face paled. "Murdered?" She crossed herself before taking the photo and studying it from all directions. "Are you certain?"

Her English had magically appeared, but not her trust in police.

"Yes, ma'am." He pulled out his phone. "I can ask the morgue to send a photo of her face, but it's not a pretty sight and I would hate for you to see something like that." The poor Princess was probably unrecognizable in her current state. One eye was swollen shut, her jaw hung at an unnatural angle, and her lip was split. The Sanitizer had taken his time for that much swelling to occur.

"No. No." She crossed herself again and shook her head vigorously. "I may have seen her, but I don't know her name. If this is the same person, she was always running, with her *mochila* full of books, bouncing against her back. Once I called to her, 'Slow down *chiquita*—little one. It is a beautiful day. Enjoy the sunshine.' She turned and gave me a smile to melt your heart. 'Maybe tomorrow, *Mamacita*. I'm late for school.'"

Had to be the same person. Small, young, always running, heading to school with a backpack full of books. Now they were getting somewhere. Maybe. "Do you know where she lived?"

Mamacita shrugged. "Somewhere around there." She pointed halfway down the street and on the left.

A neglected four-story apartment building sagged in the afternoon sun. The bottom two feet of fake stucco was covered in green mold. The entire building needed painting. Especially the warped front door.

No lock or passcode prevented Noah from entering the building. The main hallway was dark, possibly in an attempt to hide the dirty walls and peeling floor.

He'd been in many old buildings and was prepared for the rancid smell of old food and urine.

But that wasn't what he found.

Instead, the aroma of fresh chilies and spices and other good food wafted from behind unpainted doors, reminding Noah he'd skipped lunch. His stomach rumbled as he knocked on apartment 1A.

The door opened three inches and a woman peered out.

Noah held out his only photo. "Do you know this woman? She lives around here."

"*No hable ingles.*"

The door began to close, but he'd learned his lesson and spoke up quickly. "She was murdered yesterday and we're trying to identify her so we can notify her family and catch the guy who did it before he harms someone else."

The woman shrugged, but didn't slam the door. "Julio," she called.

A boy of around six or seven—shouldn't he be in school?—came to her side and she spoke to him in rapid-fire Spanish.

"We don't know her," the boy said, without looking at the photo.

"Look again," Noah said. "She lives around here and carries a heavy backpack."

The boy took the photo from his hand and studied it. "I don't know. I can't see her face. There was one lady. She kicked the ball back to me when it rolled into the street. We played for a minute before she rushed away. Maybe this is her, maybe not. But I don't know her name."

"Did she live around here?"

"I guess."

"Where?"

The kid's eyes grew sad and he shrugged.

By the time Noah reached 4D, he was tired, hungry, and discouraged. Half the apartments were empty—their occupants at work or afraid to open the door—and the other half didn't recognize her or didn't speak English or both.

He'd been trudging the dark, damp hallway long enough to feel like a fungi. He needed fresh air and sunshine to think and an open space to find a cell connection so he could call his office.

An unlocked door led to the roof and Noah opened it, hoping someone had left a folding chair or bench. Two lime green plastic chairs—one with a broken leg—and a rusted barbecue pit stood in one corner.

He eased himself into the unsteady chair and when it didn't collapse under him, he punched in Conner's number. His partner answered on the first ring.

"Enjoying the movie?" He really shouldn't give Conner a hard time, but who else did he have to torment?

"You could have at least left me with some popcorn and a Coke. Maybe some Milk Duds."

"Next time. I promise. You learn anything?"

"I've watched every frame of news footage shot at the crime scene and studied hundreds of photographs. No sign of Perry speaking to anyone except when he tried to question Lincoln Montgomery."

"So, that's it then."

"Nope. I didn't say that."

Fuck. So now it was Conner's turn to give him a hard time? "What *did* you say?"

"No one spoke to him, but a white van drove past while he was waving his hand, trying to get Montgomery's attention. With so many news trucks and squad cars, I could only catch a glimpse of it and couldn't be sure it was ours, but you know how I feel about coincidences."

The same way I do. They're a definite red flag.

"I printed out the photo, but you can't see the tires and it's the wrong side for the rust spot. Even in the daylight, the windows are too tinted to see inside."

"How's the rest of our team doing? Lefty Bob or the Lieu learn anything helpful? Any sign of the bank video?"

"I think Lefty's learned everything he can over the internet concerning R.J. Perry. Now he has a call in to the guy's boss at the *Chronicle*."

Yeah. Fat lot of good that was likely to do. Newspapers considered information their lifeblood. They could call it protecting their sources all they wanted. They didn't share. Certainly not about one of their own.

"Forensics says Perry's prints are all over the letter, along with those of the mailroom kid. Other prints are too smudged to read. The envelope and stamp are peel-and-stick, so no DNA. They've sent a copy offsite to a psychologist for an expert opinion. We'll have an answer in a week."

"Wanna bet we'll get a bill worth two weeks salary over something we could have figured out for two nickels?"

"No, thanks. I've learned the hard way never to bet with you. You already own my left nut and have a lien on my right one. However, whatever this unknown doc sends us will be worth more than a dime for the vocabulary lesson alone. You know the report will be filled with two dollar words and fifty-cent ideas."

"Ah, yes. I can learn to say *nutcase* with twelve letter words. I guess there's no point in asking if we got the bank video. You'd have told me if it came in."

"I received a text from Montgomery saying the bank promised to send it before the end of the day." Conner paused and Noah could picture him glancing at the clock over the boss' door. "It's three o'clock now. They better hurry."

Noah stood, the phone still against his ear, and the plastic chair came with him. He pried it off while Conner caught him up on the small amount Lefty had learned about Perry.

The sun felt good on his shoulders. Summer had been long and hot and he was ready for even a hint of fall. A woody smell filled the air and he peered over the corner of the building where trees and vines had overtaken a decaying tool shed.

From his angle atop the roof, he could see a faint trail in the packed dirt. It led from the street, past the apartment building, under the trees, to the door of the broken down shack.

CHAPTER TWENTY-SIX

NOAH ROUNDED THE corner with caution. Anything, or any one, could be hiding in that shack.

The building was almost totally hidden from any direction except above. Whoever made that path was up to no good.

Drug dealers? Quite possibly.

Illicit lovers? Not likely. Who'd feel romantic amid such filth?

A kid's playhouse? That's why he kept his hand free, but didn't draw his weapon. He'd rather die himself than shoot a child by accident.

Or none of the above. The shack could be exactly what it looked like. A decrepit, falling down, unused tool shed. The path probably nothing but his overactive imagination.

The windows stared back at him, dark and uninviting. His heart did a tap dance against his rib cage when he realized they were covered with blackout curtains. Should he ask for backup?

Before he left the roof, he'd called Conner with his location, denying he needed help, but leaving the line open for his partner to listen in. One word—shazam—and help would be on its way.

He remained silent.

Stepping carefully to avoid any noise, he slipped behind a tree and waited. Nothing stirred inside the cabin for several minutes. Mosquitoes made a feast of his hands and the back of his neck. A bee buzzed past his face and came back for a second look. Gnats swarmed around his ears, making a humming sound. A drop of sweat started at his hairline and rolled down his forehead and into his eye.

He didn't move.

Slowly he pulled his Glock from its holster and chambered a round. The sound might as well have been cannon fire in the hushed air. One step at a time, he eased back onto the path and raised his weapon.

He held his breath, waiting.

Five quick steps to the cabin and he flattened himself against the rough wall, between the window and door. A crude latch made from castoff wood had been hammered into the frame, holding the door shut. Noah raised the latch and the door swung open.

Nothing happened.

A deep breath and he threw himself around the corner, pointing the Glock inside the cabin. He swung the weapon from side to side, covering every inch of the tiny cabin.

Empty.

A crude bed, carefully made with a colorful quilt, stood in one corner. A desk constructed from boards and supported by two broken and mismatched nightstands held books and a hurricane lantern. In the far corner, a three-legged table was held up by the window frame. On it sat a box of granola bars, a bag of chips, three bottles of water—one empty—and a cardboard box with Sunrise Donuts printed in red.

At least they knew where she worked.

He holstered the Glock and turned in a circle. "Stand down, partner. I've found where she lived, but there's not much here."

The desk chair wobbled on uneven legs, but like the rest of the cabin, was spotless.

Conner ran a hand over the table then had to grab it before it fell. Clean. How did she do it with no electricity, no running water, no screens on the windows, dirt seeping up though rotting floorboards?

Noah had been right—there wasn't much here.

Her clothes, what there were of them, were neatly folded in a plastic bin. He didn't see any shoes so she must have been wearing her only pair. An old cigar box, its lid falling off, held letters, birthday cards, and photos.

The cards were in Spanish—someone would have to translate—but Conner knew enough of the language to recognize *Pappasito,* and *Tio Juan.* He also saw the letters were old and the photos curling on the edges.

The pictures started with a toddler sitting on her mother's knee with her father standing behind. Soon, the mother disappeared and the photos were of the girl and her father. Occasionally, an older man—*Tio Juan?*—appeared. In the last photo, the girl was alone, standing beside a small duffel bag and clutching a cigar box.

At least they had a first name: Constanza.

A lump formed in Conner's chest that threatened to stop air from passing into his lungs. What had she lived through that brought her to this point? Living in a hovel, eating scraps, doing without basic services?

Yet she smiled at her neighbors, played kickball with a kid, worked two jobs, and went to school.

Only to be taken by a scumbag who called himself the Sanitizer and claimed it was his destiny to 'clean up the neighborhood.'

The neighborhood needed cleaning up alright, but not from girls like Constanza. Or any of the other victims, no matter their life choices.

He and Noah and a team of forensic techs went over the cabin, but what was the use? She wasn't taken here. Maybe they would find her family to give them the news. But any useful evidence would come from other sources.

Lefty Bob was scouring the area, armed with drawings of the other victims, hoping to find someone who recognized them, but Conner didn't hold out much hope this was the killer's sole hunting grounds.

Only a couple of the bodies were Hispanic. Some were black, some white, one Asian. Youth, a slim frame, long hair, and vulnerability were their only commonalities. He'd taken a moment to pray for each one, but perhaps he should include those they left behind.

Those who refused to move and left a light on all night in hopes their little girl would return home.

He turned to walk outside and the table slipped off its precarious perch and crashed to the floor. Noah placed his hand on his shoulder. His voice sounded like it was filtered through gravel. "Let's head back to the office. There's nothing more we can do here."

Usually, it was his job to soothe Noah. After all, he had Jeannie and Betsy waiting at home. Noah went home to a dog. But sometimes it worked the other way around.

Conner took one last look at the tiny cabin that had held so much hope and promise for one young girl. "Right behind you, partner."

"Anyone get a copy of a surveillance video from that fucking bank?" Noah tried to keep his voice calm, but the minute he opened his mouth, all the anger and frustration of the day poured out.

Jansen stepped out of his office and scowled. He sent a watch-your-language glare Noah's way, but didn't comment. "The video came in ten minutes ago, but first I've got a couple of other things we need to discuss."

Noah and Conner headed for the Lieu's office. It had to be something important to trump the video.

Jansen parked one hip on the corner of his desk. This wasn't going to be good.

"I got a call a few minutes ago from the editor of the *Houston Chronicle*. He didn't appreciate our inquiries into his reporter." Jansen held up a hand. "Protecting his version of freedom of speech is part of his job description. I kept my mouth shut." He glanced at Noah as if he should try that sometime. "And after five minutes he wound down. The gist of his call was that R.J. Perry couldn't have killed our latest victim. He was covering a story in Austin. Spent Tuesday and Wednesday nights there. Got back in time to file his story late Thursday."

"Son-of-a-bitch. That doesn't cover him for the rest of the victims. The last one could be a copycat." Noah's breath was as heavy as if he'd run up a flight of stairs.

Conner sagged into a chair like a rag doll with the stuffing pulled out. "That's possible, and we have to keep it in mind, but we have to widen our search, too."

The Lieu straightened and stepped around the desk to his ergo-dynamic chair. "Noah, you got one other call while you were out. Some guy named Assad wants you to come over tonight and pick up a cashier's check form."

At last. Although, the video was more important. The best they could hope for on the form was fingerprints and that was unlikely.

He and Conner settled into the video room and set up the recording.

Half an hour later, Conner stretched and rubbed his back. "If Jeannie wants to go to a movie Saturday night, I might not be up to it."

What the fuck? Was his partner still planning to go out Saturday night? With this case finally coming together? Noah fought the urge to roll his eyes. Why the hell not? There would always be a case and every one was important. What were the odds they'd have a lead they had to follow that time of night?

"What time do you want me to come over?"

The relief in Conner's eyes was so strong Noah moved back in case his partner tried to hug him. "You haven't changed your mind?"

"No, I said I'd be there and I will. Betsy doesn't know what's in store for her. I'm a master babysitter."

The video started and they both leaned forward, studying every frame. The ATM was situated in the bank foyer with glass doors between it and the street. The camera angle caught only a portion of the street, and that was obstructed by writing on the bank doors.

One minute before the white van appeared on the bodega owner's video, it passed the bank heading that direction.

Driving past the bodega, turning around and coming by on the other side of the street, and passing the bank should have taken three minutes. Four tops. The van didn't appear for fifteen minutes.

Constanza never did. And she had to if she wanted to catch the bus.

Noah pushed back his chair. There it was, in grainy black and white. She was abducted between the bodega and the bank. A distance of two blocks. And not one store or house or apartment in that area.

He pulled out his cell, thumbed in the number for Crime Scene, and directed them to the correct block. "Look for anything out of place. She may have dropped her backpack, or stepped out of her shoes. Check the weeds, she may have tried to run."

Crime Scene knew what they were doing. They didn't need him to tell them. But he couldn't help himself.

Conner switched off the video. "Do you think we should go out there?"

Should they? "No. They'll do better without us getting in their way. Why don't you go home? I'm going to drive out to Katy and pick up Assad's paperwork. See if his wife got her money's worth on the dye job. Or if he's lost any more body parts since we last saw him. If the techies find anything of interest, I'll meet them back at the lab and go over it."

They wouldn't find anything. This guy was too good. He'd had plenty of practice.

CHAPTER TWENTY-SEVEN

CONNER WAS SHUTTING down his computer when Lt. Jansen motioned him to his office.

"You still interested in that bus route?"

"The one our vic was hurrying to catch?" They had her name and where she lived. Did they need more? Yes, absolutely. They needed everything about her. Especially her last name and next of kin.

"According to Houston Metro, if she wanted to get to the nearest campus of HCC, that's not the bus she'd take."

Whoa. Was there something about her they were missing?

Jansen handed him a note with barely legible scribbling. "They do teach classes other places than their main campuses. A lot of their GED classes and ESL classes are held in school cafeterias. There's a GED class on Tuesdays and Thursdays from seven-thirty to eight-thirty at an elementary school four blocks from the bus stop."

What the heck. It was only a few blocks out of the way. If he didn't go by tonight, they might not get the information before the next class on Tuesday.

He parked in front of the school at 7:15, took a minute to call Jeannie to let her know where he was, then headed inside.

His footsteps echoed in the empty hallway. Classroom doors were open and miniature desks waited to be filled. His heart gave a tug. He had occasionally stopped by the school where Jeannie taught art to pint-sized Van Goghs, but this was different.

In only five years he was expected to send Betsy off for an entire day to a place where she would be surrounded by strangers? Then what? She'd learn to drive? Go out with boys?

Oh, no. Not happening. Jeannie was smart. She could homeschool. When the time came, Betsy could probably take college classes online.

There were bad people out in this world. He was Betsy's father. It was his job to keep her safe. All these cute little signs and posters didn't fool him. They were designed to make the parents feel safe, not the kids.

That was the problem with being a police officer. You knew too much. Had seen things you couldn't forget.

He rounded a corner and found the cafeteria. Long tables with attached benches filled the room. A punk-looking kid with sleeves of tattoos and nickel-sized gauges in his ear lobes sat straddling one of the benches and chewed gum like he was forcing it into submission.

Two pregnant teenagers sat at another table and gossiped. Another girl, no more than fifteen years old, followed her swollen belly into the room and joined the other pregnant girls. "I'm sorry, Mr. McNally. My babysitter flaked out on me and I had to call my baby daddy, then listen to him bitch at me cuz he was gonna miss the football game."

Yep, he was not letting Betsy out of his sight.

The teacher—Conner refused to think of him as a professor—dropped a backpack on a table with a *thunk* that everyone ignored.

A gray-haired retiree followed a mechanic type into the room. An obviously high toker stumbled in after them. Each took separate tables.

Conner approached the teacher with Constanza's photo. The morgue had sent him a picture taken from the side that hid most of her injuries. "Mr. McNally?"

"Take a seat. You've already missed the first three classes. You'll have a hard time catching up."

"I'm Detective Crawford. I'm looking for one of your students."

The man glanced up for the first time. "Here they are. Take whichever one you want."

Conner held out his phone with the photo. "This is the woman I'm looking for. Do you know her?"

"Connie? Sure. She's not here yet. She'll run in thirty seconds after class starts. Not sure why she can't manage her time better."

Because she works two jobs and has to ride the bus you jerk.

"Can you tell me anything about her?"

"She keeps to herself but knows the answers if you press her."

"Does she have any friends? Has anyone ever bothered her?"

"Not that she's ever told me about."

Of course not. You're so friendly, why would anyone confide in you?

"Do you know her full name and address? Next of kin?"

McNally sighed and closed his eyes. "It's here in these papers somewhere but it'll take me a few minutes to dig it out. Do you need it tonight? I don't like to run late."

"You look for the information. I'll ask these students if they know anything about her." Conner glanced around the room. His opinion of the motley group of students rose considerably. They came. They put up with this teacher. They took time out of their lives to try to better themselves.

"Does anybody know Constanza? Connie?"

"She's not here yet," one of the pregnant women answered. Conner wasn't sure which one.

"I know. I'm trying to get any information you have about her."

"Why?" The mechanic took up a defensive posture.

To tell or not to tell? No one in this room would open up if they thought she was in trouble. "Constanza was murdered yesterday. I'm trying to find her killer and knowing about her habits might help."

A shocked silence filled the room before some of the women started crying.

"She was kind of private, but she'd always stay late and help you with a problem if you didn't understand it." All eyes shot glares at Mr. McNally.

Ten minutes later, Conner knew how nice she was, but not much else. McNally gave him a sheet of paper with her registration information and he left.

He needed to get home and tell Jeannie about his new plan for Betsy's future. It might be a hard sell if the baby had been crying all evening.

Mrs. Assad's hair was a flat, matte black, so dark it absorbed all light, giving off no shine, or feeling of life. She must have sat through three applications of dye to reach a color that absolute.

Whatever she paid for her trip to the beauty salon, it was too much.

The woman herself was almost as severe as her hairdo. No smile of greeting sneaked through lips pressed so tightly together they revealed only a thin line.

She put on a show of protecting her semi-invalid spouse, chastising Noah. "You had no right to demand my husband search for these records. He is not able to get up and down easily. And the dust is not good for his lungs. We had to ask our son to drive across town—bringing his fiancée after they had both worked all day—climb up a ladder, and bring down all these boxes."

Yet she made no move to help her husband as he fumbled for his crutches, leaning against the wall two feet from his chair.

Noah didn't remember demanding anything. He'd asked, rather politely, if it was possible to see the copies. And by *all these boxes,* did she mean both of them?

Assad hobbled across the room and handed Noah a yellowed slip of paper encased in a plastic baggie. "I remembered what you told me and avoided touching anything. I used a pair of tweezers to pull it out and placed it in here for protection."

The man's face lit up, waiting for praise. He probably never heard any at home.

"Wonderful. You have no idea how helpful this will be." This must be his day for letters encased in baggies. He spread the plastic on a coffee table and tried to read the faded writing.

This was definitely the correct slip. The date was right and it was made out to Trusty Property Management from Medina Properties. The problem was the signature, an illegible line of squiggles.

Noah moved the baggie closer to the light. Nope, that didn't help.

He glanced up at Assad, who waited anxiously for a pronouncement of *Eureka!* Around the man's neck hung a pair of dollar-store cheaters on a cheap chain.

"May I borrow your glasses for a moment? This handwriting is difficult to read." Mrs. Assad *hurrumphed,* but her husband balanced on his one foot and pulled the chain over his head.

With the extra magnification, Noah tried to follow the looping line. The first letter was definitely a 'C.' He used his finger to trace out the rest of the signature.

Captain America.

Shit. He should have known.

Now all he had to do was return two cardboard boxes to the Assad's attic and he could go home to Sweet Pea.

The drive out to Katy wasn't a waste. He'd learned one important thing—other than never go to Mrs. Assad's hairdresser. There was no longer any doubt. Someone had planned and prepared for these murders ten years ago.

And was still operating in his city.

Noah checked in with Crime Scene when he left Assad's house, but the news wasn't good. They had found nothing. Nada. Zip.

No indication of where the latest victim was taken. No blood. No spilled backpack. No sign of a struggle anywhere in the two block area.

About what he'd expected, but still disappointing.

He had a good idea of how the abduction went down. From the little he knew of Constanza, she was a naive, friendly girl. The Sanitizer would have approached her in a non-threatening way—holding out a piece of paper and asking directions or saying it had fallen out of her backpack.

She would let him come near and then, *POW*. He would punch her in the face, coldcock her. As she sagged or passed out, he would scoop her up before she hit the ground and shove her into the van. The whole episode would take ten seconds, maximum.

Her broken jaw and split lip told the story. He didn't want to think about what came next for her. The thirty-six hours she was missing. The swollen eye. The chaffed wrists. The bruises.

All of that could wait for morning. Now he needed to go home. Pet his dog. Check on his neighbor. Maybe call his sister. Or Laurel.

His job was to investigate, period. Yet, this time he'd discovered two of the bodies. That made it personal. Each new thing he learned about the victims—the childhood abuse, the neglect, the hope for a better future—made it harder to separate work from real life.

And everything he learned about the Sanitizer made him more determined to close this case before the killer struck again.

Conner worked the same cases he did, yet realized the importance of compartmentalizing. It was time he learned it, or relearned it, also.

All work and no play might be a cliché, but he'd found out the hard way. Never taking a break or getting his mind off murder, led him into a deep dark depression. One that was hard to climb out of alone.

Harvey the invisible cat had been fed. He'd even rubbed against Laurel's ankles while she filled his bowl. Wonder of wonders.

She'd finished her Lean Cuisine dinner and topped it off with a double scoop of raspberry sorbet when the phone rang. She was in the middle of brushing her teeth so she wouldn't be tempted to eat anything else.

Her boss was due to call and let her know if he got back into town, yet she paused to check the caller ID before answering. Last time it had been her mother and she didn't want to make that mistake again.

Daugherty, N

His landline, not his cell. Was that a good sign or a bad sign? She bit her lip as she hit *accept.*

For most people, a cell phone was more intimate, but Noah used his so much at work, she guessed it was the opposite.

"Hey, how was your day?" She really had to come up with better things to say.

"Pretty busy. We found another body yesterday afternoon."

"I saw that on TV." That's why she wasn't surprised when he didn't call last night and hadn't expected to hear from him today. "That guy had some gall, using the same burial grounds."

"I still haven't decided if he's stupid or brilliant. Conner and I shouldn't have been in that field, but this dweeby little tech guy asked us to look for cattails. A couple of the graves contained traces of them."

"So he might have gotten away with it?"

"Maybe, who knows? Can I tell you something I haven't mentioned to Conner or anyone else?"

"Sure." Half of her was thrilled he wanted to share something personal, the other half was afraid to hear what it could be.

"I've worked Homicide for a long time. I've chased killers who were nasty people full of hate or greed or envy or jealousy or just plain screwed up, but this is the first one who actually scares me. He's not like the others. He's evil. I know that's a strong word, but it's the feeling I get every time I come close to him. And I'm scared to death he'll slip away and start somewhere new."

She'd liked Noah from the first day she met him. He was sweet, helping her with her divorce and with getting Crystal's brother into rehab. He was funny, making her laugh with a dry sense of humor or an off-beat observation. He was strong, dependable, trustworthy. All attributes Paul didn't have.

But she'd never realized he was deep. And she liked it. "So far, this has been a game for me. Playing detective. Looking up records. Feeling like I'm helping. I can't imagine what you must deal with every day. It's no wonder he scares you. You know what he's capable of."

"I didn't mean to dump my problems on you." His voice cracked slightly. "That was just an observation."

"No. I'm glad you told me. I like to understand your work. By the way, I traced down that paperwork you gave me. I've come up with a list of names and have phone numbers for some of them, but not all. Not sure if my boss will be in the office tomorrow or not, but I'll finish if I can."

"Why don't you wait and give it to me when I pick you up Sunday night? We've got enough stuff to keep us busy until then."

Good thing he couldn't see her as she did a fist pump. She'd been so sure he called to break their date.

They talked another fifteen minutes and didn't mention the case once.

CHAPTER
TWENTY-EIGHT

NOAH LET THE box of donuts precede him through the door. That way, not one person in the squad complained when he was twenty minutes late. Lefty Bob was digging into a chocolate cream before Noah had time to reach his desk.

"I stopped by the donut shop where Constanza worked and got her full name and address." He slapped a piece of paper in front of Conner.

His partner studied the paper for a moment before pushing a similar sheet toward Noah. "That's funny because I stopped at the school where she was studying for her GED last night and got a different name and address."

Well, didn't that suck?

"I got Constanza Villanova on Demarte Street. But the donut guy called her Connie."

"I got Constanza Guerra with a nonexistent address on Barremore. The other students called her Connie."

"I haven't had a chance to check out the Demarte address,

but I'll buy you a steak dinner if it's legitimate. As for the name, we can be pretty sure the Constanza part is correct. She's used it twice and it's on those birthday cards."

"While both last names may be fake, I lean toward Guerra. For the GED certificate to do her any good, the name needed to be correct."

He agreed with Conner on that. Why go to school if you couldn't claim the degree? So they were back to square one. Even if they did learn her legal name, what difference did it make? They were no closer to finding her killer.

"I found something else last night that's going to be about as much help as those non-existent addresses. I stopped by Assad's house and picked up the cashier's check form. You'll never guess who signed it. Captain America."

"Great. Besides being a killer, our guy's a real joker."

"I sent it over to fingerprints. Hard to act casual and avoid touching the form when you're filling it out in public. Also, it gives us a sample of his handwriting. Maybe we'll get lucky. Might be interesting to see if any of the prints match the ones on R.J. Perry's letter. Especially those of Mr. Perry himself."

Lt. Jansen appeared in his doorway. "Daugherty, Crawford, Hernandez. My office."

Noah followed the others as they took their usual places. Conner and Lefty Bob sat, Jansen parked a hip against his desk, and Noah leaned against the wall.

"Where are we on the Sanitizer case? The *Chronicle* published the letter this morning and I'd like to be up-to-speed when the calls start flooding in."

Noah waited, but neither of the other detectives jumped in. "We've got the name of our latest victim. We know where she lived and where he abducted her, but that doesn't put us any closer to finding him. We also know this was all planned ten years ago. We don't know if he actually owns the land, but he's been paying taxes on it this whole time. We suspect he had something to do with the ownership of that apartment building, but don't have any proof."

"Well, get some proof. And track down the owners. You've had a week. You'll have to do it on your own. Earl flunked his tests and will be taking disability. He's coming by this afternoon to clear out his desk and complete the paperwork."

Damn. He'd like to dig up Aldo Rogers and kill him again. For what he'd done to Earl and what he'd done to Conner.

Noah cleared his throat and hoped no one would ask too many questions. "I have someone working on tracking down names and numbers on those properties. I understand real estate can be tricky if you don't know the ins and outs."

Jansen and Lefty Bob nodded, not interested in the details. Conner turned his head and Noah could have sworn he was holding back a laugh.

"Okay then." Jansen crossed behind his desk and sat. "Get out of here and get to work. Bring me anything you have the minute you have it."

"We need a plan. Anyone have a suggestion?" Noah wasn't above asking for ideas. He was certainly short on them at the moment.

He, Conner, and Lefty Bob sat around a table in the break room, holding cups of bad coffee. Noah took a sip and pushed it away. It didn't even smell like real coffee. More like toast burned to a crisp and dunked in water.

Lefty Bob finished his coffee. Didn't the guy have any taste buds at all? "Why don't I go back to Constanza's neighborhood with a photo of that van? See if anyone noticed it prowling the area."

"Good idea. I doubt our guy was dumb enough to let his face be seen, but you've got to try. I'd love to know if he scouted areas first or if it was all random. Conner, you got anything?"

"We still need a positive ID on Dancing Queen cheerleader, but for the moment any information on Constanza is more time sensitive. Why don't I phone Lincoln Montgomery and have him follow up with the prison. Meanwhile, I could head over to Demarte Street and ask around. Someone might know Constanza. She got the address from somewhere. It won't help us solve the case, but I'd like to be able to notify her relatives, if she has any."

Noah waited, but Conner didn't move. He knew that look. "You have something else on your mind?"

"I do, but you're not going to like it. What do you think about releasing the drawings of the victims and the white van to the news media? If we could get an identification, we'd have another area to search. I'd sure like to get a better fix on this guy. Does he hang around one part of town? Does he have a favorite hunting ground we could stake out?"

"You're right, I don't like it, but I'll go along with that. I hate to give those vultures anything, but it's time. We can't keep them off our backs forever and with that letter from the Sanitizer out there, they'll be after us like a pack of hungry dogs. Ready to go for our throats if we don't feed them something. But only the last three victims. Their drawings are the most accurate and the most likely to bring results. And not the van."

Conner scooted his chair back and dropped his half-finished coffee in the trash. "I understand the victims, but why not the van?"

"It's our only solid lead. If the guy ditches it, we may not be able to prove anything, even if we catch him. We can always put it out there in a day or two. You guys head out. Fingerprints promised to call me by noon. It'll take me that long to get the drawings sent to the right people."

It would also give him a reason to call R.J. Perry. He didn't trust the guy. Any excuse to keep close tabs on him was a godsend.

~

Two hours later, Noah had sent the forensic artist's renderings of Joyce, Kathy, and Lucy to local, state, and national news outlets.

The crazies had started calling about the Sanitizer's letter. Noah took five calls and quit. The man might be Satan, but that didn't help in locating him. And the calls claiming the man was doing local communities a favor by cleaning up trash, well, he didn't care to speak to those people.

Fingerprints hadn't called yet, but they had another hour until their deadline.

Any logo identifying the maker of the white van was missing or not visible in the photos, but the department had stacks of books with photos showing examples of cars and trucks and vans.

Noah sat with two photos of the van beside him and studied every example. After an hour, his back hurt, his eyes burned, and his stomach rolled from too much coffee.

But he might, just maybe, have an answer.

Now what? Everyone questioned so far claimed not to have noticed the van at all, so that was no help. There was one phone call he could make, but odds were slim after all these years.

"Sleeman Cement." The pink-haired girl sounded just as perky as she had the day he and Conner went out there.

"Hi. This is Detective Noah Daugherty. My partner and I were out there last week. I hate to bother you, but is Luis on the lot today? Could I speak to him? It's important."

"I'll get him for you. It may take a few minutes." She didn't sound nearly as excited as when she thought he was a customer.

Before she put him on hold, he could hear her on the intercom. "Luis, please report to the office. Luis, to the office. Thank you."

At least she added the thank you before the elevator music started.

Luis must not have felt the need to hurry, because Noah quit timing the wait after five minutes.

"Good morning, Detective. This is Luis." He sounded pleasant at any rate. Probably happy for the excuse to come into the air conditioning.

"Morning, Luis. I had one question I didn't think to ask you before and you may not remember. Do you have any idea the make or year of the van Big Dick drove?"

"Brand spanking new Mercedes, white as my mamma's hair. That was the joke around the lot. Who would drive a Mercedes where they were pouring cement? New car, new tools, new clothes. Someone sent their baby boy off to his new job well-equipped. Too bad he was useless as tits on a shark."

"You only told me he was a jerk. You never mentioned he didn't know what he was doing."

"Oh, yeah. Had us pour in the wrong place a couple of times. Then wanted us to correct it for free. Old Mr. Sleeman told him to f-off. He didn't put up with that type of *mierda*. Whole project was riddled with errors. One of the reasons it went so far over budget."

Noah felt a smile threaten for the first time that day. You never knew when the pieces would fall together.

The plastic cover of Conner's cardboard vending machine sandwich peeled away with a *sluppp*, allowing the disgusting odor of day old pimento and cheese to drift out. Irritation gnawed at him as Lefty Bob bit into pulled pork barbecue on a hamburger bun. The man must have stopped at a drive thru on his way back to the office.

Would he have bought something for himself and not the others?

No, but Lefty had four kids and an ex-wife. Was that the reason he was cheap or the reason he had an ex-wife?

Lefty wiped the sauce off the corner of his mouth with a napkin the size of a Post-it note. "I'm tired of busting my butt for nothing. Nobody admitted seeing the van. Claimed the area was swimming with vans and they didn't know one from another."

Conner couldn't blame him. A working-class neighborhood. Lots of self-employed yard men, window washers, painters, handymen. Plenty of vans. He'd had a little more luck, but so what?

"Constanza did live at the Demarte Street address." He

glanced at Noah. "So you owe me a steak. Three girls, same last name, supposedly cousins, shared a two-room apartment, bathroom down the hall. The other two girls worked in a sweatshop and were caught up in an immigration raid and sent back to Mexico. Constanza worked somewhere else, maybe the donut shop, but she hid out. Never came back. The landlord, creepy guy. If I'd had a warrant, I'd have checked the bathroom for a camera. He kept a box of the girl's belongings. I brought it back to the station. Maybe I can figure out where they went."

He already knew the box didn't contain a toaster, a coffee pot, a sauce pan, or a warm coat. Anything worth more than two dollars was undoubtedly in the landlord's pocket.

Noah tossed his tuna sandwich in the trash and opened his bag of chips. "The Lieu assigned that rookie, Kevin Gilmore, to take the calls about the Sanitizer. Poor guy, he's going to learn fast. I only took a few of them and want to wash my ears out with lye soap. Latent prints called. They didn't pull up any fulls from the cashier's check form, but got a couple of partials and they don't match R.J. Perry or any from the letter."

Conner perked up. This was something new. "So we're eliminating Perry?"

Noah sighed and pulled on his ear. For some reason, his partner had a hard-on for Perry and wasn't going to give up on him easily. "Not eliminating him, but dropping him to the bottom of the list."

"List? We have a list? Last I heard, Perry was it." Had Noah learned something he hadn't shared yet?

Noah opened a notebook to a page full of vans and set the photo they had taken from the bodega video beside it. "Everybody agree this is a 2007 Mercedes van?"

They looked the same to Conner, but he let Lefty Bob study the photos.

"I'd like it better if we had a good shot of the front or back, but from what I can see, yeah You found it. Good work." Lefty pushed the book back toward Noah.

"Luis from the cement company says the job foreman on the apartment project, Big Dick, drove one like this, white. I know it's been ten years, but this type of van would last that long, easy. Especially if it wasn't driven that often. I think we're looking for a tall Caucasian male in his mid-thirties."

Lefty Bob wadded the remains of his lunch and hurled them into the trash. "What now? We got no solid leads, no suspects, and no place to start."

Noah slammed the auto identification notebook shut with more force than necessary. The sound echoed through the suddenly silent room. "We go back to the beginning. Who owns the field and the apartment building? Also, we wait for identifications on the other victims. Maybe the guy made a mistake with one of them. If none of that works, we go to the media. Ask for help."

A twenty-pound weight settled on Conner's shoulders. Noah must be growing desperate to suggest going public. And he had every right to be.

Friday afternoon. Innocent young women, their lives ahead of them, would be planning their weekend, looking for fun, with no idea what—who—was waiting for them.

The Sanitizer could be out there tonight. Stalking his next victim. If he found a new disposal site, the bodies might not be found for another ten years.

CHAPTER
TWENTY-NINE

S ATURDAY MORNING NOAH mowed his and Mrs. Powell's yards. Then he drove her to the store for groceries and her medications.

"I'm not an invalid, you know. The doctor didn't tell me I couldn't drive."

She looked like one. Her face was thinner than he'd ever seen it and she hadn't bothered with makeup.

"Hey, I need food, too. There's nothing in my fridge but dried out lunch meat and one of Rachelle's casseroles."

"I thought you said her cooking had improved."

"It has. This is one of the old ones. I took it out of the freezer."

"Lord help you. Don't eat it by accident."

She *hmphed* and *shushed* while he carried her groceries inside and helped put them away, but took his hand before he left. "I have a favor to ask you."

His breath caught in his throat. He could count on one hand the number of times she'd asked for his help in the four years he'd lived next door. This had to be something important.

"Have I ever told you how much you remind me of my Andy? Oh, you don't look like him, he was on the small side, but your dedication to duty. To right and wrong. He dropped out of school and joined the marines after 9/11. Not a day goes by I don't think about him. Next week will be seven years since he died. Would you drive me out to the Veteran's Cemetery? With this surgery coming up, I feel the need to sit by his grave and talk to him and I'm worried if I get down on the ground, I won't be able to get back up."

Now it was Noah's turn to *hmph*. He wasn't sentimental. Betsy had been cremated as per her wishes. He'd sprinkled her ashes off a pier in Galveston at sunset. He didn't visit his parents' graves, but Rachelle did. She'd told him how much it helped her.

The Sanitizer had yanked a dozen women—possibly more— away from their families and buried them in unmarked graves.

How hard must it be, not knowing what happened to someone you loved?

Conner eyed the folders under Noah's arm and laughed. "Good luck with that."

A flash or irritation shot up Noah's spine. He'd done plenty of babysitting with Emma and Iris and no one complained.

Betsy sat in a jump seat swing, rocking back and forth, sucking on a pacifier. He rubbed the back of her hand with one finger and she reached up to him and giggled.

He shot Conner a so-there look. He could handle this. Piece of cake.

Jeannie came in, her face glowing and the back of her hair

damp, as if she'd just gotten out of the shower. "Hey, Noah. I thought I heard the doorbell. I was worried you'd changed your mind."

"No. I swung by the office to pick up some work."

She glanced at Conner and sputtered out a laugh.

"There's a bottle in the fridge and the warmer's on the counter. She'll probably want to eat in an hour. Don't feed her too fast. She gets gas. I left an Italian cream cake in the fridge if you get hungry." Jeannie grabbed her purse and they were out the door.

Noah eyed that sweet baby, swinging contentedly. She eyed him back.

Two hours later he was pacing in front of the window, jiggling the baby as if he were trying to churn butter. But that was the only way she'd stop crying.

How long did it take to eat one fucking dinner?

And how on God's good earth could a baby the size of a teddy bear produce so much gas? He didn't even want to think about that diaper. He'd never smelled anything that foul in his life. And it had only been a week since he'd stepped on a decaying body.

Fortunately, by the time Conner's headlights swept across the ceiling, Betsy was sleeping contentedly and he had his file folders spread out on the coffee table.

He had no intention of telling them if they had returned ten minutes earlier, it would have been a different story.

Conner opened the door and Jeannie glanced around the peaceful room in surprise. "Where's Betsy?"

"Sleeping,"

Noah's pretend nonchalance didn't fool Conner for an instant. He could see the line of sweat along his partner's forehead. He turned toward his wife. "Why don't you check on her and change out of those shoes you've been complaining about? Noah and I will go in the kitchen and cut the cake."

If Noah had managed more than five minutes to himself, a slice would be missing. Conner opened the refrigerator door. The cake was intact.

"Now you want to tell me what's up with all the files?"

Noah went to the cabinet, lifted out three plates, and carried them over to the kitchen table.

Conner stood rock still. He could out-wait his partner.

"Before I transferred to Homicide, I spent six months in Missing Persons under Garrett Lewis."

Conner knew Lewis. Talk about a blowhard. That lazy loser spent more energy avoiding work than doing his job. He'd run through more partners than Betsy went through diapers.

"He went to great lengths to teach me that any teenager who went missing had simply run away from home. They were all on drugs, you know. Even when there wasn't any evidence. He'd been there for years. I figured he knew what was happening. He claimed he had a nose for it. Took me longer than it should have to realize he swept more cases under the rug than he worked."

Noah took his slice of cake and sat in his usual chair. "I tried to press for some of the cases, but he pulled rank on me. The one that did me in was a young girl named Felicia Vickers. I didn't realize it at the time, but she was the younger sister of a girl Rachelle knew in college. Felicia was a typical high school senior. Chaffing to get out from under her parents' thumb."

"Was she doing drugs?"

"A little, but not enough to mess up her GPA. She would have graduated in two months. She had this boyfriend her folks hated, so they grounded her. Then she started slipping out the window at night. One time she didn't come back. Lewis claimed she'd run off with the boyfriend. Only he was out of town that weekend, touring college campuses with his parents."

"That's when you transferred?" He was starting to understand what had been on his partner's mind for the last week. That didn't make him any less pissed the guy was keeping secrets from him.

"Not immediately. I tried to work the case myself, but Lewis kept piling shit work on me to keep me busy. An opening came up in Homicide and I jumped for it."

Conner tapped the pile of folders. He'd known something was up when Noah brought them over. "And you think this Felicia Vickers might be one of our killing field victims?"

"Doc M thinks her dental impressions probably match the body he named Cloe."

"And you didn't tell me? That's unacceptable. How can I work the case if you're keeping secrets from me?" Conner clamped his teeth together to keep from saying something he'd regret later.

"Doc told me not to mention it anyone yet. We can't go public with it until the official report from the forensic dentist, but I trust the doc."

"I seriously doubt he meant to keep it from me. Partners have to act as a team. You know that. Any other way doesn't work."

"I do know that. Not telling you right away was a bonehead move on my part. It's been hanging over my head for days. I think I was embarrassed to admit I let Lewis pull that shit on me. The thing is, I've seen what waiting, never knowing, does to families. Felicia's parents got a divorce. Her sister dropped out of college. What if there's another one in the cases Lewis filed and forgot?"

"You don't think a match would show up when Doc or Lincoln Montgomery finished entering information in the computer?"

"Are you kidding me? With all the missing persons in Harris County, not to mention the rest of the state, the nation? It could take a year, probably longer. Their families shouldn't have to wait that long. In half an hour, I can pull out any young girl between the ages of seventeen and twenty-two, slight of stature, long hair, who Lewis shoved to the back of the pile."

Noah placed his hand on top of the stack of files. "I owe them that much. I failed them the first time." The pain in his voice was palatable.

Jeannie walked in wearing sweats and a T-shirt. She saw them staring at each other, not speaking. With an exaggerated sigh, she grabbed her slice of cake and headed toward the bedroom. "Shit," she muttered. "Don't be too long."

Conner pulled half the pile his direction. "Let's make it between sixteen and twenty-three. Just to be on the safe side."

Noah studied the display of weapons. Which was more important, ease of use or amount of ammunition?

He laughed and reached for the orange plastic water gun. This wasn't rocket science, but he wasn't going back to Rachelle's without protection.

Ten minutes later he stood on her doorstep and waited while she answered the bell. He put his finger to his lips and held up the orange menace. "The girls in?"

The edges of her eyes crinkled. "They're in the backyard. Are you sure you're willing to take them on? Two to one and they've had more practice."

"Yeah, but I'm ready for them now."

In no time he was drenched and out of breath from laughing. Exactly what he needed after two weeks of death and destruction plus a well-deserved dressing-down from his partner. And another waiting from his sister when she found out what he'd avoided telling her.

Sweet Pea had given him her patented 'poor pitiful me,' look when he'd started to leave the house, so he brought her along. Now she was running in circles, trying to trip him. "Whose side are you on, Pea? Have you forgotten who feeds you?"

She barked and tugged at the hem of his jeans. Ungrateful little stinker.

He was on the ground with two little girls standing over him when Rachelle called out. "Okay guys. Time to get ready for Mackenzie's birthday party."

"But Mom. We're having fun with Uncle Noah," Emma whined.

"And you'll have fun at Mackenzie's. Her feelings will be hurt if you don't go. And Iris, remember how excited you were to be included in the invitation? Your clothes are on your beds. Go change and your daddy will drive you over there."

Noah French-braided Emma's hair, a skill he'd mastered on Rachelle when their mother was ill, while his sister got them dressed and out the door.

She led him to the kitchen and made them both a cup of tea. "Now, you want to tell me what's on your mind? Why you turned up at my door unannounced? I'm not complaining. I love to see you anytime and so do the girls, but I know when you have an ulterior motive."

He kissed the top of her head and pulled out a chair. "Sometimes I need to see you and the girls to remember that some things in the world are good and clean. But you're right, there's more on my mind than that. Do you remember Felicia Vickers?"

"Of course I remember. Her mother telephoned me the day you showed up on the news with all those dead bodies. She was afraid you'd ignore her if she called you herself. I swore to her you wouldn't let her down and I'd keep her informed if there was any news. Is there? Any news?"

"Maybe. Probably. But the identification isn't official yet so I can't let her know. Saying we'd found her daughter and then having to go back and admit we were mistaken would be worse than not knowing. I remember how torn up they were and not being able to tell them is killing me."

"When will you know for sure?"

"A day. A week. A month. Who knows? I asked for a rush determination, but I don't have any control over the situation."

"I'll call her today and tell her you've sent in Felicia's information and will let her know as soon as possible, one way or the other. Simply knowing you're checking will make her feel better."

"When I get the final report, will you come with me to notify her? Our last conversation didn't go that well." That was an understatement. The woman had yelled and cursed at him and he was afraid the dad might hit him. The thought of having to arrest a grieving father had hung over him for the last ten years.

"You didn't need to ask. I was already planning on it."

Half the weight on his shoulder had lifted when he played with his nieces. The other half lifted now. He'd known Rachelle would help him figure out what to do. The one thing he didn't understand was how she got so smart and why none of that talent came to him.

CHAPTER
THIRTY

NOAH SAT ON the floor playing tug with Sweet Pea. After the workout she'd had at Rachelle's, she didn't need a walk, just dinner and fresh piddle pads.

He started out the back door for Laurel's townhouse when his eye caught on his favorite picture of his nieces. Every year for Christmas, Rachelle gave him a calendar with different photos taken of Emma and Iris.

This one showed the girls in last year's new back-to-school outfits. Emma, the prissy one, had on a blue dress and leggings. Iris wore jeans and a red top. He'd taken them shopping for their backpacks.

He stopped abruptly when he realized the photo was for September. Already into October and he'd never turned the page. He flipped over to the next month and the new photo, ringed with orange leaves and pumpkins, showed the girls in their Halloween costumes.

The photo wasn't what caused his heart to slam against his

ribs and try to escape.

That would be the date circled in red. October 26. Fourteen months to the day since Betsy's death. The day he'd chosen to join her.

How the hell could he have forgotten?

Now what? He couldn't depart this earth with the Sanitizer on the loose, preying on unsuspecting women. And he couldn't leave Rachelle. Or Emma and Iris. Or Conner. Or his new Goddaughter. Or ignore the next lowlife who showed up.

Then there was Sweet Pea. He didn't want to leave her—she'd already lost too much—and he didn't want to take her with him like he'd planned in the beginning.

Which left the big question. After fourteen months, had he made a decision?

Noah had mixed emotions when he got to the office on Monday morning. The Yin and Yang of his weekend left him antsy. His conscience had told him he should be at the office, yet there was nothing he could do there.

Sunday night was fun but still unsettling. The dating world had changed over the last years and he hadn't kept up with the newest etiquette. What was he supposed to do? Not do? Had he been too pushy? Did she expect more? Less? What was it *he* wanted from this?

Laurel made it easy. She chattered about her day and the kooks she had to deal with until he was laughing. They went out for a nice dinner, held hands on the way to the car, watched a ball game at her place.

He never saw Harvey. Maybe the cat *was* invisible.

Before he left, she gave him a printout of the phone numbers she'd uncovered. He'd even kissed her goodnight on his way out. More than once. They'd lingered in the doorway until he worried about nosy neighbors but decided he didn't care.

And that was the problem.

Because he did care. He loved Rachelle and his nieces. Was devoted to his friends and his work. But that was half a life, not a full one. He needed more if he planned to stick around another forty years. He hadn't known Laurel that long, yet every time he was around her, he caught a glimpse of what life could hold, given a chance. But was he being fair to her?

She didn't fit into his plan. If things didn't work out and he decided to take his original route, would it hurt her? Would she blame herself?

So many questions, his head wanted to explode.

He was almost glad to get back into death and murder. That's where he belonged. Not on a comfortable sofa with a beautiful woman curled up against his shoulder. Making him laugh and forget there were things he didn't deserve.

Conner came in with a smile. Apparently, he'd forgiven Noah for keeping secrets. "What's up, partner? Any word on… anything?"

"We have multiple identifications on all three of the victims whose drawings appeared in the paper. We can let our rookie check out most of them, but we've got three similar hits for Lucy and two for Joyce. How about we track them down and see what we can find?"

"Sounds good to me. What about Lefty Bob?"

"He caught a new case last night. He's going to work on that, but we can have him back if we need him." Life—or death—went on. More murders to investigate. If they did need Lefty, would it be because they had new evidence or a new set of problems?

The drive over to Cypress Creek Parkway took thirty minutes once rush hour traffic had passed. Conner was driving a nondescript motor pool car that for once didn't scream 'Cops.'

They parked in front of a rundown motel sitting back half a block behind a tobacco shop. The manager, a potbellied man in his fifties, had a name tag that read Herman.

"I thought the call was supposed to be anonymous," he bitched. "That'll teach me to do my civic duty."

"It is anonymous. No one will know except the three of us. Now, how did you meet this woman and what can you tell us about her?"

"Is there a reward for information?"

"What happened to civic duty?" Noah glared across the counter and the guy seemed to get the message.

"She called herself Cinnamon, but I think her real name was Stella. She worked the street around here. I haven't seen her for several weeks. I thought she had moved on to another area."

"Did she have a pimp?"

"When she first started coming around here she did, but he got busted for something and she was on her own. He was here day before yesterday, looking for her. I thought she knew he was due to get out and that's why she disappeared."

Conner had his spiral out. "What's his name?"

"Tito. Skinny guy with tattoos."

"Tall, short, Caucasian, Hispanic?"

Herman shrugged. "Ugly."

"Any of her tricks a tall white guy named Dick?"

"I didn't keep track of her johns. She met them outside or

took them straight up to her room. Either way, I wouldn't have seen them."

"Have you noticed a white panel van hanging around? Has mismatched wheel rims and a small rust spot on one door?"

"Must be twenty panel vans an hour go past on this street. I work inside. I wouldn't know one from another."

Noah wasn't ready to give up. The guy must know something. "Did she work the street or get a room?"

"While Tito was around, she only sprang for a room if the guy paid for it. Lately, if I was on duty, she got a room for the evening. Don't know what she did on my nights off."

Disgust filled Noah's belly. Herman was doing her for the price of a room. Otherwise, she took her chances getting in a car with strangers.

Noah dropped his card on the counter with instructions for Herman to call if he heard anything.

Two more stops and they had a real name, although her belongings had disappeared in the weeks since she'd gone missing.

She had roomed with another one of Tito's girls at one time, but moved out when he was busted. Her real name was Stella Fitzgerald and she'd followed a boyfriend out from Abilene. For a while, she worked flipping burgers but when the boyfriend left, she couldn't make the rent and took up hooking.

They had enough information to find Tito and probably her parents to make sure they had the right woman. More than that, they had an idea of where she'd been snatched and it wasn't in Constanza's neighborhood.

The area of the Sanitizer's hunting ground had increased to include not only all of Harris County, but probably Galveston,

Chambers, Liberty, Montgomery, and Fort Bend counties as well.

Didn't that just make his day?

Noah jumped out at the front of the building while Conner returned the car to the motor pool. They'd made two more stops, checking out calls regarding Joyce.

Both callers were convinced the drawing represented someone they knew well, but both had different ideas of who she was.

One could have been correct, but not both.

He was already checking the census in Abilene for an eighteen-year-old girl named Stella Fitzgerald by the time Conner got back inside.

Noah finished with the girl while his partner started tracing her pimp.

Fifteen minutes later, Conner had located Tito, and Noah had an address for Stella's mother. She wasn't a paragon of virtue, having served one ninety-day stretch and a couple of overnights for DUIs, but better than the father. He'd been in prison for manslaughter for the last twelve years.

He tried to foist the notification call off on his partner, but Conner refused. Noah found the mother, he'd have to deal with her. Next time he'd make sure Conner found the phone number. He was better with that sort of thing.

Noah stalled, planning what to say to the bereaved mother while Conner tried Tito at the number his parole officer had given, at his mother's house, and at the place where he was supposed to work. No luck.

The guy was in the wind.

Noah gave up and called Stella's mother, who seemed more interested in recovering her daughter's things than her remains.

"If you can send us a sample of your DNA so we can make a positive ID, I'll have the items shipped to you right away. There's also the possibility you would qualify for our local Survivor's Benefits Fund." No point telling her there weren't any items *to* ship and that fund had gone broke. She might not bother to cooperate with the identification. "Now, if you could help us, we're trying to piece together your daughter's last days. Do you know if anyone was bothering her? Following her?"

He made notes on his memo pad while she complained about her daughter's behavior.

"It's been that long since you've heard from her? Well, I can see that you wouldn't be able to help us."

He swiveled toward Conner. "Mother hasn't talked to her in two years."

"I just love a happy family. While you were chatting with the World's Best Mother, I tracked down our Dancing Queen cheerleader. She's now Darlene Ainsworth and lives in River Oaks."

"I've dealt with all the lowlifes I can stand for one day. Let's head home and call on her first thing in the morning while we're fresh and terminal pessimism hasn't had time to set in. I can't wait to hear how she managed to misplace a daughter and never realize she'd been dead for two months."

CHAPTER
THIRTY-ONE

"WANT TO CHECK in with the boss or scoot out before he sees us?"

Noah thought for about two seconds before answering. "Do I want to? Yes. Should we? No. We've ditched him too often lately. This time we actually have progress to report. We'll save the scooting for some time when we don't."

He almost changed his mind when he realized the Lieu's blinds were closed but it was too late by then. The door was open and Jansen had seen them. "Good, you're here. Come on in."

"Morning, sir. We wanted to bring you up-to-date before we headed out." *Just smile, give the report, and get out before anything happens*

"Excellent. Glad to hear it. Especially since I'm so seldom honored in that manner. But first, let me bring you two in on what's been happening in my world this fine morning."

Ah, shit. Here it comes.

"The mayor called the Chief. At home. Before seven o'clock.

The Chief called the Chief of Detectives. And the Chief of Ds called me. Imagine how happy that made me."

He didn't have to imagine it. The closed blinds were a dead giveaway.

"Would you care to guess who called the Mayor?"

Not really.

"Someone from the *Chronicle*?"

How did Conner figure that out?

"Seems R.J. Perry objects to being followed. The mayor objects to being awakened. The Chief objects to being told what to do. The Chief of Ds objects to wasting his limited budget following a man who knows he's being followed. And I object to having a man who calls himself the Sanitizer running around my city unimpeded, killing people at will. Do you two numb-nuts have anything to add?"

Holy crap, this was bad. "We identified one of the victims yesterday and have a strong lead on another one we're about to follow up on now. Doc M has promised us more DNA and possible fingerprints shortly."

"That's great. I'm sure those young women's parents will be glad to have some closure. But do you have any leads on the son-of-a-bitch who is actually doing the killing?"

Conner stepped forward. About time he shouldered some of this. "We believe him to be a large white male named Dick, in his mid-thirties, has worked construction, and drives a ten-year-old white Mercedes panel van. We've hesitated to post photos of the van until this point, worried he might destroy the only piece of evidence we have. If we haven't made any more headway by this afternoon, we were considering releasing the photos to the media. Do you concur with that plan?"

Good job, partner. Put the decision back on him and get us off the hook.

Jansen stuttered, knowing he'd been snookered. Either decision held risks. Pick wrong and the blame fell square on him. "Do…do you have any other leads you're working besides the next identification?"

Thank goodness for Laurel's help. "We have a list of phone numbers of people who were once part of a corporation that at one time owned a portion of either the vacant lot or the apartment building."

"Get to it, then. We'll meet back here in the morning and discuss our options."

Noah recognized a dismissal when he heard one and was gone before Jansen's wooly eyebrows settled back into place.

Something better break before morning or they'd lose their best lead.

Darlene Ainsworth's home was nice by any standards, but not a McMansion. This was the "old money" Laurel had talked about. Not something Noah thought about consciously, but knew instinctively.

The Lexus SUV in her driveway had a bumper sticker touting The Kinkaid School.

Apparently Lamar wasn't good enough for her kids. Or was it the memories of what happened to her when she was a student there?

So how did her daughter become one of the Sanitizer's victims? Did the apple not fall far from the tree even in the rarified atmosphere of a premier private school?

And how did someone in her early thirties end up living in a part of town reserved for crotchety old millionaires?

If the house screamed 'old money,' the woman who answered the door corroborated his assessment. She wore camel-colored slacks and a white blouse, yet somehow he knew they cost more than his suit and Conner's put together.

Her hair was in a simple style, but the blond highlights gleamed. The rock on her left hand would have weighted down a less athletic-looking woman.

Conner held out his memo pad as if unsure they had the right house, although the former cheerleader was still evident in her face and bearing. "I'm Detective Crawford and this is my partner Detective Daugherty. We're looking for Darlene Quinlen Ainsworth. Is that you?"

If the idea of two detectives at her door bothered her, it didn't show. "Yes. May I help you?"

"May we come in and speak to you for a moment?"

"About what?"

Noah didn't like to deliver bad news while standing outside, but she wasn't budging from the door. "There's no easy way to put this Mrs. Ainsworth, but are you the same Darlene Quinlen who had a baby eighteen years ago with Roscoe Madison?"

All that poise and self-confidence dropped away like a giant hand had reached in and pulled the plug on her life. She blanched and made a sound like a cat coughing up a furball. Two seconds later, the mask was back in place. "I'm sorry. You must have me mistaken for someone else."

"That's not what Roscoe told us, but we can come back later with a warrant for your DNA if necessary." Fuck her and the SUV she rode in on if she thought she was going to cut him off.

Professional con men had tried and failed.

The hand resting on the doorframe began to tremble. Blue eyes lost their fire. "Follow me," she said, her voice a case study in resignation.

She pivoted on one ballet-slippered foot and strode toward the back of the house.

On the left, they passed a darkened room with a giant TV tuned to the CNBC. A running stock market report crawled across the bottom of the screen while Jim Cramer yelled and pounded on noisemaker buttons.

An elderly man—Darlene's father?—sat ensconced in a throne-like leather chair. The lights of the TV bounced off his bald head. Without turning he ordered, "Who was at the door?"

"No one, dear. Just a couple of men soliciting another donation for Robbie's school."

"Whatever you can afford from your checking account. I'm not giving another penny until they prove they can whip his useless ass into shape."

She led them through a living room that had never been lived in and out the back door to a patio with nicer furniture than anything Noah had ever owned. He sunk down into a cushioned lounge chair and waited for her to begin.

"You'll have to excuse my husband. Our son was expelled for three days for hazing a freshman. With the money we give those people you'd think they'd be more understanding of childish hijinks. It's not like the boy was physically harmed."

"We're much more interested in your daughter." Noah watched the fear flash across her face.

"Please! Keep your voices down. My husband has no idea of my youthful indiscretion. That was another time. Another life. I really can't help you with that. I've moved on."

She'd *moved on?* Just like that. She wrote off the life of another human being?

She smoothed back her perfectly coifed hair and lifted her chin. "I was guaranteed all of that would be kept confidential. If she thinks she can approach me now, she has a lot to learn and if you or anyone else is considering blackmail, forget it. You can see that my husband keeps me on a tight leash financially. I can't spend more than five hundred dollars without his permission."

Noah couldn't resist seeing what she'd say. "What if we tell your husband?"

"Then he'd know so what would be the point of paying you?"

She was sharp, he had to give her that. "My partner and I are Houston police detectives, ma'am. We're not in the blackmail business. We're looking for any information on a female, approximately seventeen years old, whose DNA matches Roscoe Madison. Her body was discovered last week. An identification might help lead us to her killer. A forensic artist has made a drawing if that would help your memory."

"So she's dead. That part of my life is truly over." She heaved out a heavy sigh. "I was always afraid she'd show up, try to contact me or Robbie. With the 'Search your DNA' malarkey on TV all the time, who knew what could happen?"

Noah had come across cold people before—those who committed homicide seldom expressed remorse for anything other than getting caught—but this had to be a record on the kelvin scale. Even Roscoe Madison, who set fire to an apartment full of rival drug dealers, mourned the daughter he never knew he had.

Conner tapped the memo book he'd been silently holding.

"We still need to identify her. Can you tell us where she was born? What happened to her?"

"I was very athletic in those days so I didn't show. I graduated with my class and announced I was traveling to New York to spend the summer with my aunt. My folks drove me up to Ft. Worth and checked me into the Edna Gladney home. The one here was out of the question. Someone might recognize me."

"And that's where she was born?" Noah recognized the contempt in Conner's voice, but Darlene was completely oblivious.

"The child was born near the end of July. I forget which day. Then I went to Bryn Mawr exactly as planned. The incident was never spoken of again. Two years later, my parents were killed in a boating accident. Martin, as my father's best friend, took over handling my finances. It seemed natural to marry him after I graduated."

Noah pushed a pen and paper her direction. "We'll need your permission in writing for the release of information from the Gladney Home." He had no idea if that was true or not. He just wanted her to admit the *incident* had happened.

Her hand hovered over the pen, but she didn't pick it up.

"Or we could come back with a warrant."

She scribbled a few words and shoved it back as if the paper itself was contaminated.

Noah folded the paper and placed it in the folder with the drawing she had never asked to see.

In the car, Conner made a note in his pocket spiral. "I'll get started with the Gladney Home, but then what? Even if we identify her, odds are against it leading to her killer. If we don't come up with something solid by morning, the Chief might insist we go public with the little information we have. When that happens, the Sanitizer could decide to fade into the night, pulling up stakes and moving on to a new killing field. How do we prevent that?"

Noah switched on the engine, but Lola's familiar roar failed to offer any encouragement. "Damned if I know, but we better think of something fast."

CHAPTER
THIRTY-TWO

"I'M NOT GETTING anywhere with these calls. You got any better suggestions?" Conner tossed his empty coffee cup into the trash with a solid *thoip*.

Noah stretched his aching back and eyed Jansen's darkened office. What were the chances he could snag the Lieu's ergo-dynamic chair for a few hours without getting caught? "I don't know. We still have a few hours reprieve before the boss gets back. The way I see it, we've got three choices—hope a reasonable tip came in overnight on the hotline, identify another victim, or locate the owner of the vacant field. Because if we don't come up with something by the time he gets back, we'll have to post that photo of the white van."

"I've checked out a dozen of these tips and I've got to tell you. We have some crazy people in this city." Conner rubbed his eyes and drew a line through another name and phone number.

"This city, Hell. I've had calls all the way from San Diego." Noah studied his emails in hopes some new lab or DNA report had come in within the last ten minutes.

Nope. Nothing.

"I have that list Laurel sent over with phone numbers for the officers of the various corporations that owned the apartment complex. It's not the field, but we could try them anyway."

"Feels like a long shot—bunch of rich dudes who live two hundred miles away and never set foot on the property—but what have we got to lose? I'm sick of talking to weird conspiracy nuts who think aliens came down, abducted our victims for examinations, brought them back, and buried them."

Noah pulled up the list on his computer, printed it off, and gave half to Conner before easing back into his rock-hard chair. He'd made one call, only to be hung up on after his first question, when his cell rang. He glanced at Conner before answering. "Hey, Laurel. What's up?"

Her voice was hesitant, unsure. "I know you said not to make any calls, but I found the name of the real estate company that handled the last sale on the vacant lot. I'd never heard of it, so I called to see if it was still in business. I left a sort of generic message saying I had a client interested in buying the property and were they still the agents."

Noah's heart began a slow climb up his throat and he strained to take a full breath.

"After I hung up, I started thinking about the name. Several of the corporations involved with that apartment building were named after Texas rivers: Frio, Salado, Blanco, Llano. And then this agency named Comal Realty. The thing is besides being an odd coincidence, all those rivers are west of here. Closer to Austin and the hill country. If you wanted to name a business in Houston after a river, wouldn't you pick one closer, like San

Jacinto or Brazos or even Neches?"

Fuck. Fuck. Fuck. Why hadn't he noticed? The cashier's check for the tax payments came from Medina Properties. Wasn't that a river near San Antonio? Noah forced himself to speak calmly. "Did you identify yourself?"

"Only as Royce Elkins Realty."

Not good, but better than some creep knowing her name. "And no one has called you back?"

"Well, I had one odd call. Some guy asked about a property we have listed on Brier View Drive."

"Don't people call in about that kind of thing all the time?" Why else did realtors put ads in the paper?

"It's a beautiful property, right off the bayou. But the owner's a privacy nut, doesn't want his neighbors to know he's selling, so the ad didn't give any particulars. Just said call for information. I started describing it and he cut me off. Wanted to know if there was anyone else in the office he could talk to."

"Was your boss there?" There were still men who preferred to do business with another man so the call wasn't *that* odd.

"Yes, but he was in a meeting with a client."

Okay, calm down. She wasn't alone and the guy knew it. "And that's what you told him, right?"

"Not exactly. I asked him to leave his number and said Royce would call first thing in the morning. He laughed and hung up on me."

"How long ago was this?"

"An hour or so. About ten minutes after I left the message."

The volume knob on his voice shot to *high*. "Why'd you wait so long to call me?"

"I didn't want to phone till Royce left. He took the client to look at another property."

So she was alone in the office?

"There's one other thing I've been thinking about. Did you ever read the stuff I sent you about Tom Meyers' client?"

Shit. He'd been too busy trying to solve *this* case. Plus he didn't like Meyers and especially didn't like being maneuvered into doing something to help the guy. A clear case of his ego getting in the way when he knew Meyers wouldn't have called him if it wasn't important.

Luckily, Lauren barreled on without waiting. "His client was the son of a prominent Austin businessman. He was accused, along with one of his frat brothers, of raping and strangling a prostitute. Tom proved his client was out-of-town at the time so charges were dismissed and it all fell on the frat brother—Jeffery Landers—who was released two weeks ago. The client's name is Richard Bachman, Jr. Bachman is a lake up near Dallas, but it comes off the Trinity so I guess it qualifies as a river."

"Hold on a minute." Noah set down the phone and tore through his notes. Where was the information from that banker who signed off on the first loan? Papers scattered across his desk.

Conner hung up on his last call and hovered, waiting. They'd been partners long enough for him to know something important was going down.

There it was. In his pocket spiral. He ran a finger down his notes. What was the guy's name? Yes, the corporations were all rivers. And the officers were… *Oh, shit!* Bradly R. Bachman, Junior and Senior. What had the guy said? Junior had dropped out of school. He was totally useless.

Because that was the same description Luis from Sleeman Cement had given about the construction foreman. Had Bradly

R. Bachman, Senior tried to keep his son busy by giving him a job at the apartment?

Did the R stand for Richard? As in Dick. Big Dick?

He glanced at the clock over the Lieu's office. Almost four o'clock. Rush hour traffic was already underway. "Go right now. Lock the office door. Turn out the lights. Wait in the bathroom if you need to. Stay out of sight. Your office is on Memorial Drive, right? It'll take me at least forty-five minutes—"

"Lefty Bob," Conner interrupted.

"What?" Noah tried to make the leap in his mind.

"He's working a case on that side of town. He could be there in ten minutes."

Noah's heart slowed down. That would work. "Did you hear Conner? I'll send Lefty Bob to pick you up. He's a big guy, dark hair. Don't unlock the door until you see his badge and identification. It'll say Roberto Hernandez."

CHAPTER
THIRTY-THREE

WHAT THE FUCK had just happened?

Medina Realty was not listed anywhere. That number never rang unless it was a robo call. Some machine going down a list of numbers in order with no idea who or what they'd reach.

That bitch had not only known the name of the agency, she'd known the property.

And no one in their right mind would want to purchase that property. Not after it had been featured prominently on the news. Along with its multitude of occupants.

Something was up and he had to find out what, and he had to do it fast.

The call didn't seem to be police related. A Google search led to a webpage for an actual company with two agents. Laurel Newcomb must be the woman who left the message. She seemed to be a real person with a Facebook page showing friends and photos going back several years.

Much too cute to be an undercover cop. She'd be his type if she were a few years younger. Although he was willing to make an exception if necessary

Laurel. The name felt good on his tongue. From the Greek if he wasn't mistaken. Meaning strength or courage. Not that either one of those would do her any good.

He'd wasted fifteen minutes panicking when he checked the message. His blood pressure had skyrocketed to dangerous levels and his shirt soaked through with sweat before he came to his senses. He had everything he needed to take care of the situation.

His private playhouse didn't look like much from the curb. But why should it? No one drove down the dead end street. A four car garage with an equipment shed attached was nestled behind an abandoned mansion whose ownership would be tied up in court for years to come.

The garage was four-star all the way, but the equipment shed was an add-on. No electricity, but lanterns worked fine. No running water, but a bucketful of bayou water was all he needed for washing his visitors.

His name appeared on no document. There were no utilities to trace. Considering the nature of the old wooden building, one match would destroy any evidence should anyone come too close.

He eased back behind the empty house and into the garage where his van waited.

The white paneled van had served him well over the years and he took good care of her. She was fully equipped with everything he might need. Waiting comfortably behind her tinted windows was no problem.

If he couldn't get to the woman now, he'd follow her home.

Royce Elkins Realty was located in a stand-alone building next to a quiet side street. On the opposite side, they shared a parking lot with a three-story brick structure with no windows facing that area.

The late afternoon sun glared directly into the windows of the building he parked in front of and all the blinds were tightly closed.

The first thing he noticed was the woman pictured on the agency website. Using the binoculars he kept on the front seat, he could see her through the glass panel on the front door.

She talked on the phone. She worked on her computer. She walked to the file cabinet.

He was right. She did have a cute ass.

The second thing he noticed was a man who looked similar to the owner pictured on the company website. So her boss *was* in.

The bitch had lied to him already.

What else did she know? Given time, he could find out. All he needed was to get her alone.

After twenty minutes, his attention waned. He watched a woman walk a poodle with a pink bow out of the dog grooming shop at the end of the block. He couldn't stand dogs, but the woman had nice legs. A flurry of movement caught his eye.

The owner and an elderly couple were leaving the realty office and he almost missed it. His father's words echoed in the back of his brain. *Loser. Lightweight. Can't control yourself long enough to finish anything. Big disappointment.*

He slapped the steering wheel then yanked his hand back. He'd ruin everything if he hit the horn.

He glanced back into the office and Laurel was still there, talking on the phone.

The elderly couple inched down the sidewalk and toward the parking lot while the owner tried to pretend patience. The old woman clung to her husband's arm. Squeezing her fat ass into the rear of the silver Infiniti took both men. Then the husband worked his way to the front passenger seat and eased inside.

Some discussion must have followed—Seat belts? Destination? Air Conditioning? Radio Station?—because the car didn't move for an excruciatingly long time.

Meanwhile, Laurel had hung up the phone. When had that happened?

The Infiniti backed out at one-mile-an-hour, then stopped at the edge of the driveway, waiting for nonexistent traffic to pass.

Finally! He eased out of the van, being careful not to slam the door and attract attention. He casually strolled across the street when a beat-up Volvo approached from the opposite direction and turned into the lot.

A hefty guy with a good start on a beer gut heaved out of the car. His sport coat flapped as he speed-walked across the lot, showing a gold badge attached to his belt.

He couldn't let the cop see his face, so he bent to tie his shoe.

The cop skidded to a stop as he reached the sidewalk and eyed his white van.

How the hell did the cops know about his van? He was in deep shit now.

The fat cop swung toward him but he had already reached for a loose brick lining a flowerbed. He hurled the brick into the cop's face.

The blow stunned the man but didn't take him down. He

reached for the gun on his hip, but it tangled in his sport coat. By the time he got it loose, the distance had been closed.

The cop was stronger than he looked. He struggled to regain control of the gun, but it was too late.

Pulling that trigger was a thrill he'd never experienced before. So much power at his fingers. The gun bucked, but the sound was muffled by the press of their bodies. The cop stared into his eyes as if surprised. His ragged breath grew faint.

Now what? He couldn't stand in the middle of a parking lot holding a dying man.

Weren't cops supposed to stay in good shape? This guy weighed a ton. The cop began to sag and he dragged the body behind the flowerbed.

A quick glance around the street said he was hidden from view so he took the opportunity to help himself to the guy's badge and identification. Roberto Hernandez.

Well, his own hair and eyes were dark and he was tan from spending time outside. If he kept his finger over the photo, he should be able to pass.

While he was at it, he relieved the guy of his cash, too. That might confuse any investigation. Besides, to the victor belonged the spoils. And he was definitely the victor. No point in taking the detective's gun. It was covered in blood.

Besides, he already had his own.

Fortune had smiled on him this morning when he'd put on a maroon shirt. Any blood splatters shouldn't be easily visible.

He took a deep breath to calm his racing heart, smoothed down his hair, and strolled toward Royce Elkins Realty with his back straight and head held high, only to find the door locked and the lights off.

Where'd she gone? Her car had to be in the lot. There was no parking on the side street. He'd checked. If she'd passed, he'd have seen her.

He cupped his hands and looked through the windowed door into the office. Enough of the afternoon sun filtered inside to make out her desk, a file cabinet, visitor chairs, a potted plant. A thin line of light seeped from under a closed door in the back.

He pressed tighter against the cold glass and saw something sitting on the edge of her desk. Her purse.

No woman went anywhere without her purse.

She was in there. He knew it. He tapped on the window but nothing happened. He knocked harder, rattling the glass in its frame. Had she met Hernandez before or was he just coming to question her? No way to know for sure. Best not to use his name.

"It's the police, Ms. Newcomb. I know you're in there. Please open the door."

Several seconds passed before a door opened and light spilled into the room. He could only make out the woman's silhouette as she leaned around the corner. "Detective Hernandez?"

"Yes, ma'am. I'm right here." He held the badge and ID against the window, making sure the photo was obscured by the agency name painted on the glass.

"Noah said to expect you."

Job one as soon as he had her secured: find out who Noah was and how much he knew.

She edged closer, examining first his ID and then him. The door was flimsy. He could kick it in if necessary, but he preferred that she come willingly, so he held still under her scrutiny.

"Wait a second, let me get my purse." She twisted toward her desk.

He fought back a smile. They never went anywhere without their purse.

Laurel was still digging in her purse for the office key when Detective Hernandez took her arm and tried to pull her away. "Give me a minute. I have to lock this door or my boss will be furious."

"I don't like you out here on the street, exposed."

A car came around the corner and he twisted, turning his back to the street and blocking her from view.

Wow. Noah must really be worried about her.

The instant the lock clicked, Hernandez hustled her away. His hand was rough and calloused, and his grip a fraction too tight for comfort.

He rushed her across the street to a white van. Not what she expected, but then Noah drove a pickup.

A *chip chip* sounded as the door lock popped open, and he all but shoved her inside.

Geez. She knew he was concerned for her safety, but he didn't have to be so rough.

The back of the van was neat and orderly, but held all types of equipment she didn't recognize. Lefty Bob must be an amateur handyman. Wouldn't that be nice in a friend? She had half a dozen things in her townhouse that needed to be fixed and she really wanted an arbor and porch swing for her patio.

She glanced over to see if he had on a wedding ring. He didn't, but he wore his watch on his left arm, not his right as she did. Some people did that, but it always felt awkward to her.

Noah had told her the man was big, but she had no idea he meant huge. The guy wasn't simply tall, he was muscular. He

reminded her of a football player with all his pads on.

She clicked her seatbelt and twisted toward him. "So where are you taking me?"

"Didn't Noah tell you?"

Had he? "I don't think so. Only someplace safe while he figures out what's going on. I thought his office."

"No. Too many people there. We have a safe house where you'll be comfortable until he can come."

That made sense.

Noah glanced at his phone. It stared back at him, cold and silent. Sure, Lefty Bob drove like an old man, but how long did it take to get from Dairy Ashford to Memorial?

He was supposed to call as soon as Laurel was safe in his car. Not wait until they got back to the station. He glared at the phone again. Daring it to ring.

And it did.

He grabbed it up without thinking and shouted, "Where have you been?"

"Nebraska."

What? "Who is this?"

"Lincoln Montgomery."

Shit. He'd yelled at the FBI. Way to go when he was asking them to help. "What's up, Montgomery? We're in a rush around here."

"I've got the information you've been asking for."

About time. "Spill it."

"First, Stella Fitzgerald's mother sent in a sample of her DNA. It'll take a while, but I'll let you know if it matches the body you've been calling Lucy."

That was good, but he already knew the woman was her mother, so the DNA was only a formality.

"The dental records you sent for Felicia Vickers were a positive match."

Did that make him feel better or worse? The Vickers's daughter was definitely dead, but they could quit searching now. If his neighbor Mrs. Powell was right, having a grave to visit was some comfort.

So how did he feel about his part in dropping the investigation? Like that piece of gum you stepped on in the parking lot and never got rid of.

"There's one more thing."

He didn't like the sound of Montgomery's voice. Another shoe was about to drop.

"Forensics found matches for two of the seven cases you sent over."

Damn the lazy Garrett Lewis. How many cases had he swept away because he couldn't be bothered to investigate? If they'd spent more time looking into them at the time, would they have found a connection to the man in the white van?

"One was in Ft. Worth and the other in Abilene. I've contacted the sheriffs in both counties. You'll probably be hearing from them."

Son-of-a-bitch. The Sanitizer hadn't taken a break for ten years. He'd just moved around the state.

Why did he turn out to be right on the times he most wanted to be wrong?

Noah disconnected, grabbed his phone and thumbed in Lefty Bob's number. Again. Where the hell was the guy and why didn't he answer?

CHAPTER
THIRTY-FOUR

"D ETECTIVE HERNANDEZ?"

"Call me Roberto."

Sure, he probably thought that sounded more professional than Lefty Bob.

She could use a friend right now, and this guy wasn't as friendly or warm as Noah and Conner. Maybe because he was on the job.

But then so was Noah when he questioned her and the Hudsons' maid Rosario. And when he helped her find a decent divorce attorney. He might have been off duty when he drove her to the prison to visit her dead friend's brother, but he was when he used his influence to help the guy get into rehab instead of jail.

That didn't make Noah cold like Roberto. Where was the funny Lefty Bob Noah kept telling her stories about?

Idiot. He's not going to tell jokes when he's trying to rush you to safety.

She'd feel better if his eyes weren't so dead. He'd smiled at her a couple of times, but it felt forced. Like something that didn't come naturally to him.

He glanced at her again with that fake smile. "Did you need something?"

"Wondering how soon until we get there. I guess that makes me sound like a kid on a car trip." She tried to laugh, but it didn't come out.

Roberto looked at her like he didn't get the joke. They stopped at a light and he pulled out his phone. "At least forty minutes with this traffic. I'm texting Noah right now to let him know we'll be a little late."

Pretty fast texting for his right hand.

The light changed and he slid the phone back into his pocket, pulled out a comb, and ran it through his hair.

Again with the right hand?

Maybe he was ambidextrous? She tried to think of everything he'd done since she'd met him. He'd opened the car door with his right hand although his left was closer to the handle.

He wore his badge and gun on his right hip and he didn't wear a jacket to cover them the way Noah and Conner always did.

Had she actually *seen* the photo on his ID?

She tried to study his face for any sign of Hispanic heritage. He had several tiny spots on his cheek, near his ear. Moles? No, two of them had run slightly, leaving a barely visible trail of dark red.

She twisted further toward the back to avoid looking at that thin red line. A knot formed in her throat and she swallowed it back. She had to say something casual, but what? "You must be quite the handyman to have so many tools."

"Yes, it's my hobby. I was woodworking earlier today." For the first time, his smile seemed genuine.

All this playing detective had messed her up big time. That wasn't blood and if it was, the woodworking was a reason for it. She sighed and studied the tools, lined so carefully against the side of the van.

Tucked safely into the rack where it couldn't spill out was a pair of right-handed scissors.

Her mind flashed back to a documentary on snakes she'd watched last week in an attempt to overcome her unrealistic terror of them. It hadn't worked, but she'd learned a lot. Boa Constrictors didn't kill their prey by crushing them. They squeezed until all blood flow to the heart and brain were cut off, causing death.

That was how she felt now. No blood. No air. No escape?

Noah stabbed at Lefty Bob's number on his cell so hard his finger hurt. Where the hell was the guy?

He wasn't having any better luck with Laurel. Both their numbers went straight to voice mail and he was tired of leaving messages no one answered.

Conner paced behind him and peered over his shoulder. A sure sign he was just as worried. "Do you think one of us should stay here and the other go to her office or both go and ask the Lieu to let us know if they show up?"

"I can't sit here waiting another minute. We need to track down that guy Laurel gave us—Bradly Richard Bachman, Junior—but if something's wrong, we should both go. And something's definitely wrong. Let me call and leave a message so Lefty will know what we're doing." Not that it mattered. The guy wasn't picking up so what were the odds he was checking his messages?

At some point during the last ten minutes, Earl Sparks had arrived and was clearing out his desk. "Let me help. I can hunt down the address and any other information on that Big Dick character. It'll be my last official job before I sign my retirement papers in half an hour."

"While you're at it, check out that massage parlor we visited last week." Conner slapped a sticky note on Earl's desk.

"We don't have time for that now. If you're worried about it, we can give the name to Vice later." Given the chance, Noah would grab the note and toss it in the trash. Sure, Conner was a choirboy and those things bothered him, but he needed to get his priorities straight.

"Fuji Massage and Spa. That's a river in Japan."

"I thought Fuji was a mountain."

"A mountain and a river."

Fuck. Did he need to check every business in the city named after a body of water? He twisted toward Earl. "See what you can find, then turn it over to Vice. There's no way we can get a warrant with the information we have, but if they raid the place, who knows what they'll come up with. For now, we've gotta find Laurel and Lefty Bob."

Conner opened his desk drawer, grabbed his weapon and spun around. "I'll get my car. Meet you in front."

Noah tried to protest. He'd rather take Lola, either because he drove faster or because he needed to feel in control of something, but it didn't matter because Conner was already out of sight.

One more useless call to Lefty and another to Laurel where he got a message that her mailbox was full—had he called that many times?—and he spun toward the door.

He'd returned his cell to his pocket when it started ringing. Lefty's name appeared on the screen. About. Damn. Time. The bellow in his voice echoed across the room. "What the fuck have you been doing? You were supposed to call me the minute you got to her."

A youngish voice with a heavy Hispanic accent answered. "Yo. Settle down, man. It's all cool."

Something cold and dark tried to slither up Noah's throat, but he forced it down. "This is Detective Noah Daugherty. Who is this?" If a voice could streak through a phone and grab the person speaking, his would have.

"Sorry, sir. This is Officer Chaz Perez. My sergeant told me to see if I could get the person who keeps calling this number to say anything helpful." All traces of an accent were gone.

"And I'm trying to figure out who has Detective Hernandez's phone and why."

"Oh, shit. Our vic's a cop?"

That cold, dark thing in Noah's throat exploded, wrapping its tentacles around his neck and chest and gut so that he couldn't breathe or speak.

Lieutenant Jansen stepped out of his office, his face the color of the paper gripped in his left hand. "Just had a call from dispatch. Shooting victim on Memorial. Isn't that where you sent Lefty Bob?"

Noah managed a nod and squeezed out a few words. "Male or female?"

"Male."

Noah held up his cell. "I've got a young officer calling me on Lefty's phone, talking about *our vic.*"

"Go. Now."

~

Conner screeched to a halt in front of the Headquarters building. Noah jumped in, a panicked expression on his face.

What the hell happened in the five minutes it took to get his car?

"There's been a shooting on Memorial. Sounds like Lefty Bob."

Conner's breath *whooshed* out as if someone hit him in the gut. "Do we know how he is? What about Laurel?"

"Bad enough he hasn't identified himself as a police officer. And no one has mentioned Laurel."

Had they allowed the Sanitizer to shoot their friend and make off with their only witness? Not that she'd witnessed anything, but she knew which direction the investigation was heading. And if he had her, he'd know soon. "We need to put out an APB on the white van."

"Already done. The Lieu took care of it. And Lefty's car also. We don't know what vehicle he took."

Was there anything else they could do while driving? "You've tried her office?"

"Half a dozen times. All I got was a recording. The Lieu is trying to find her boss. Last I heard, the uniform on scene was at the office door looking for emergency contact information."

Conner didn't often drive with lights and siren going. Most of their victims were already dead. Weaving in and out of traffic, noise throbbing in his ears, flashing lights assaulting his eyes, worry about his friend burring into his brain, had his heart doing summersaults.

None of this mattered. People were depending on him. He couldn't let them down. His foot pressed harder on the accelerator and he roared through an intersection, ignoring Noah's tight grip on the armrest and the incongruity of the infant seat bouncing behind him.

He reached Royce Elkins Realty in twelve minutes and slid to a halt behind an ambulance as two dejected-looking EMTs loaded their equipment back inside.

Noah didn't wait for Conner to come to a complete stop. He threw open the door and jumped out. Most of the activity seemed to be to the side of the office, in a parking lot. He ran that direction.

A group of uniformed officers, and jumpsuited techies huddled near a flowerbed.

Noah's feet gained ten pounds with every step. Benny Schroeder, the pint-sized, Bozo-haired techie held up his hand. "You don't want to go any closer."

The hell he didn't.

He pushed forward and the group stepped aside. Doc M knelt over a prone body. One glance at the cheap sport coat and worn shoes and he knew it was Lefty Bob.

For the first time since he'd known Doc M, his eyes held warmth. "Stay back, Noah. You can't be involved in this case. You're too close to the victim. Even I'm gonna get someone else to do the post."

"Fine. I'm not working this case. I'm working the case he

was working. Now, give me everything you've got." That ploy might work for a few minutes, but not once the Chief of Ds got involved.

Conner was beside his shoulder and he could feel the sharp intake of breath when he recognized Lefty Bob. Within two seconds, his partner was back on the job. "Any sign of the woman he came here to see?"

A uniformed officer with stripes on his sleeves and a *SGT Rusty Bourgeois* nametag stepped forward. "The realty office is empty and locked. We found an emergency number. My boss tracked it down and the owner is on his way back. Sorry we didn't identify the detective sooner, but we just found his wallet. It was in the flowerbed and blended with the mulch. The gun on the ground made us think he might be up to no good."

So the guy took Lefty's badge and ID, hid his wallet, but left his gun? Why? Did he come prepared with his own? "Have you started canvassing the neighborhood? Did anybody see anything?"

"Not so far."

Conner had his spiral out, taking notes. "What about the white panel van? Did you know to look for that?"

"Just found out. Haven't asked anyone yet, but the old Volvo is here in the lot so they cancelled the BOLO on it."

"When you do ask, add a tall white guy in his mid to late thirties, to the list. Might be the driver."

"Anything else you want me to check on?"

Noah wanted to knock the guy across the parking lot. "Well, there's the missing woman. You might want to look for her. She's blond, slim, about five-four."

"Any distinguishing marks?"

None that he'd had a chance to check out yet.

Crime scene tape had been strung around the area and a silver Infiniti drove up to it and stopped. After a short discussion with one of the uniforms, the car pulled forward.

A puffy-faced man with bad skin waved them over. "I'm Royce Elkins. I got a call. Did something happen to Laurel?"

This was Laurel's boss? She said he wasn't too healthy. Easy to believe. "She's missing at the moment. Do you have any idea where she might have gone? Were you expecting a client?"

"No, we were pretty much done for the day. She only needed to man the office for another hour."

"She was on the phone."

"I beg your pardon?" Noah turned toward the back seat. An elderly woman the size of a blimp glared out at him, her lips compressed into a disapproving line.

"She was all nervous and sneaking looks around before we left. As soon as we were out the door, she picked up the phone."

"How do you know if you were outside?"

"Could see her reflection. Couldn't wait for her boss to leave."

"That was me she called. Wanted to report a suspicious call earlier."

Noah twisted back to Royce. "Did you see a white Mercedes panel van around here anywhere? Or a tall guy. Mid-thirties, white?"

"No, but I wasn't paying attention."

"It was parked across the street." The woman pointed to three-story brick building. All the windows in the front had closed blinds. "Facing that way." She motioned with her head.

"Did you see the guy inside?"

"Kind of. The windows were tinted. I think he was tall. He

skooched down when we passed like he didn't want us to see him."

"What about his face? Beard or clean shaven?"

"Looked clean to me, but he could have had one of those ridiculous little tuffs of hair under the lip."

A soul patch. Noah wouldn't want the judgmental woman for a neighbor, but he loved her for a witness.

Conner tugged on his arm. "Earl texted me with Bachman's address. He sent a patrol car to check it out and another to check out Laurel's townhouse. Here's his driver's license photo." He held his phone in front of the woman. "Is this the man you saw in the white van?"

"Certainly could be."

A positive ID would have been better, but that might be enough for a warrant if Earl worked his magic.

The guy with the sergeant's stripes looked their way while talking on his cell. Noah caught Conner's eye. "Let's get out of here before the Chief of Ds shows up and takes us off the case for good."

CHAPTER THIRTY-FIVE

"WHAT ARE YOU doing?"

Laurel didn't like the sound of the guy's voice. She hefted her purse onto her lap. "Looking for my phone. I think I left it at the office. Can we go back and get it?"

The sound he made was probably supposed to be a laugh. "Noah would have my balls for breakfast if I did that. I'll text him and see if he'll stop and pick it up on the way to the safe house."

"But he can't get in. I have the keys here." She held up the office key on its flashlight key ring.

"My mother will have a fit if I don't call her soon. She's been trying to reach me all day. I had to turn my phone off and stick it in a drawer." That much was true. She'd switched it off and hidden it. Out of sight. Out of mind. Only she'd grabbed it and stuck it in her jacket pocket when she got her purse.

Her left-hand pocket.

The one nearest the driver.

And she couldn't get it out without some sort of distraction.

She clunked her heavy purse on the center console and began digging through it.

"What are you looking for now?" His voice wasn't as rough, but it still held an edge of warning.

"My lipstick. Whenever I get nervous, my lips get dry." She moved things randomly in her purse until he quit staring at her. She flipped down the visor and made a show of putting on lipstick, returned the tube to her purse, and waited until he switched on his blinker for a left turn. Using her purse as a shield, she slid the phone out of her pocket and into to her right hand.

Now what?

The volume had been turned down, but did that affect anything but the ringing? Could you still hear the voice of the person speaking? There was space between the seat and the door so she held the phone down there and used her fingernail to turn it on.

Trying to hold the phone in her right hand while pressing Noah's name with her thumb was tough and took all her concentration. The ringing sound was faint, but she could hear it.

"Everything okay?"

The sound of the driver's words caused her to jump. The phone slipped out of her hand and fell under the seat. "Oh, I'm fine. Just wondering why I carry so much junk in this purse." Was her voice a little too loud? Shaky? That shouldn't seem too odd, considering she was supposedly being whisked away from a dangerous situation.

"Look at all this *stuff!* I've got three lipsticks, lip balm, sunglasses, a package of cough drops, allergy medicine, a coin purse I never use because there has to be two dollars' worth of change floating around the bottom, the case my phone is *supposed* to be in, my key ring, the office key ring, and all these receipts! What are they all for, anyway?"

How long could she keep this up? She was running out of things to list in her purse and she didn't even know if she'd managed to dial Noah's number.

The driver guy, Bachman, if that's who he was, looked disgusted at her prattling but if he heard a voice coming from under her seat, what would he do?

"Do you mind if I turn on the radio?"

He shot her an icy glare. "It doesn't work."

"Stop here for a minute." Noah pointed toward a grocery store parking lot well away from the activity around the realty company. "My phone's blowing up and so is yours."

Conner pulled into a spot away from other cars with easy access to the exit. "Yeah. We need to figure out where we're going before we drive any farther."

Noah's phone went off again before he had time to answer the first call. "No one answered at Laurel's townhouse and her car wasn't there, but we knew that because it was parked next to Lefty Bob's." His throat tightened at the effort of saying his friend's name.

"They didn't have any better luck at Bachman's place. Kind of like R.J. Perry. He lives in an apartment in the Galleria area. On the seventh floor. A quick search of the parking garage didn't turn up any sign of the van, either."

Noah's phone continued to buzz. "Oh, shit. It's Laurel. Finally." He took a deep breath. He had to be careful. He'd yelled at Lincoln Montgomery and at the officer he thought was Lefty Bob. He couldn't afford to yell at Laurel. They had no way of knowing where she was, what had happened to her, or if she knew about Lefty Bob. Whatever was going on, he needed her to be calm and in control.

"Hey, Laurel, I've been trying to contact you. Where did you go?"

The only answer was a loud, uneven hum. A car? Had she butt dialed him? If so, he needed to get her attention before she disconnected. He drew in a breath to shout when he thought he heard her voice.

"No CD player, either?"

He couldn't hear an answer over the roar of the road.

"Well, what type of music do you like when you have a radio?"

He turned toward Conner and lowered his voice. "Call Montgomery. See if they can get a trace on this call."

Conner worked his magic while Noah held the phone close to his ear, listening for any tell-tale sound.

"I don't blame you. I don't care for rap either, but I like most other kinds. I hate to admit it, but I have a thing for Rachel Platten. You know, *Fight Song*?"

She didn't sound frightened. Was that because she didn't know what was going on or because she knew what was at stake?

She started to sing. Something about a boat, then yelling *FIGHT SONG* as if leading a charge. He'd never heard the song and off key the way she sang it didn't make him want to.

He listened closer to the words. Ocean. Waves. Was she trying to send him a hint or was the reference to water a coincidence?

And how could he spend his life with a woman who could murder a song that badly?

Whoa! Where the fuck had that come from? He'd only had three dates with her. And why the hell was he worrying about a lifetime when he hadn't figured out if he'd be here next week?

Maybe he had decided, gradually, over the last year, without realizing it.

For now, he had to find Laurel. Then he could decide what to do.

Laurel gave another off-key shout that might be part of a song and he tried for a calming breath. *As long as I can hear her voice, she's safe.*

Conner placed his phone in the cup holder between them. "Montgomery says they can get us in the vicinity using the cell tower her signal's bouncing off, but not to the exact spot. If she has a Find My Phone app turned on, he can get us closer."

Did she have one? And was it on? How was he supposed to know?

"What do you want to do?" Conner sat with his hands on the wheel, waiting.

"Let's take the Westpark Tollway to 59. The killing field is that direction. So is the place Constanza was abducted."

"So is Trusty Property management, but not the convenience store where he purchased the money order or the motel were Stella Fitzgerald was last seen. Let's head north toward I-10. Then we'll be ready to go either direction as soon as we hear back from Montgomery."

"That motel is near I-45 which would give him a clear shot south where we know he feels comfortable. South to Westpark, then east. That's the way he'd go. I can feel it. It's easier to drive a long way when you're looking to buy a money order than when you're carrying a dead body."

At the last two words, a shiver shot up Noah's spine. At least he knew Laurel was still alive. He could hear her singing.

She'd moved on to one of Adele's songs. He recognized that one by the words if not the way Laurel sang it. *Water Under the Bridge.*

~

The woman was hurting his ears. If she didn't quit that screeching, he might have to take her out now. Or at least give her a punch to the jaw to shut her up.

That had always worked before.

He wasn't used to making nice with one of his special projects. *Pow* and they were out. Secured by the time he had them in the van. But he hadn't been able to do that on the street by this one's office. Too many windows. Too many eyes. Too big a risk.

He forced his hands to grip the steering wheel until they ached, but it was the only way he could keep from hitting her.

Finally. She stopped the caterwauling and leaned back against the seat.

"Sorry."

She didn't sound sorry to him.

"I guess I'm nervous. Maybe if I could talk to Noah. Can I borrow your cell phone?"

A laugh threatened to bubble up, but he swallowed it back. "He's driving. He can't answer the phone. Regulations. Besides, cell service is spotty out here. That's why they picked this place.

Less chance of someone tracing a call. We're only a few minutes from the cabin. They have one of those secure SAT phones just for that reason."

"What's a SAT phone?"

Did she have to talk that loud? God, he hated pushy women. Maybe she wasn't a tramp like the others, but she was still a bitch with a capital B. The type who led a man around by his cock until he turned into a groveling mass of jelly, willing to do her bidding. "A SAT phone. They work off satellites instead of cell towers. That's why they can't be traced or hacked. They're much safer in this type of situation."

What a bunch of crock. But it sounded good. All those forensic programs he watched on TV were worth the price of cable.

A car pulled next to them at a light and he could see the driver talking on his cell. If she noticed, she didn't comment. He wasn't used to coming this way during the day. The amount of traffic was an unpleasant surprise.

She picked up her purse again—what was it with women and their purses?—and set it in her lap, next to the center console. Her hand slid under the purse, close to her seatbelt buckle.

The light changed and he floor-boarded it across the intersection.

If he didn't get to the cabin soon, she was going to become a real problem.

CHAPTER
THIRTY-SIX

"SHE QUIT SINGING."

Conner watched as Noah pressed the phone against one ear and covered the other with his free hand, trying to shut out traffic noise.

"Are they still moving?" He eased the speedometer from eighty-five to eighty-seven. His hazard lights were flashing, but if he flipped on the siren, Noah would never be able to hear Laurel. God he wished he was sure they were traveling the right direction.

His radio crackled and Montgomery came on before Conner could say a word.

"We have her." Excitement flooded the Feebie's voice. "They just passed Montrose and I-59. Looks like they're headed east. Judging by the time it took them to get from Kirby to Montrose, he's driving about five miles over the speed limit."

How the hell did Noah figure that one out? The man must be psychic.

"Keep us posted." Any minute now, the Sanitizer, with Laurel aboard, would hit the downtown interchanges and could take off any direction.

"I will. I contacted your boss. Jansen has an APB out on the white van and SWAT is under orders to be prepared for immediate deployment."

Noah leaned over and shouted into the radio mounted on the dashboard. "Lotta good that'll do us if they sit at headquarters and wait to find out where he lands. Tell them to saddle up and head toward the killing field. He'll be somewhere in the area."

"Will do. I'll check back as soon as I have the next update."

Conner eased his speed to eighty-nine and swerved around slower cars, although in Houston, that wasn't everyone. Once they got closer to downtown, the traffic would pick up and he'd have to slow down. Maybe he'd use the siren then. "Can you still hear her?"

"I catch an occasional word. A few minutes ago I think she asked about a SAT phone."

"If she's asking for a phone, do you think there's any chance she's not with our killer? Maybe driving with someone else?" But who would she be with? And why?

"Her car was in the lot and her phone's turned on. Probably under the seat judging from the road noise. I think two songs about water was the best hint she could give us. And we have to find her, no matter who she's with."

"Elgin and 59." Montgomery's voice sounded through the radio.

"Check." Conner was too busy navigating through increasing traffic to say more.

"If he turns onto I-45 south, let's take Elgin as a shortcut.

Maybe shave off a few minutes."

"Wouldn't the freeway be faster?"

"Not if you use lights and siren. I'll sacrifice hearing Laurel to close the gap."

It was risky. They could get caught behind a truck. But if it worked…

Laurel was done. She couldn't sing anymore—her throat closed up and any sound that came out was more of a squawk. She could no longer carry on a casual conversation with a man who had abducted her for who knew what reason and wouldn't be able to think of a subject if she were able to.

She wasn't even positive this man *had* abducted her. He could still be Lefty Bob. If she knew what to do, she'd do it. But she was out of ideas.

If only she could ask Noah.

Face it, she was on her own. No one knew where she was. Hell, she didn't even know where she was. She'd never been anywhere around here.

She sat in silence. Praying Noah had heard her. Praying Noah didn't say anything her abductor could hear. Praying Noah would send her a sign of what she should do next.

After several minutes in which no one spoke, they passed an exit sign for University of Houston. Finally, something she recognized. Was that the sign she had prayed for?

"Did you see the U of H game last weekend?" What had Noah said about it? "They always play best when they have the home field advantage and they were on fire Saturday."

Bachman, if that's who he was—why hadn't she clicked on

the photo of him?—didn't answer except for a noncommittal grunt.

Had Noah heard her? Was he even there? She had an idea they were on the southeast side of town, but what good did that do?

Another five minutes of silence and she thought ants would crawl out of her skin. They crossed over a short bridge and she recognized her surroundings. "I've been to that restaurant before." What the hell was the name of it? She strained to read the sign but could only make out *Crossing*. "Peter brought me here for a client's Christmas Party. The food was delicious. It's getting late and I never had any lunch. They have a crab bisque that's to die for."

Shit. Had she actually said that? Poor choice of words. "Can we stop here to eat? I know it's expensive and might not be in your budget, but I'll treat. I have a credit card and know how to use it."

But they were already past the restaurant, heading the opposite direction.

There was only one way on and off the island, so this had to be the place he planned on taking her. Her heart raced. Each second was an hour. Every move in slow motion.

Was this barren deserted spot where she would die? It couldn't be. She'd only started to live.

She felt under her purse for the cold metal of the seatbelt latch and snapped it open as the van lurched over the rough roadway. Her purse was still unzipped and she lowered her head as if digging through it.

He switched off the engine and turned toward her. *GoGoGoGo* ran in a constant loop through her frozen brain, but her body didn't respond.

For the first time, she saw his true smile, and it sent chills all the way to her toes. He pulled back his fist—his right fist.

Without hesitation, she screamed and threw her purse his direction.

Noah jumped an inch off the leather seat of Conner's car. His hand flew up and he nearly lost his grip on his phone. His heart ping-ponged between his ribs and backbone until he thought something would break.

"What happened?" Conner's eyes were wide, showing too much white.

"She screamed." He had to force the words out. "One minute she was talking about going to lunch. The next she screamed." The sound had turned his blood to ice.

"Can you hear anything now?"

"No more road noise so the car's stopped. Some type of movement inside the car. Maybe door's opening? Yes! That's it. There's a pinging sound, like he left the door open with the key in the ignition."

Montgomery's voice filled the car. "La Porte Highway onto Broadway."

Noah placed his phone on his knee and grabbed Conner's. Using the app for maps, he pulled up the area. He'd be ready the moment Montgomery gave them the next street name.

"He's somewhere near Broadway, but I can't be sure where." For the first time, the ever-cool FBI agent sounded frustrated.

Fuck. Just when they needed specifics most.

Shortcutting on Elgin and using the siren meant they had

gained seven or eight minutes on the van. But that still left Laurel on her own for at least ten minutes. "She talked about a nice restaurant. This doesn't look like the part of town with one on every corner. Maybe Siri can find it."

He sent up a silent prayer and pressed the *Home* button. "Four star restaurant near Broadway and the ship channel."

Several came up. Three were closed. One was a sushi place. Not the first choice for a Christmas party. He'd found one that sounded right when Montgomery came back on the radio.

"Guys? I think he crossed onto a strip of land jutting out into the ship channel called San Jacinto Peninsula."

Noah tapped Conner's phone. "San Jacinto Crossing, Seafood and Steaks."

Laurel flew out of the van and into the woods. Her head start on Bachman wouldn't last long.

Plus he had a gun.

Two steps into the dense undergrowth and she wished she'd run the other direction. That way would have led back to the restaurant and civilization but she'd have to cross an open space and race past Bachman to get there.

There was nothing this way except vines that tangled around her legs and soggy earth covered with leaves and full of hidden stumps.

She had to lift her feet with each step to avoid sinking into the marshy ground. What a day to wear a skirt and heels. Her calves already stung from a multitude of scratches.

The air reeked of rotting leaves and little light filtered through the trees. The area was too dark to see where she was stepping, but too well-lit to hide undetected.

She glanced back to see if Bachman was following and ran into a low hanging limb. Her hair caught in a mass of twigs and she yanked it away.

"Ms. Newcomb. Ms. Newcomb. What are you doing? I need to get you inside the safe house. Noah will have my ass if I don't take good care of you. Come back now, before you hurt yourself."

Could she be wrong? Was all this her overactive imagination? Was this man actually Lefty Bob? A watch on the wrong arm, a gun on the wrong hip, and a pair of right-handed scissors could all have a reasonable explanation. Maybe he pulled back his arm to reach for something in the back.

Why would Bachman want her anyway? She didn't know anything or have any power. She hugged the back of the tree and tried to make herself thin while she caught her breath.

She was a fool. Was it too late to come out and beg Lefty Bob not to tell Noah? She glanced down at her torn skirt and bloody legs. No way to hide this.

Heavy footsteps startled her and she crouched behind a bush. To her left, the man pushed through an open spot between the trees, his gun held in front of him. In his right hand.

A surge of fear ran through her and she wet her pants. Great, now she stank of dirt and rot and sweat and pee. He wouldn't have to see her. Another couple of minutes and he could smell her.

His foot crashed through a decaying log and he bellowed out a string of curses. When he worked it loose, he waved his gun and shouted, "You better come out, you little bitch. Every minute I have to spend hunting through this filthy jungle is going to cost you."

The place was dirty and smelled bad and things caught at her from every direction, but it was hardly a jungle. Just a small patch of overgrown trees that would run out if she went too far in any direction.

She tried to stand and something moved beside her foot. She wanted to scream more than she'd ever wanted anything in her life. She forced herself to look down. Hidden among the leaves was a snake.

Okay. Take a breath. Don't startle it.

Was it poisonous? What had she learned in that documentary? Check for slit eyes and a triangular head. Great. Why didn't she just ask him to stay still while she looked at his face?

The snake uncoiled and slithered through the leaves, giving her a chance to see its markings. Little Hershey Kisses shapes ran along its side.

ShitShitShit. A copperhead.

A soft *eeeeee* escaped from between her clinched lips. Her teeth chattered. She couldn't breathe or move.

The snake slid through the undergrowth and she took a step back. And another. And another. Until she backed into a tree and a limb crashed to earth.

Noah bit his lip as the car caught air bouncing over the one street leading onto the peninsula.

His partner's head swiveled from right to left. "Which way?"

Yeah. That was the question. And the wrong answer could cost Laurel her life. According to Conner's map, the peninsula was long and narrow, lying on its side like a flower with a broken stalk. The restaurant was on the left, where the broken stem would attach to the land. "Right. They kept going for several minutes after she mentioned the restaurant."

Conner spun the wheel and swerved right without slowing down.

Noah grabbed the door handle and held on. Had he really accused his partner of driving like an old man? Never again.

The peninsula had few roads and fewer places a white van could hide, yet several tries left them at a loss. Conner threw up his hands. "We've been down every street. Now what? Want me to head back to the restaurant?"

"Let's see if the fucking FBI can earn their pay." Noah keyed the radio. "Montgomery. What'd you see?"

"You're close. That's all I know. They're pinging off the nearest cell tower."

"Are you sure they're on the peninsula?"

"I'm not sure of anything. Just that the signal's not moving."

Fuck. A hundred things could have happened. Bachman could have found her phone, tossed it, and driven the opposite direction. He could have planted it on one of the restaurant's delivery trucks at any time since leaving the realty office.

No, he'd heard her voice and she'd mentioned a fancy restaurant. A couple of minutes later the van had stopped and she screamed.

What if they'd changed cars and weren't in the van? If so, he had no idea what to look for.

He opened the car door and stepped out. The air smelled of saltwater. Cranes dotted the skyline. Nothing on the land moved. A cry sounded in the distance. A scream? A seagull? Barge traffic on the ship channel? "Let's start over and take each street slowly. Maybe we missed something."

Conner crept down one street after another as they each craned their necks. At one point, they cruised the parking lot of a ship repair business, even checking out a metal hanger-shaped building. Boat equipment, but no cars or vans.

Noah motioned an employee leaving the building. "We're looking for a tall man and a short, blond woman. He might have been driving a white panel van."

The guy took off his hardhat and wiped his forehead. "I've been here all day. The only woman I've seen is Mrs. Hicky in accounting. She's African American and nobody *ever* described her as short. Sometimes vans go past. I wouldn't remember if one was white."

Not much help, but the guy would have noticed a woman screaming so Bachman wasn't hiding inside.

The last street was a dead-end, its surface a crumbling asphalt full of potholes. Conner stopped in front of the only house, a decaying mansion guarded by an eight-foot wrought iron fence. The oversized double gate was secured by a thick chain and padlocked closed. Weeds grew abundantly through the ornate brick driveway. "No one's been here in years," he said, backing up the car to turn around.

"Wait. Drive to the end of the street."

"We're *at* the end of the street. There's nothing more. Ten feet of dirt, then trees."

"Humor me. Did you see the sign over the gate?" Noah pointed to the arch above the entryway. Blending in with the curlicues of the design was a name, spelled out in cursive.

San Saba Estate.

CHAPTER
THIRTY-SEVEN

THE CRASH OF a falling tree limb stopped Bachman. She was here, somewhere. The thick brush muffled the noise, making it impossible to tell which direction to look.

He froze, waiting for another sound. Was that something, over to the right? He pivoted, trying to keep silent. The deep shade made observation difficult.

He held his breath, waiting, until he could make out a form that didn't belong. Was that her? A spot of green like the woman's blouse instead of brown like the bark of a tree.

Had she seen him? If he moved, would she run? On a street, in the open, he could outrun her any day. Here in this overgrown hell hole full of briers and spider webs and rotten leaves, she had the advantage.

The disarray of downed limbs and tangled vines and the abject filth of every surface made him feel like tiny demons with pitchforks were digging their way into his soul. He hated dirt and disorder.

As punishment for disobedience as a child, his stepmother refused to let him bathe instead of forcing him to as other children were.

As soon as he had the woman secured, he would strip off and wash with the river water. Disgusting as it was, that was better than being coated with dirt.

He switched the gun to his other hand so he could smooth back the hair that had fallen in his face and tuck in his shirt. Those small moves restored his sense of dignity. He could stand this long enough to grab her.

Because he couldn't kill her...yet.

He had to discover what the police knew. If they didn't have his name, would it be safe to stay? Carry on?

Probably not.

Best to start over in a new city. Maybe even a new state. He'd done it before. He could do it again. Find a good place. Get the lay of the land. Start slow and see what happens.

If they did know his name, that would make things more difficult. He'd have to leave with nothing.

Then, once he was settled, it might be time to pay a midnight visit to his stepmother.

She'd been enjoying poor health for more years than he could remember. A migraine when he had a school activity. Nerves when he needed her support. Lightheaded if he had bad news. Stomach problems if he needed money.

Yet none of these things seemed to kill her. She was strong as a bear when she wanted something. A trip to Europe? Sure, but only first class. A new car? Of course, if it was a luxury model. How about two week cruise? Only if she could have a suite.

But she couldn't afford to give him an extra cent of his own father's money. She was ill, you know. She might need it.

But after years of playing the invalid, would anyone be surprised by her death? He knew the way inside even if she had changed the locks. He also knew where she kept her medications, her emergency stash of cash, and his own mother's jewelry.

For now, he had one fucking job. Find that bitch!

A smile creased the corners of his mouth. She looked like the type who wouldn't answer right away.

Conner crept forward until he reached the end of the road. Nothing in front of his car but a wall of trees. What did Noah want him to do now?

"Over there." Noah pointed past his shoulder to a barely visible dirt path.

"That's not a road. It hardly qualifies as an animal trail." He made a sharp left and eased onto the trail. If he blew a tire or busted a shock, the department would never reimburse him.

But it was the only spot on the island they hadn't checked.

Fifteen feet later the path curved and led to an opening behind the main house. A stand of cattails indicated the nearness of the water. A building, half garage and half equipment shed, sat behind a line of trees, completely hidden from the road or house.

Beside it sat a white van. Both doors stood open.

Damn the tires. Damn the shocks. Conner stomped on the accelerator, shooting down the path until he reached the van and threw on the brakes, stopping in a shower of dirt.

Noah was out before he switched off the engine.

Conner ran to the passenger side. A woman's empty purse, its contents spread over both seats, lay crumpled on the floorboard.

Noah began shouting into his phone, "Laurel. Laurel. Where are you?"

The sound echoed in Conner's ears from two directions. He reached under the seat and pulled out Laurel's phone. If he'd harbored any hope they'd made a mistake and she was somewhere safe, they deflated like yesterday's party balloon.

In the heavy shade, the back of the van remained in shadow. Conner slid open the door and climbed inside. Against one wall was a coffin-sized wooden box with a shiny new padlock.

Noah already had out a hammer, swinging uselessly at the latch. Conner pushed him aside and fitted a crowbar under the loosened hinges. He pressed back once and wood splintered but didn't part.

He readjusted his grip and tried again. This time the hinge popped free. Noah was so anxious he was dancing from foot to foot. The instant the lock was loose he jumped forward, throwing open the lid. Inside lay a neatly organized tray with nails, screws, washers, bolts, molly bolts, and drill bits.

Noah lifted out the tray and flung it to one side, its contents flying through the van, bouncing off the metal floor and walls like an indoor hail storm.

Under the tray was nothing but an empty box lined with thick padding. The tray had come to rest upside down and the bottom was also covered with padding, but its material was ripped in long gashes.

Fingernail tears?

Conner shuddered. "SWAT won't be here for twenty minutes, earliest."

"We can't wait that long."

"I agree. I'll take the cabin. You take the woods. We'll keep our phones on in case one of us finds something."

Noah was gone before he had time to climb out of the van.

The garage portion of the cabin held a late model, dark Suburban. Almost as good as a panel van for transporting unwilling occupants.

Conner shot a prayer of thanks to Jeannie for nagging him about wearing his vest as he pushed open the door connecting the garage to the tool shed. Heavy curtains covered the windows, leaving the cabin midnight dark.

He fumbled his way to one wall and yanked them open. Pale afternoon light filtered inside. He opened another window covering and could see rudimentary furnishings: an antique clawfoot tub with a drainpipe that disappeared into the floor, a narrow bed, its mattress covered with a plastic sheet, and two chairs, one of which was bolted to the floor. A set of chains was neatly coiled on a table next to a hurricane lantern.

Two industrial sized hooks hung from the ceiling. In one corner, a square of the floor had been removed and a bucket on a pulley system could be lowered into the ship channel for water.

Conner hovered over the opening and vomited into the slow moving current.

Noah ran full speed toward the line of trees. Halfway there, he began measuring the area with his eyes. Where would Laurel have entered?

The nearest point from the van was close to the water and the tree cover was thin. If she headed for the thickest part of the woods, she'd have to cross too much open ground.

There. Between those two trees. Still on the outer edge, but leading into a more forested area. If she'd had time to plan ahead. Hard to do when running for your life.

He crashed through the tree line into another world not twenty yards from one of the busiest shipping lanes in the world. The sinking sun turned the area into a shadowy maze where trees looked like giants reaching out with wooden claws.

Spider webs coated his face and thorny vines grabbed at his ankles. Every nerve in his body yelled *hurry,* while his brain cautioned *slow down.*

Where was she? Did Bachman have her? Should he yell out? No. Not yet. Stealth was a better ally, if that was possible where sounds telegraphed every move.

As he adjusted to the darkness, shapes became clearer and the forest sounds settled into a recognizable rhythm. A breeze off the water swayed branches overhead. Squirrels or birds scurried away. Footsteps sent out a *crack* of broken twigs or sent up a shower of rustling leaves.

Noah stepped as softly as possible for a two-hundred pound man. Something moved to his left and it wasn't a squirrel. Could a deer live in this small patch of trees?

He bent low under a branch and eased that direction. The trees parted and he could see Bachman. Three feet past the killer, Laurel huddled behind a bush that only covered her from the front. And Bachman was approaching from the side, a gun pointed at her head.

Neither saw Noah as he worked to find a clear shot at Bachman.

"Get up, bitch." Disgust coated Bachman's voice. "I told you not to hide from me."

He yanked her up and she stumbled against him as she fell

forward. He took several steps backwards as he struggled to maintain his balance while holding her arm.

He let out a surprised scream and jumped from one foot to another, pointing his gun toward the ground and firing off several rapid shots. He screamed again and held up a bloody foot. The gun in his hand swung toward Laurel. "You fucking bitch. This is your fault. First a snake bit me, then I shot my own foot. You're gonna pay for this. I'll—"

Noah's bullet cut off the man's words before he could say what he planned to do.

Bachman's eyes widened in surprise as he gasped for air, a thin trickle of blood running from between his lips. He sagged slowly to the ground like a feather floating to earth.

Noah lifted the gun from his lifeless hand and stuck it in his belt. Laurel stumbled toward him, her hair wild with leaves and brambles, the sleeve of her blouse torn, scrapes and scratches on her arms and legs.

He pulled her close and whispered in her ear as she shuddered. "You may be the smartest, cleverest, most beautiful woman I've ever met, but you're the world's worst singer."

CHAPTER
THIRTY-EIGHT

LAUREL TURNED THE cup of pumpkin spice latte in her hands. Since the moment she entered the coffee shop, Noah had fussed around like a cat near a campfire. He took her coat, pulled out her chair, returned to the counter to place her order, then jumped up to retrieve it.

He was nervous. Anyone could see that. Well, she was too.

They'd texted since the shooting, but hadn't talked on the phone or seen each other for a week.

Sure, he'd been busy—filling out reports, working with other agencies—but if he'd wanted to see her, he would have. Right?

Had he chosen this almost deserted coffee shop to break up with her? Her actions directly led to him killing a man. If she'd minded her own business instead of trying to play detective, maybe they'd have caught Bachman without any violence.

Or maybe he didn't care for the new Laurel. When they first met, she'd been lost. Unable to function because her louse of a husband had dumped her. Left her broke and alone.

Since that time, eight months ago, she'd found a new job, a townhouse, and her backbone.

She wasn't the person he'd been attracted to then.

Well, too damn bad. She liked him—a lot—but she liked herself better. She wasn't turning back into Lost Laurel for anyone.

As if reading her thoughts, he reached over and squeezed her hand. "I'm sorry you had to go through such an ordeal. I'd give anything if I could have taken him any other way. Are you okay? Having any aftereffects?"

"I'm doing all right. If there were a pill to make me forget those few hours, I'd take it in a flash, but lying on the sofa with Harvey the invisible cat in my lap, purring, works fine."

"I'm glad Harvey decided to accept you. Sweet Pea does the same for me."

"Have you talked to anyone about what happened?"

Noah twisted his coffee cup. "The department is trying to make me, but so far I've resisted."

"I had a couple of sessions and they helped me. You might want to give it a try."

"I'm not sure anyone else can understand what killing a person does to you. That's what I wanted to talk to you about."

Here it came. Her foolishness had led to him taking a life and he couldn't forgive her.

He'd dropped her hand while they were talking and he took it again. "I have secrets no one in this world knows. My sister thinks she does, but she's only guessed half of it. I told Betsy when we first started dating because I wanted her to know what kind of man she was involved with. We haven't gone out that many times, but keeping this a secret wouldn't be fair to you. I trust you or I wouldn't share this with you, but if you ever tell anyone, I could go to jail."

Oh God. She *really* didn't want to hear this.

"I told you my father was murdered. A guy tried to steal his violin and he refused to let go. The son-of-a-bitch shot him. Right there beside the concert hall. He was heading home after rehearsal. The police were sure they knew who did it—a part-time mugger and full-time drug dealer that worked the downtown area—but they couldn't prove anything. It almost killed my mother. Well, I guess it did kill her. She'd been free of cancer for seven years, but it came back with a vengeance. Within three months, she was bedridden."

"Oh, Noah. I'm so sorry. Losing both your parents so close together. I can't imagine." Her parents' divorce had devastated her and they were both still alive.

"We could control her pain during the day, but the nights were awful. I begged the doctors to give her something stronger but they refused. When I doubled up the dosage on my own, they wouldn't refill her prescription. They thought I was taking the pills. That left her with nothing but aspirin."

This was tearing her up. His father. His mother. His wife. She knew he had a dark corner he tried to hide, but she had no idea.

"She kept begging me to find Dad's violin. Said she could sleep if I'd play. I took all the money I had, sold my guitar and amps and went to the guy's house. I offered him a little over a thousand dollars for a violin worth more than twenty grand. He laughed at me. I don't know if it was anger, frustration, exhaustion, but I slapped the money on the table, shoved him over a chair, grabbed the violin, a couple of bottles of oxy, and ran."

"That's it? You knocked a guy down and took something that belonged to you? Okay, and a few drugs. But what the heck?"

"That's not it. The guy died from hitting his head. A subdural hematoma, bleeding of the brain. They found him two weeks later and thought it was a drug deal gone bad. There's no statute of limitations on murder. I've stayed away this week because I didn't feel I could start a relationship with you until I came clean about the type of man you'd be getting."

"Are you kidding me? You were how old?"

"Nineteen when my father died. Barely twenty when I lost my mother. A legal adult."

"And you've been carrying the guilt around all these years? You shoved a guy, Noah. It was an accident. A bad guy, perfectly capable of hurting you the way he hurt your father and probably others. I'm not worried this makes you an evil person. You were protecting yourself and your mother. But I am worried you might be a fool. How do you know you're the one who killed him?"

They were leaning their heads together, whispering, although no one else was in the shop.

"He died, honey. From a knock on the head. The kind that takes several days to kill you."

"Several days. Not several weeks. He was a drug dealer. Bad things happen to them. Have you ever checked to see if they arrested anyone?"

"I never saw anything about it in the paper, but my mom died the next day and with the funeral and all..."

"You're not a kid anymore. You have access to records. Look it up. No matter what you learn, it doesn't change my opinion of you. I had a lousy husband and recently spent some quality time with a serial killer. Trust me when I say the man I'm looking at now is the best man I know. If you're interested in me, think we might have a chance at a relationship, I'm willing to try. If you're not, I'll understand. Let me know when you've made a decision."

She grabbed her purse and walked out. Not looking back was the hardest thing she'd ever done, but too damn bad. She liked him—a lot—but she liked herself better.

She wasn't turning back into Lost Laurel for anyone.

Noah rounded the corner to his office with every intention of asking Jansen for time off. Too many thoughts were swirling around in his mind. He needed a chance to sort them out.

Instead, he found a county sheriff waiting with one hip parked on his desk.

"Detective Daugherty? I'm Sheriff Guerra. I read about your Sanitizer case and wondered if you could help me. We had a rash of missing women four years ago. A couple of bodies turned up strangled. It seems a Richard Bachman worked for a local construction company around that time."

An hour later, the sheriff left with an armload of file copies. Noah felt like banging his head on his desk. He couldn't take time off. The Sanitizer case wasn't over. It was just beginning.

If he planned to sort out his own life, he better get to it. Avoiding his problems wasn't working.

Noah glanced around the squad room.

No matter how often he saw it, the sight of Lefty Bob's empty desk caused a rope to tighten around his chest, cutting off the ability to draw a deep breath.

A thousand Lefty Bob jokes swirled in his brain, but he'd

never tell another one.

Did some of the responsibility for Lefty's death fall on him? He had involved a civilian in a murder case then sent Lefty Bob to protect her. Or was Laurel right and he tended to blame himself for things that weren't his fault?

He risked a quick peek over his shoulder at Jansen's office. The blinds were closed. His boss was either working or napping.

Earl, now a part-time civilian clerk, was on a coffee run.

Lincoln Montgomery had called earlier to offer Noah a job with the FBI. Noah had managed his first good laugh in two weeks—what idiot thought he'd be a good fit for the Feds? He told the agent he'd reached the wrong partner and handed the phone to Conner. After five minutes spent encouraging his partner to accept, Conner had gone home to discuss the possibility with Jeannie.

That left the room as quiet as it was ever likely to get.

Decision time. How badly did he really want to know?

He could have looked any time since he transferred to Homicide, but he hadn't. Why? Because he didn't want to know. Didn't want to see the crime scene photos.

Didn't want to face what he'd done.

Noah's chair squealed when he pushed it back and he froze, waiting to see if anyone noticed, but the sound was muffled by daily office noises.

For a nanosecond, he almost changed his mind. Then what? Keep living half a life?

He strolled past the break room and down the hall to Records where he pulled out the murder book for his last case and the one before that. A quick glance around the area showed he was alone.

Holding the two thick case files in the crook of his arm, he moved farther down the line until he reached books from sixteen years ago. They were thinner—there were fewer scientific tests available at the time—and dustier, but worked on the same principle.

His hands shook as he reached for the book labeled *Charlie Avondale.*

The door to Laurel's townhouse was painted bright blue. Pansies filled terracotta planters on either side, their colorful faces smiling up at Noah as they bobbed in the autumn breeze.

Was it an omen? Would Laurel smile when she saw him? He eyed the bouquet of yellow roses he clutched in one hand. *What a lame idea.*

A surprised smile flitted across her face when she opened the door, then disappeared almost before it registered. She reached up to smooth her hair and then her T-shirt. "Oh, Noah. I wasn't expecting you." She glanced back into the room.

Does she have company? Should I have called?

"Come on in. Harvey and I were watching a movie. He seems to prefer the old classics because they don't have as many shootings or car crashes." She stepped aside and he could see her sofa with an afghan thrown back as if she'd just gotten up. An oversized mug sat on the floor beside a pair of fuzzy slippers.

There was no sign of the cat. Maybe he really was invisible.

"I felt bad about how I acted last time we met. I brought these by way of apology." He thrust out the flowers.

"You didn't have to do that, but…"

But it didn't hurt.

She offered a weak smile as she took the flowers and headed for the kitchen. "I don't think I have a vase, but this might work." She placed the roses in the bowl of a blender and carried it to the coffee table.

"I wanted to tell you that you were right." He stumbled over his words.

"Well. That's always a good way to start." Her smile was genuine, reaching her eyes as well as her lips. She even offered a small chuckle which felt like a warm blanket on a cold night.

Maybe he did have the nerve to get through this. "First, I didn't kill Charlie Avondale. It was a drug deal gone bad, although the perps heard a rumor he had a valuable violin. One of the men responsible confessed and testified against the other two for a lighter sentence."

"I'm so glad you found out and could let that go."

"That's why I had refused to see the department shrink. I couldn't talk about one killing without talking about the other. Once I got going, it all spilled out. Charlie's death wasn't the only secret I've been hiding. Betsy and I had been trying to get pregnant when she died. When we saw the plus sign on the plastic test stick that morning, we were both elated. Seeing her all excited turned me on and I started kissing her and…stuff. Even knowing I'd make her late for work. An hour later, she was speeding through a yellow light when an eighteen-wheeler hit her. The driver was asleep, but still, I've always blamed myself."

"Oh, honey."

"No. I need to finish this. You have a right to know. I've been trying to make up for killing Charlie Avondale so I'd be allowed in heaven with Betsy. I'd picked the date, fourteen months after she died. October 26th."

He hadn't realized how tightly he was gripping her hands until she yanked them away. "Three days from now? What am I supposed to do with that information?" The anger in her voice was like a slap in his face.

"That's just it. You encouraged me to talk to the department shrink and she helped me admit I'd already decided not to go ahead with it. I was hesitant to face it because I felt disloyal to Betsy. My parents' death, Charlie's death, Betsy. The baby. I've held it all in so long it turned toxic. I've had three sessions with her so far and each one makes me feel like I've lost twenty pounds. She wants to see me one more time in about a month. You said you were willing to give me a try at a relationship. I hope I haven't waited too long or scared you off."

"Nothing scares me. Not anymore. Not after I faced down a poisonous snake, two of them if you count Dick Bachman." The teasing tone to her voice was a ray of light.

"You got the best of Dick Bachman, no doubt about it, but I think the snake was a lucky break." If she could tease, so could he.

"Are you kidding me? There wasn't any luck involved. I hadn't taken my eyes off that snake for ten minutes. I knew exactly what I was doing when I pushed that creep back against the tree. As for you, I sure hope Harvey approves and you like classic movies."

Wow. She was tougher than he thought. And he already knew she was plenty tough. She might be more than he could handle. But it sure would be fun trying.

Ten minutes later, they were cuddled on her sofa watching Gary Cooper in *High Noon*.

A tiny black cat-face peeked around the corner, whiskers

twitching. Before the final credits rolled, Harvey was standing on Noah's chest, purring. Looked like he'd passed the ultimate test.

Despite monumental screw-ups, he'd been accepted by both Laurel and her cat.

He slipped his arm around her shoulders. Laurel had given him a second chance at life and he didn't plan to waste it. He'd learned his lesson.

No more secrets.

ACKNOWLEDGMENTS

A special Thank You to my son, Ron Muller, for answering questions ranging from "Do kids still chase Pokémon?" to "Who is in charge of foreclosed buildings?" and "Where would I find legal records over ten years old?" or "What's the fastest way to get through downtown?"

To my daughter, Angela Rehm, my son-in-law Jason, my daughter-in-law Karen Muller, and my grandkids, Andrew, Sam, Caroline, and Bode. You are in my heart at all times.

Thank you to J.E. Handcock for teaching me how to use Google maps.

Thank you to Jami Crumpton for showing me how to use Instafreebie and other things.

Thank you to Shauna Allen and Christie Craig for many insightful comments.

Thanks to Delma, Mary, Paula, and all my friends.

Thanks to Marti for you-know-what.

Thanks to B.N. Squire for your friendship and encouragement.

Thanks to Carla Rossi and Kimberly Dawn. You made the process easier and better in every way.

Thanks to all the members of Susan's Clue Crew. You're the best!

Thank you to the members of Northwest Houston RWA, Kiss of Death RWA, Houston Northwest Medical Center Auxiliary, my fans and supporters, and to you the reader.

Dear Readers,

I hope you enjoyed this book as much as I enjoyed writing it. If you did, please consider taking a moment to leave a review. Authors live and die by reviews. Reviews don't need to be long. A single paragraph works better than a long retelling of the story. Just say what you liked about the book. How it made you feel. Did it offer heart-racing excitement or heart-tugging emotions? Did the characters come to life? Were you invested in the outcome? Did the villain give you the creeps?

If you are interest in seeing what else Noah and Conner are up to, check out the rest of the books in the Seasons Pass series. Remember: Murder is always in season.

WINTER SONG

Homicide detective Noah Daugherty is on a mission: solve cases, lock up murderous scum, and get on with what's left of his life. He's on the clock, and his time is steadily ticking away. His path leads him to an icy Houston street, where a car has careened out-of-control and crashed, its driver, a beautiful young socialite, is dead. All the clues lead straight to her husband, but Noah's intuition screams the case is more than meets the eye.

Not willing to give up until he solves this cold-blooded murder, he finds the unthinkable . . . a hitman no one saw coming, with a chilling personal agenda that now targets Noah.

Can he solve the case and save himself before winter is finished singing her song?

SPRING SHADOW

Homicide detective Noah Daugherty finds purpose in solving the most horrendous of crimes. The last thing he wants is to babysit some spoiled country singer, but that's exactly what his lieutenant demands.

Posing undercover as a member of the singer's band, he makes it his mission to protect her from a stalker whose ominous threats have become increasingly personal. As things heat up, she hides a piece of her past that is key to solving the case, ashamed of the part she plays.

Can Noah unearth the painful truth before spring casts its dark shadow?

WINTER STORM

It's a scorching Houston summer, and homicide detective Noah Daugherty's only consolation is his life's work: solving crimes to atone for the sins of his past.

When the high-powered CEO of Beneficial Products, a company dedicated to the production of healthy foods, is discovered drowned in her hot tub, what appears to be either an accident or suicide, quickly escalates into something much more sinister. As the body count rises, the link between victims becomes all too clear.

Can Noah find a killer bent on vigilante justice before the storms of summer strike?

Check out my website at: www.SusanCMuller.com

Or join me on social media.
Facebook: Susan C. Muller, author
Twitter: @SusanCMuller

Sign up for my newsletter to learn about new releases and to be eligible for prizes. http://eepurl.com/cibhMn

Love reading? Join my review crew for ARCs (Advanced Reader Copy) of my latest novels.
https://goo.gl/forms/BW55alj8iSjAjCCB2

Happy reading, and remember:
Life is a Mystery
Reading is the clue

Susan